GREG AT THE STATION

The Nick & Greg Books #7

Other published works by John Roman Baker

The Nick & Greg Books
Nick & Greg
Time of Obsessions
Nick's House
Greg in Paris
Love & Cowardice
Nick's Fugue

Other Novels
No Fixed Ground
The Dark Antagonist
The Paris Syndrome
The Sea and the City
The Vicious Age
2020

Short Stories
Brighton Darkness

Plays
The Crying Celibate Tears Trilogy
The Prostitution Plays
Prisoners of Sex

Poetry
Cast Down
The Deserted Shore
Gethsemane
Poèmes à Tristan

GREG AT THE STATION

John Roman Baker

WILKINSON HOUSE

Greg at the Station
Part 7 of *The Nick & Greg Books*
Copyright © John Roman Baker 2024

Published by Wilkinson House Ltd, November 2024

FIRST EDITION
978-1-899713-67-7
(Trade Paperback)

Wilkinson House Ltd.,
20-22 Wenlock Road,
London, N1 7GU
United Kingdom

www.wilkinsonhouse.com
wilkinsonhousebooks@gmail.com

Cover design: Rod Evan

British Library Cataloguing-in-Publication Data
A catalogue record for this book is available
from the British Library.

"Contrariwise," continued Tweedledee, *"if it was so, it might be; and if it were so, it would be; but as it isn't, it ain't. That's logic."*

Lewis Carroll
Through the Looking-Glass

Dedicated to the memory of Julien Green

CONTENTS

Part One:
Gare du Nord

April 2019. A clear sky over Paris, and yet, to Greg, a large dark cloud appeared to cover the light. The city was no longer its shining self, and the walls were briefly blackened. Then the cloud passed, and he wiped his eyes with his hands as if it was within himself that the shadowing of light had come. An inner giddiness temporarily shook his body. Recovering, he made his way towards the entrance of the Gare du Nord, and once inside, dreaded with every step that he took the checking-in back to England, and all its inevitable routines. First, the waiting around, packed with others, unwanted heat shared between them in the cramped spaces. The giddiness returned, violently and savagely. Escape, I have to escape, he thought, struggling to retain his consciousness and his sanity. He pushed towards the station's exit, accidentally hitting into a young child who burst into tears.

"Can't you be more careful?" The cry of an outraged woman's words pierced his ears. He turned to look at her, but he saw two of her, his vision blurred, doubling everything he saw.

"I need—I need to get out. Out!" he shouted.

The tearful child only sobbed more loudly, attracting the attention of others. Somehow he made it, and finally the escape was achieved, and he was outside and the cage of his captivity opened.

"I need an ordinary café," he whispered to himself, and his hands were covered in sweat as he still clung to the luggage he had taken with him.

"Tout va bien?" a voice said to him as he bumped into a man who was around his own age. He replied that he was just a little tired, and the man moved away.

In the distance, he noticed what looked like a reasonably

inexpensive and old-fashioned café, and tentatively made his way towards it. He paused before crossing the traffic and turned to look at the façade of the station, seen so many, many times before in his life. As he studied it, his eyes focusing, a young man came into his line of vision. He was hurrying towards the entrance and Greg could not see his face completely, only the side of it. This glimpse of the man's good looks was like a trip on a step, a lunge forward, and at the same moment a lunge backwards into time. The man was dressed in a deep blue suit, his sturdy, strong body, tightly compressed into it. But this was not the only compression that Greg perceived; the man was a compendium of all Greg had known of beauty in compact form. It was enough, this sideways image of his dark blond, finely set features, and despite the inherent contradiction that physically he did not resemble all of them, he was *all* of the past, all those faces that Greg had loved and that he saw no more. The young man was graceful and masculine in his overall physique, and Karel came to mind. In his sturdiness, he was Bart, and also in the whole of these added parts, he was Nick. Nick *totally*, and at the same time, held together in form by the impress of the other essential men in his life, and in his precision of destination and the march of his step, he had Nathan's thrust forward towards whatever destination he had chosen. Nathan, the last in this construct of impossible, but possible beauty, and in the fire of them all, himself included, he was the sum being of desire and past holding. This was all in a few seconds imprinted upon Greg's eyes and mind. The youthful testimony of them all, was in this living, fleeting body, and then was gone, disappearing into the mass of others, as they hurried towards their respective trains.

"I love—I loved," Greg murmured, and he had to gather enough strength to return into that mouth of the station to try to get just one more glimpse of this man. It was futile, useless, but he had to do it; an ageing obsession, to add to all his former obsessions. The interior of the station was packed;

scurrying legs rushing to trains to lead them to family weekend visits or marriages or clandestine lovers. How could he possibly see that blue suit and dark blond flesh again? How could he hope to fasten once more the clasp of his glance upon this unknowing emblem of all that life had meant to him in that house he had called, Nick's house? Unreconciled, he knew the stranger was gone. Had he been imagined? Had he really seen all this in one single body? He questioned, despite the fact that his mind was now becoming blank, like a white sheet of memory that had been written upon and then progressively wiped away. A train to Lille was just departing. Was he on that train? Was he crushed between other strangers who would not notice him at all, or would he become suddenly the passion of another and for it to be reciprocated in this new century that Greg held tenuously on to? Greg would never know.

"The years," Greg murmured, and slowly he returned to the light of the exterior. He made his way to the café that had not been altered with the years. But truth could not be avoided. In this desert, the full force of present reality hit at him. He *had* been leaving Paris for a reason; there *was* someone in Paris for him, and he was escaping. This man was all that the stranger he had seen was not; the same age as Greg, and in his youth hauntingly beautiful. How many times had he, this man Renaud, haunted the dreams of others? And had not Greg himself seen the images, flickering, of this captive self upon a screen? Handsome even in his older years, he had been venerated and had received messages of longing from others. Renaud in colour and in black and white, weaving his fictions like a spider to draw others into his many different lives. Greg too, had been drawn in, driven by the power of the image. And the reality? The reality had sat next to him, and with hands now mottled, had clenched Greg's thighs. A mouth desired by millions had kissed his lips, and the taste had been good, and the feelings good, until these last long days of mental pain which had stripped bare Renaud's decay and his desolation, and the part in it Greg had played. But now was not the time to recall this. He entered the cool interior of the café, ordering first a coffee, then a glass of cognac.

Minutes passed, perhaps an hour, and after a few drinks, Greg raised his head from looking down at the table and looked towards the café door. Nick walked in. Was this a day of miracles? Had the young man in blue metamorphosed into Nick himself? Greg found his voice and cried out Nick's name loudly, but there was no response, and Nick ignored him.

"Nick, Nick," he repeated loudly, so loudly that there was a response, and the face that he so loved turned towards him. Greg felt faint with hope.

"*Oui*?" Nick responded.

"Don't ignore me. Please don't ignore me," Greg cried back in English, and perplexed customers around the two of them stared and murmured. Nick came to the table and smiled down at Greg.

"Please sit down," Greg said.

"My name is *Nicolas*," the familiar voice replied. "Do you really want to talk to me?"

"But it's you—of course—and why? How? What are you doing in Paris?"

"So many questions," came the reply, and Nick sat at the table.

"I thought you were—" Greg paused. "Nick, I thought you had gone forever."

"Really?"

Nick looked amused as Greg asked this, and his eyes that had not aged at all stared back at him.

Greg asked, "Why did you disappear to Paris? You could have found me in England, or did you hope I would find you here? Perhaps you wanted to hide from me forever? Is this a dream?"

There was desperation in Greg's voice as he questioned,

and then he grasped at the table tightly. He was about to pass out, and was afraid that his head would collapse and fall forwards. He could not do this. He would not do this, and his body, drained of energy, managed to cling on to the marble tabletop. He tried to focus on the glass of cognac, now empty of alcohol except for a thin film of liquid at the bottom of the glass.

"You look ill. Are you ill?" Nick asked.

"Yes."

"I will help. Stay there."

Greg felt Nick's presence move away, and he uttered a small cry, a cry of fear that Nick would not return. Minutes passed.

"I noticed it was cognac you were drinking. Here, I have bought you a double." Nick had come back.

"You shouldn't have."

"I do not like to see a person like this. I too have been there."

There was a long silence, and Greg said, "Do you think I have become an alcoholic?" and managing to focus, he stared into Nick's eyes. The intense stare was returned.

"Tell me about *me*," Nick said slowly. "When you are ready. When you have steadied yourself. I am intrigued about this person called Nick."

These words were said with such precision that Greg asked, "First tell me why your English is so exact? So precise? Almost as if you are translating it from the French? What has happened to you—and why have you come back into my life like this; in this way of just walking into the same café?"

"I cannot answer the last question. I would like you to remind me of who I was. I *did* visit England—and maybe we met. Maybe you remember me from there."

"You lived in Brighton."

"Did I?"

Greg felt a little drunk now, and he got up and went to the

bar and asked for a large, strong, black coffee. He had to be aware of everything; because the mystery of this incredible meeting; this wish above all his wishes had to make sense to him. It was not a miracle. He could not be that deluded. Carrying the black coffee back to the table, he apologised to Nick for not asking if he wanted a drink.

"I drink only juices. They are mixing me my favourite blend of several fruits. I am a regular here. I like to look at the station."

"When did you stop drinking alcohol?"

Nick did not reply to this. Greg stared again at his face. How young he still looked. How unlined his features were, and the eyes showed a youth that he, Greg, knew he no longer posessed. Greg felt as if he was talking to a man at least twenty years younger than himself, and even then he looked years younger than that. Thirty-five? No, it was ridiculous. That was the youngest Greg could go, and that was well below the subtracted twenty.

"You look young," he said to Nick.

Nick laughed, and still laughing, went to fetch his drink. Returning, he sat at the table and looked down at the colourful mix of juices. "Here, taste it," he said, and pushed the glass towards Greg.

This sign of unforced intimacy which recalled the past, made Greg feel freer in what he was going to say. He took the drink and drank some of it.

"It tastes good," he said. "I tasted mango—"

"Yes, you are right," Nick replied, and reaching out, drank from exactly the same spot Greg had drunk from.

He tastes me, Greg thought, then said, "So tell me why you have this accent?"

"I am French," came the simple reply.

"Yes, but your English accent is too perfect. And how did you know I wasn't French?"

Nick smiled.

"You called out Nick in such an English way. Such a

desperate call. I was moved. Touched. No one has ever abbreviated my name, not even in England. At least I think not. At least I do not recall it ever happening. You see, it's because of my memory—"

Then Greg understood. Nick had lost his memory. That is why the things that had happened, had happened. That is why he had not read a letter or received a call from him for so many, many years. He reached across the table and placed his right hand on Nick's right hand.

"I understand," he said.

Slowly, Nick withdrew the touched hand and looked down at it with a distinctive look of amazement that Greg remembered from their past together, a puzzled look as if he had been lied to, or cheated out of something and did not know why anyone would have wanted to do it. In his mind (developed over years of separation) Greg had built many fantasies about how Nick was, how he behaved. This amazement and its look that was specific to Nick was one of them.

"I am sorry if I touched too soon—you look—" and Greg said no more.

Nick was now staring at him again with a smile and a hint of laughter. "It is just that I have not been touched in so long. At my age, one is not touched so freely."

"I said I was sorry."

"A man of my age is seldom touched with such a sense of spontaneity. There are so many lines on my hands now. I can remember how my hands *were*—that is something so clear in my memory."

"And *my* touch? Do you recall in any way our intimacy? I am Greg, Nick."

Nick shifted uneasily in his chair, and to distract himself from the question, drank the juice down in more or less one go. He got up.

"May I get you another drink? I certainly need another of these. It is my main food. You have noticed I suppose that I am more than slim; I am thin. A thin man, just a whisper of life—*un soupir de la vie.*"

"Nick, you are English. Try to—"

"Impossible," Nick said brusquely, and returned to the bar.

Greg watched him walk, and yes, his body was very slender, almost the body of a boy. Even his buttocks were still tight and firm and he held himself with an uprightness that is associated with youth. Greg knew that he could make love with him, and that with a minimum of encouragement from Nick, he would take him to a nearby hotel. He wanted Nick. How could it be otherwise? The desire had not dimmed and even if he had looked very old it would not have mattered.

"*Enfin!*" Nick said as he returned with the second fruit juice. "I did order you another drink. The waiter, a friend of mine, will bring it over."

"He's your friend?" Greg asked.

"Albert? Yes, of many years. This is my favourite bar. I've been a customer here for at least twenty-five years." He paused, and then added, "Now what was the year exactly? Oh, to hell with it," he concluded, smiling.

"So, you always come here when you come to Paris?"

"Greg, I *live* in Paris. I have lived here for just over twenty-five years. It is long enough to call it my city, *non?*"

"And before?"

"Before what?"

"The twenty-five years. Where were you before?"

"In the provinces. Angers to be exact. The Loire valley. I was born near to Angers in a small village. It is called—"

Greg could stand this no longer and almost shouted at Nick, "How is this loss of memory so real if you can recall that village? If you can recall that, why can't you recall that you lived in a house in Brighton, England?"

"Brighton?" It was as if Nick was savouring the word, playing with its flavour in his mouth. "Is it as bright as its name? I imagine white. The sun. Is my imagination correct?"

"You know it is, Nick. You had a house there. It was left to me, but so much happened within its walls. Can I give you names? People you knew? Loved?"

"Loved?" Nick questioned back.

"Yes."

"But I do not know who I loved. How can I when there is no memory of the words, I love you. And yet, I have photos of myself. Taken when I was young. They are cut-outs. All of them. I have cut out all the background. Who I was with. Where I was. I don't know why. I was good-looking then, by the standards of the day of course. Not now. Beauty has changed I think in this twenty-first century. Don't you agree with me?"

Greg sat back in his chair. "Can we leave this place? This café?" he asked.

"To go where?"

"Take me to where you live. We have to talk seriously. I have so much to say to you. I was about to return to England for good, but that is another story. When I arrived at the Gare du Nord with my simple luggage here, I suddenly decided to stay on in Paris."

"You are a fascinating man. If that is what you want, come to my place. I live nearby in the Rue La Fayette. I only have a small apartment. Two rooms. What else should I need?"

Greg wanted to say, *me*, but said instead, "I would like to go there with you."

"I think I can trust you," Nick said with a smile. "After all, I have nothing you would want to steal, and why kill me? That is a joke, Greg. I can make very dark jokes." Then he looked down at the luggage, and added, "But you cannot move in. Okay? I have always been alone, and even if we become friends, there must always be a distance."

Greg said nothing to this except to murmur softly as if it was a revelation to a stranger, "I am homosexual," and he stared into Nick's eyes as he said the words.

"So? We are brothers in that. But you know, I cannot recall what it felt like—I mean in real terms. I watch porn sometimes. I only know watching, and as for my youth—well, that is lost to me."

"You asked me to tell you about yourself. I will."

"Make it good, Greg. I want your fantasy of me to be good because I am sure you do not know me. We have never met before. Maybe for an instant I reminded you of someone called Nick, and as it happens my name is Nicolas, N-I-C-O-L-A-S!"

"You *are* Nick!" Greg insisted, and the cognac had done its work. He was refreshed and all doubt was gone. He had found the other side of himself. It was only a matter of giving time for Nick to recall; to open the box of himself with care and gentleness. To release all that he had gone through, and all that Greg had meant to him and would mean to him once he remembered.

"I will pay for the drinks," Nick said, and although Greg resisted, he was touched by the way Nick took control, and after paying the bill, Nick steered Greg out of the café in the direction of Rue La Fayette. "It is not a long walk."

Greg saw how Nick walked with the same strong determination of the young man in the blue suit.

"I would not have chosen this *quartier*," Nick said, "but it was chosen for me. It is near the tracks that cross the Gare de l'Est. Fifth floor. Here we are."

They had walked more quickly than Greg was now used to and he stared up at the building, noticing the long, elegant balconies on its lower floors, and above, window railings that could only be leant against with caution.

"I like to look at the railway tracks," Nick said, "and I confess I love to read Zola. Not for intellectuals you may be thinking, but I do not think I ever was one."

"Yes, you were," Greg interrupted.

"Was I? Never mind. Zola suits me fine. Have you read *La Bête humaine*? I read it often. When you have loss of memory repetition is normal. I have few books, but I read them again and again."

"I have read it," Greg said truthfully. "A pessimistic book, but a fine one."

"Pessimism, optimism. All words to explain that we can rise and flourish or fall into material and mental despair. I have been told that I had a serious breakdown. The man who found me this apartment all those years ago tried to explain the causes, but my mind could not absorb those so-called facts. Maybe you have other facts. You know me, or so you think, so tell me a story worthy of Zola."

"You have a sense of humour—as always," Greg said as they ascended in the lift. After the lift stopped it was a brief matter of time before Greg was inside the apartment. He looked first at the windows. The shutters were closed, and the curtains drawn. "I'd like to see the view, Nick," he said.

"Never before evening. I cannot explain why, I do not like natural light in this apartment. It is something to do with the past."

Without asking if he could, Greg sat in one of the low, soft chairs which had wide arms and a cushion to rest his head on.

"Yellow is my favourite colour," Nick said. "Bizarre, isn't it? I do not like the light of day coming in, but I love the sight of yellow beneath the light of lamps."

Nick went into a small kitchen area and started to fill some bread with meat and cheese. He also brought out several bottles of juice.

"The café we were in bottles this especially for me. I am sorry there is no alcohol, but then I never have guests. You are, believe it or not, my first in all these long years."

Greg listened carefully to this, and thought, how am I to begin? To begin to relate to Nick all those years he has somehow lost? Then the fantastic side of the whole story took hold of him. How could Nick believe he was French, considering how the Nick he knew had been indifferent to France? He had after all not visited Greg once when he had lived in Paris. After he had disappeared, Nick had gone to an unknown place in England to live, not Paris. He had gone to live with what he had then called the love of his life. What was the man's name? The name was lost.

"I can hear you thinking," Nick said, looking over his shoulder as he put the finishing touches to the food.

"I wish you could read all my thoughts," Greg replied.

"I do not think in silence. I talk aloud when I am alone," Nick said as he walked towards Greg with the food.

"Surely that can't all be for me," Greg said.

"You must be hungry," Nick replied and sat in a twin chair to the one Greg was sitting in.

With a sudden surprisingly intense sense of loss, Greg thought of an old couple who had been forever together sharing their usual and punctual meal.

"Do you always keep this much food?" Greg asked.

"I bought my whole week's food this morning. You came at the right time, that's all. You see, Greg, my life is a ritual. I shop rarely, and I also have other regular patterns. I go to bed around eight. I read a little, and try to recall the details of the day, and then I turn out the light. I sleep until six in the morning. I get up, listen to some music, mostly Fauré and César Franck. And then I have my bath around seven and am out around eight. I walk around the city, taking various routes and always end up at the café where we met. I talk to Albert if he is not too busy, then I walk a little more and come back here for an afternoon rest. Then, around four, I go and look at the trains coming in and going out. And yes, I have a very small portion of food every day. This lunch for example at midday, but today it is for you. I have my juice an hour before I go to bed. That is my day."

"Always?" Greg asked. He could not touch the food.

"Since I can remember moving in here. It keeps me stable. I show no signs of senility, and my doctor comes to see me quite regularly. I've had no need for hospitals. Not yet." He looked over at Greg and said softly, "Please eat."

"I really am not hungry. I mean it was good of you to make all this, but really—"

"Please," Nick replied. "I want to watch you eat. Here in this apartment, I make such small amounts. And I do not mind that, but sometimes—yes, sometimes, there is a fleeting memory of others, and large meals. Shadows. Shadows of people and things. I cannot make out their faces but we are all sitting at a long wooden table—" he paused and then reached out and just very gently touched Greg's plate. He then withdrew his hand and seemed to go into a sort of trance.

"Go on, go on," Greg said as eager as an impatient onlooker who sees a closed mysterious box beginning to open; a box sealed down so firmly that it appeared to be closed forever. Nick was in it, and now he was just beginning to release the clasp, rusty with age, or a hidden lock to bring the content of his true self out. It would open, it would. And Greg looked on, concentrating on the act. Nick had to release himself. "Just try to remember more," Greg said, and Nick, coming out of his trance, looked back at him.

"I can't. I feel as if I will disappear if I attempt more."

"No you won't. One more attempt. Release the shadows and they will tell you their names. Shall I remind you of them?"

It was as if Nick had not heard this, for he said, "It was in Angers. Yes, there was a man there. He was standing over me when it hit me—"

"What hit you?"

"I don't know, I don't know," and there was anguish in his voice. "Loss. Pain. I don't know."

Nick got up then and paced the room and as Greg looked on, he noticed that same walk; that same movement of limbs that he had loved so much. He watched as Nick went to each object in the room, touching first a lampshade, then a chair, and at last an empty frame where a photo should have been. He picked up the frame, caressing the glass as if he saw a photo within it.

"Who is it?" Greg quickly asked.

"I have no idea why it is here. Why it is kept. And what

photo it contained—or was to contain!"

"Was?"

"I don't know."

The way he said these three words was a cry of despair and he put it back onto the side table where it had been, but face down.

"Did *you* buy the frame?"

Nick did not reply but came back to his chair and pushed the plate of food to one side.

"Please Greg, I know you don't want to, but reach out and just eat a little. Just so that I can watch."

Hearing Nick say his name made Greg pick up his plate and begin to eat. Nick was watching him intently and on his face was an expression that could only be described as tenderness, but perhaps more than tenderness, an astonishment that someone else was in his apartment eating in front of him. He was smiling. Greg could interpret the smile either way and despite his lack of appetite, and the food that tasted strangely bland in his mouth, he smiled back.

"You must fetch a plate and eat a little of this with me," Greg said.

"Yes, yes," and Nick went slowly back to the kitchen and bringing another plate over, picked out a couple of slices of cheese with his fork, then lifted a slice of tomato to his lips. He ate slowly.

Greg finished first, and pretending that he was not a guest, and that this was his apartment as well, took the plate back to the kitchen. He was conscious of the way he was acting, trying perhaps too obviously to show Nick that this was only natural for him to do; that it was the right thing to do as it had been done before in the distant past.

"Will you pour me some juice while you are there?" Nick's tone of voice was natural, as if the request had been asked so many times before, and the tone was light, free of all uncertainty and questioning. Greg, hearing this, reached for one of the bottles of juice, and bringing out a glass, half-filled it before going back to the chair where Nick was seated and handing it to him.

"So, now you know how much I eat," Nick said.

"Yes," Greg replied.

Greg returned again to the kitchen and emptied the few remaining contents of the plate into a bin. As he finished, he knew the act of normality had to end there and that he had to challenge Nick again.

"Can't you remember names at all?" he asked.

"No. No."

The reply was like a shudder. It quivered invisibly in the space between them. It was definitive. Greg sat down, not in the same chair as before, but on an upright one that looked as if it had come out of a church. The back was high and made of dark wood, and the seating was made of rush. He felt empty, and suddenly wanted to leave.

"I cannot do a thing about this," he said slowly, more to himself than to Nick.

"What can't you do?" Nick asked, his voice trembling.

"Open this—this box you are in."

He then looked at Nick and saw that his eyes were full of tears.

"I am so old," Nick said. "It has been too long. I am an unknown self. I will die like this." He paused before adding, "And that will come soon enough. The box will open my death."

"You—we, we have many years left," Greg replied suddenly. He had to stay. He could not leave Nick.

"The mathematics would deny that," came the slow reply. "I am at an age to die. I am at an age to die, complete in myself or not."

"Same goes for me," and Greg got up and went over to where Nick was seated. He pulled a handkerchief from his trouser pocket, and reaching out with it, dabbed at the tears that had not formed. As he did this he said, "But the years grow more precious. The older you are, the more precious they are. If you recalled the past, you would know that. Our lives are in no way finished. Your doctor finds you in good health, and so does mine. The fight of youth is still in us. I wish you could remember us running down Trafalgar Street in Brighton. The escapades we had in that town—"

"Were what?" Nick interrupted and asked.

"I was a great thief, for starters, and I knew every swearword that was not in the book. Would you like me to remind you of a few?"

It was then that Nick laughed.

"With *your* accent?" he said. "I know enough about the English to recognise a posh accent when I hear one. You'd be no good at swearing. It would sound so inauthentic."

"Well, I didn't have a posh accent as you call it back then."

"And are you now imagining that I was with you, using the same words?"

"You did your best."

"Where did we meet?"

"In a park. It is called St Ann's Well Gardens. It still exists."

"A large park?"

Greg moved away and put the handkerchief back in his pocket. As he did so, he thought how papery thin Nick's skin was.

"No, not large, but it had so many vistas that it gave the illusion of being bigger than it was—is," he added, finding it hard to realise himself that the actual park, more or less as it was, was only a day's journey away. "Pack a bag and come with me, Nick. I will show it to you. You are sure to recall everything there."

Nick got up and moved towards Greg.

"It's no use, Greg. I will never be able to remember, simply because I am not that person."

Greg, frustrated and showing his frustration, cried out, "How do you really know you are not that person? You could have visited Angers after we parted. Maybe with someone.

Someone who was your lover."

Nick passed a hand across his face showing how weary he was.

"I'm tired."

"I know, and I'm not making it any better. But you are Nick," Greg persisted. "Even tired, you make the same gestures that you used to make. Like that gesture of showing tiredness by passing your hand over your face, so lightly, so lightly. The face does not lie, and your face is Nick's face."

"I have no real face. I must lie down. Do you want to come with me. I know we are really strangers, but I do not mind resting beside you. That too is something that solitude steals from one; the presence of another, lying beside you on a bed."

Greg reached out then and took Nick's hand within his own.

"I will go with you," he replied.

Nick led the way, and a tall white door was opened, and together they crossed over its threshold into Nick's bedroom. The bed was a double, covered with a light green cover. Beside the bed was a book. Greg went over and picked it up. He did not look at the title.

"Oh dear," Nick said, "I exaggerated. I do read other authors aside from Zola, but my memory plays tricks on me, and out there on the street, his was the only name I could recall."

Nick lay down first on the bed, fully clothed. The windows in the room were not as shielded as those in the living room. A feeble light came in through the semi-closed shutters. Greg lay down beside Nick, then leant up and looked at the book on the side table. It was a book of poetry.

"You like Rilke? And you like to read him in English?"

"I find him better to read in English than in French. The translation is better, and I do not read German." He paused, and then said, "I like his inward objectivity. Take his poem *The Panther* for example. The vision of his later poems is already there, but he *sees* outwardly and clearly. His objective poems are most important for me."

He then recited a few lines from *The Panther*.

His sight, from the constant passing of the cage bars has grown tired; so tired that it cannot perceive anything else. It appears to him there are thousands of bars; and behind these thousands, no world."

He paused after that and then said slowly, "It is as I said, a sort of inward objectivity—as if the objects, the people, and the places of the world come to him spontaneously—it's hard to describe. It's like he was writing with his eyes closed so as to let the subject exist in its own right. Of course, that sounds absurd, and it is. He had his eyes wide open. But he allowed what he wrote to be itself, of itself, as if it was somewhere in the atmosphere around him, just waiting to be put into words. He allowed all things to be what they were and not to be anything else other than what they were, and yet transformed. He did not create; he recreated what was already there and waiting to be revealed."

Greg thought how much this was Nick as he was. The same passion for poetry, and he remained quiet.

"Open the book and read one of the poems," Nick said.

Greg took the book, and leaning up, placed the book on the bed and opened it at random. A page fell out of it. It had been written upon in Nick's hand.

"What is this," he asked, holding it up.

"My version of *Autumn Days* from Rilke's *The Book of Pictures*. Read it, Greg."

Greg looked at the lines and read aloud:

Who has no house will not have one.
Who is alone will remain alone,
will sit, read, write letters through the night
and walk on the boulevards, up and down
without rest, while the dried-up leaves are falling.

"Is that how you see your life?" Greg asked, replacing the paper in the book.

Nick smiled, "It is a translation of *my* Rilke. I am trying to get to the essence of the poem. Simply, for myself."

"Don't you remember your own poems? The published poems? Do you have them here?"

"Did I write poetry?" Nick asked. "Poems that I created?"

"You cannot have forgotten."

"Well, there are none here. You can look through all my things. I have nothing to hide."

"But you *have* hidden them," Greg said. "Or destroyed them. The bookshop? The poetry readings? Try, try to recall."

"I have Rilke. That is all I need. Not the *Duino Elegies*. I cannot read those. I do not understand them anymore."

"Why do you say *anymore*?"

"Don't interrogate me, Greg!" Nick cried out "What is gone is gone. These poems, these few poems of that great poet are all I have, all I need. They are objective, and only slightly touch me within."

"Do they never touch you in the depths, Nick?"

"Stop it, Greg. You have more images of the past and the people to draw down than I have—and this, and maybe this *is* the truth—what is to be gained by total knowing? Believe me, Greg, we cannot know, neither you nor I."

"Know *me*." Greg said.

As if in a trance, Nick whispered, "This is Rilke again. Listen."

World was in the look of the beloved—,
but blindly it poured out and was gone.
World is outside....
It cannot be grasped.

"Once more, Greg, not an exact translation."

Greg replied, "Imagine your past as poems. Poems to be recreated. The past has not gone from you. It can be grasped.

It is waiting to be written." He touched the book and replaced it on the bedside table.

"And then?" Nick asked.

"You will know."

"I lie here beside you. I am glad of that. You are familiar to me as a stranger is familiar to me, and I am thankful that you are here. I can feel the warmth of your body beside me, and there is a wonder in your presence. A mystery presence. I want it to be like that."

There was a long silence between them. A clock ticked in the room, and as Greg looked sideways at the shutters, he thought he saw a flash of white, the white of a bird's wing? He thought of the seagulls in Brighton, and rough seas, and all that Nick and he had shared there.

"Nick, I love you," he said at last. The silence was only slightly rippled by the sound of his words. A gentle wave on the water of memory. "I love your face. You say you are Nicolas, but that is the same as Nick. I do not see you as Nicolas, but only as Nick. I explain you to myself as Nick. I love what I see."

"It cannot be grasped," Nick replied. "And what if what you see is an illusion?" Nick's hand gently and yet firmly reached for Greg's hand as he asked this.

"It is not illusion."

"You cannot be sure."

"But I tell you, it is not."

"And was it a man, Greg, that you left, and did you love him? Were you going to the station to escape from him? Or was it simply to leave?"

"His name was Renaud. An actor, an elderly actor. I thought I needed him."

"And do you still think that now?"

Greg did not answer, and Nick whispered as if they were children revealing secrets, "And is it possible to need more than one person—at the same time?"

"*Tu demandes ça?*" Greg replied.

"It's just a question. You do not have to answer."

"But *you* know it is possible, Nick. You have experienced it."

"No."

Nick withdrew himself slightly away from Greg.

"Karel. Bart," Greg said. "And then there was Nathan. We all of us made love together. It was sexual love, but it was a sincere love."

"I know nothing of this."

Nick's voice was cold. He then leant up and looked down at Greg, and his still handsome face looked paler than before, stretched thin in its tiredness.

"I was not there in Brighton. I am not this man. I never had a house there. I never knew a Bart, a Karel, or the other one, Nathan. The names mean nothing to me."

"But you said yourself you felt, or was it saw, shadows at a long table. There was a long table in the house you owned."

"There are long tables in the Loire Valley as well. It was there, not the place you describe."

Brutally, the gentle wave rose up, higher and higher, and Greg was afraid. A storm was about to break within his body. Brighton itself rose up with the wave, threatening to crash down. He cried out, and Nick put a hand over his mouth and told him to calm down. The immense wave, the whole of Brighton, moved, rising up like a sea cobra to strike. No, no, Greg thought. Stop this madness. Nick held on to him and slowly, very slowly, the panic receded.

They stayed like this for a long while, Nick looking down at Greg, watching him, and then as time passed, Nick asked, "Can we end this subject? I like you. I am glad we have met, but my loss of memory is *real*. It is not fake. I cannot remember. I had a breakdown, and yes, there are shadows. I want you to try to understand me for *me*, as I *am* in the *present*. Can you accept the present?"

Greg closed his eyes and then he let go. He fell asleep and when he awoke the room was in almost total darkness, and he heard music coming from the living room. He heard Nick walking around the room. He realised he needed to go to the toilet, and he had no idea where it was. He went into the living room, his urgency for the toilet, embarrassing, as he felt a slight dribble begin.

"I need the toilet," he said bluntly.

Nick showed him where it was, and Greg closed the door behind him and faced a simple toilet and stark white walls. He pissed, then pushed down his trousers and masturbated, but the emptying out made him feel faint. He sat on the toilet seat for a long while, not flushing, incapable of moving even an arm. Eventually there was a tap on the door. He heard Nick ask if he was alright, and unsteadily getting to his feet, he flushed.

"I am sorry I took so long," he said when he returned to the living room.

"Next to the toilet there is a shower room. Would you like to take a shower?"

At first Greg felt like saying no, but realised that he did need one and said yes.

"I have clean underwear as well. Please accept the offer, Greg." Nick's voice was gentle as he said this.

"I will accept the offer," Greg replied, and Nick showed him the shower. Then he discreetly left him to take off his clothes and after he had done that and placed his pile of clothes outside the shower, he stepped in and turned on the water. He let the water run cold, adding only a little heat to wash off the soap. And afterwards, outside, he found two pairs of underwear to choose from, and two pairs of socks. He bundled his own used underwear into his trouser pocket, trying to flatten them out.

"I will throw them into the kitchen bin," he said quietly, suddenly ashamed of himself.

"Do you feel refreshed?" Nick asked. "I have made some coffee."

"Thank you," Greg said, and returned to the yellow chair

with the soft light of the lamp beside it. Nick brought the coffee to him, then went over to the other chair and sat down.

"I want to talk to you." Nick looked across at Greg as he quietly murmured the words.

Greg sipped at the coffee, then put it down and slowly nodded his head.

"We are old men," Nick began, his voice still low, "and it can be for some a time of forgetfulness. Yes, I do want to know more about who I was, but I thought while you had your shower, what can I really make of that knowledge? I live quietly. The man who found me this flat told me that it had been bought in my name, and I have the papers to prove it. The name on the papers, I have looked at, and they must be my real name, and if they are not, it has not prevented me from living here all these years."

"Did you have money to buy it?" Greg asked. He felt calm, and the wave had not moved, had not threatened. It was fixed inside of him, holding him together in its stillness.

"Apparently yes. There was a house just outside of Angers that was sold. Apparently mine. With that money, this rather run-down flat was bought, and when I first moved here it needed a lot of renovation. It was cheaper than most because of the state it was in. This man, whom I can no longer remember, saw to it that it was plainly redecorated, and over time I have given it—a certain warmth. The chairs, the yellow that I love, all bought second-hand. And I have a pension that I would not have if I was the Nick that you think I am."

It all sounded plausible, but the Nick before Greg *was* the Nick he knew. He clung on to that, otherwise he would drown; go under completely.

"Papers can be faked. Identities—" he said feebly.

"Not so successfully that I have a pension. The French may be foolish, but they are precise, and nothing gets through the net of bureaucracy."

"Yes," Greg said, and he closed his eyes. He saw a fake Nick suddenly—an exact copy of Nick, but not Nick. He started in his chair, almost jumping out of it. The wave was about to fall. "And you?" he cried out. "What is your full name?"

"My full name is Nicolas Ghéon," Nick said.

Greg stared at Nick and said, "You are not Nicolas Ghéon. This name seems too fabricated, or rather, given. And please, no fake papers to try to prove otherwise. You are *my* Nick. The other side of the same coin. Remember?"

"No."

The word was said slowly, stretching out the 'O' to its maximum length of sound. As he said the word, Nick got up, and Greg watched as he went slowly into the bedroom. Just after he had crossed the threshold, he turned and with his left hand, beckoned for Greg to follow him. Greg felt the wave move a little inside of him, and then with caution he followed. Once inside the bedroom, Nick closed the door.

"I want—" he began.

"What?" Greg asked.

"For you and I to throw all this finally away. What we think we know and what we do know. I will never show you the papers to prove my name. They are not here, so don't look for them. I am just me, and because you want it, for you I will be Nick. I will be Nick for you, because absurd as it may sound, in just this one day, you have made me want to come alive again. I want a lover. And I want that lover to be you." He paused. "And have you wondered, since you met me, why I smile so much? It is to hide the wounds. It is to hide the sorrow beneath the mask. They gave me room for that."

These enigmatic words disturbed Greg, and looking at Nick, he saw that he was not smiling. A shadow fell on Nick's face and Greg felt his head was playing tricks on him. How young and how beautiful he looked. And as he thought this, Nick moved towards him.

"Hold me in your arms," Nick said, "but gently. My body is frail—this paper self."

"We are young again," Greg replied.

"Such a beautiful thought," Nick said, and raising a hand he caressed Greg's face.

"I am already your lover," Greg murmured. "You have miraculously returned. The café door had to open. You had to walk in. Mystery? Coincidence? Fate? It does not matter. I have been returned to you, and you to me."

Nick moved backwards then, and something happened that seemed very strange to Greg. The room appeared to grow longer, and Nick was moving into a part of it that was in total darkness and he realised that he could not walk into that place of darkness Nick had retreated into. He was afraid of what he would find.

"Please—" Greg said. The 'please' seemed distant, faint, even to himself, like an echo that can be barely heard. "Return to me here," Greg asked.

"I can't," Nick's voice said.

"I will not follow you into that deep shadow. How big this room suddenly seems that it can hide your face from me like this."

"You will not see my face if you come to me."

Out of the darkness, Greg saw a hand stretched out, and the hand beckoned. Greg went into the darkness. He did not want to, but his legs seemed to move of their own volition, and when he arrived in that darkness he saw there was a light, a green light, and what he saw, he blocked out of his mind completely. He heard himself scream and it was as if it was another him who screamed, coming from far away, on the further side of death. The wave had fallen, and he ran from the room, out of the apartment, and instead of the lift which he perceived as a trap, he ran, legs unsteady, down the stairs and out into the street.

Greg walked in darkness through the lighted streets of Paris. He had left his luggage behind him in the apartment, but it did not matter. He had his passport on him and his money and his bank card. The hours passed and it was late and he felt hungry. The fear that had walked with him was still there, but diminishing, and by the time he arrived at the Bastille, too exhausted to walk further, he felt calmer, and yet cold inside.

"I must eat," he said to himself, passing a cinema that was disgorging its public. As he struggled through the crowd, who were moving it seemed uniquely in his direction, he tripped and fell. At first, no one came to help him. He was incapable of getting up and he did not want to get up, and this urge to remain down disturbed him. Did he want to be crushed by them? Did he desire for this to be a form of suicide to end it all? He lay on his front, waiting for feet to trample all over him. His head pounded, and his ears rang with fear. Then he felt himself being raised up, and the arms that raised him felt firm and strong. A voice in his ear, neutral yet forceful, told him not to resist and that he would be alright. Suddenly vertical again, his eyes attempted to focus, but giddiness and a lack of will to do anything to aid his situation made him totally passive.

"I cannot see; I will not see," he said to himself.

"*Ça va mieux maintenant?*" the voice asked.

He heard the deep, masculine sound, but did not answer and he allowed his body to be forcibly dragged towards the bright light of the cinema entrance. As he was dragged, he saw the title of the film being shown, and it was something about *Avengers* but then again, he had no desire to know more. Slowly regaining their focus, his eyes saw the red plush of seats, and his flesh allowed itself to be seated on one of them. He made as if to fall forwards again.

"*Non, ne fais pas ça,*" the voice insisted.

He was then pushed back into the chair which was wide and brazenly red as if blood had been splashed all over it. He now willed his body to move, and he clutched at the armrests. He heard the words, "Thank you," come out of his mouth.

"You are English?" the voice asked, and with a sudden force to know who his saviour was, he stared up at the face of a handsome man dressed in black. He noticed the clothes first.

A suit cut to measure. And then moving his eyes upwards, he stared at sharp features, carved by nature to a precise perfection.

"I again thank you," he said.

"You must rest for a while. I do not think the crowd would have harmed you, but people rarely look down when they have just been thrilled by a film. As the film had bored me, I did, and I acted quickly."

"I am sure I am fine now," Greg said, moving himself into a respectable sitting position and trying to release his body from its state of being a victim. He had the urge, sudden and almost brutal, to take control. "You must understand that I am not in the habit of displaying myself like that for all to see."

His voice was hard and controlled.

"It could happen to anyone of your age," was the equally hard reply. Greg had the impression that they were both trying to brush off the indignity of the situation. An elderly man falling in a crowd is always an indignity.

"The cinema must be closed now," Greg said. "I do not want to hold them up. Does everyone who works here know what happened."

"No worries," the young man said, and the expression, which clearly had been picked up from modern English usage made Greg feel a moment of dislike. He had hoped to escape common English terminologies, and now this young Frenchman (if he was French) was forcing it upon him. The next thought that came to his mind was a thank you to himself for not having done the obvious thing, and that was to have waited for the next train back to England.

"I will get you a drink."

"Here?" Greg asked.

"I know the manager. He is friendly with the bar next door. Most of the staff have a drink there after the cinema is closed, and he has said he will keep the lights on in the foyer and bathroom until you leave."

"Clearly he is a kind man."

"He is a client of mine. Now, what will you have to drink?"

"A cognac," Greg replied, and despite the fog that remained in his mind, he took in clearly the word 'client'. And it was not difficult to work out the meaning, but he had to be sure. "I assume, when you use the word client, that you do not mean that you supply things for the cinema, like drinks or popcorn?"

The cold features of the young man cracked a little with the strain of laughter.

"Oh no, not that."

"Drugs?" Greg was now bold enough to ask but knew instinctively that it was not. Or if it was, it was only part of the service.

"You are being too serious," came the reply, and with a strained smile, the elegant body walked away.

The foyer was empty, and listlessly Greg looked at the posters of forthcoming attractions. The films were all American, but the titles were in French. This was certainly not a cinema *d'Art et d'Essai*, but then Greg had to remind himself it was 2019 and that that sort of cinema was in decline, and in any case, the vulgarity of the plush and the touches of fake gold here and there all too clearly overstated its place in the sphere of populist cinema.

"I bought you a double," the young man said.

"I really must pay you," Greg said.

"Later."

Then returning to the seat, the handsome figure relaxed in the chair, his long muscular legs stretched out and the heavy bulge in his groin distinctly visible. Greg sensed that this part of the young man's anatomy was clearly trained for business and always alert.

"I have had a shock," Greg murmured, moving his eyes away from the perennial obscure object of desire. "Do you have a name?" he asked, raising the cognac to his lips.

"Bryce."

"That is not very French."

"All the same, Bryce is my name."

"Is it a fashionable name to have?"

"I do not adhere to fashion."

"But you've clearly adopted it, and it must comply to some desire, as do your clothes."

Bryce stretched his legs out further, and the bulge, in its self-indulgence, grew larger. At the same time, his face stared coldly into Greg's and Greg knew that they were now politely at war with each other, sparring verbally for conquest. He felt a rush of energy, driven on perhaps by the double cognac.

"So how shall I thank my rescuer?" Greg asked.

"There is no obligation, and speaking of clothes, yours are very dusty. Don't you think you should go to the bathroom and tidy up? There is one just behind you to the right."

Greg now felt like telling him to fuck off, but despite his weariness and the despair in his mind, he realised that he would give in to useless desire. He knew he would rub against marble, but eventually the marble would become malleable and even, if Greg was lucky, burst into flame.

"And the manager is alright about this?" he asked.

"You're not his customer, but you are with me, and he always complies with my wishes. Even to leaving all the lights on here, which is improbable in Paris—but then we live in improbable times, don't we? We take what we can."

Greg stood up and his legs did feel weak, but he was determined not to show it. He looked down at the improbable Bryce and smiled.

"I have no place of residence in Paris," he said coldly. "I was about to leave the city, then decided to stay. It's not a story you need to know, but as fortune is kind, I do have any price that is necessary."

"No luggage?" Bryce asked.

"Left behind somewhere. I can buy again what is inside it. My clothes are not too fresh or anywhere near to the same standard as yours, but I do have clean underwear and socks, and only a short while ago I had a shower."

Bryce looked up at him, and Greg saw the glint of greed in his eyes. He saw quite clearly that this mannequin was the purest white of individualism, and would have passed any Ayn Rand test. Only time, as it did for her, would make him break into small frozen pieces to be picked up by the trashcan of the common lot.

"Then you can work out a price and a place, and I will as you suggest, dust myself off. I will try not to fall down again, as I am sure the human element of rescuing someone in a toilet—which is of course by definition a place of unwanted waste—would be distasteful. That you rescued me from the feet of the crowd is now quite clear in my brain. It could have been *you* there, in years to come, and the only humanity left in you, realised that. You rescued me from the cattle as you would hope someone would do for you. Perhaps you even sensed I am a man of quality who is as equally naked in his hostility to the cattle of mankind and their existence as you are."

"I have never offended," Bryce replied, "and I admire your capacity for oratory. I too went to an elite school. It always shows."

Greg laughed down at him. "No, I went to a school called the Knoll, which was quite, quite ordinary, and the boys there spoke in a dialect that would be quite alien to you. My long life has taught me to adopt a façade and to become a chameleon. You know, that creature of nature that always changes?"

"I don't like creatures or any kind of animal."

"Not even the superior ones?"

"Oh dear, I see some lack of wisdom has led you into the stupid but now universal belief that we are animals. I believe that I am made of different—"

"—stone?" Greg interjected.

"Oh please, now go and do what you have to do. I like the fight, but it will tire both of us. Can't you see that behind my blue eyes I am inwardly bored and yawning?"

Was this how Renaud used to be, Greg wondered, before he too became aware of the fallibility of human flesh, human time and need?

"Don't suffocate, Bryce, on the natural act of breathing while I'm away," and after a short pause, Greg added, "Just turn on the computer within and calculate, and do not distress yourself if you have any fears of robots taking your place, you are already imitating them. They will in fact fear you."

Bryce now glared at Greg.

"How old are you?" he asked.

"Too old for any contact. I would estimate you are about twenty-two."

"How did you manage to calculate that, so accurately and so quickly?"

"Experience. A human thing. All young men are now twenty-two to me."

Bryce made an impatient wave of his hand. "Go away," he said. "Take your time. I will chat to the manager for a while. You see, I do have a heart after all. He is wasting light on us, and I think it is not right for him to do that without a reward."

"Will the reward take time?" Greg asked.

"I will make sure it is quick, and to rinse out my mouth afterwards."

Greg then walked away, finding the bathroom with its long row of glistening white sinks and golden taps. He went at once to wash his face and his hands. He was exhausted and despite the dark victories of their communication, he wondered if he could go through with any act of sex. He had wanted it desperately with Nick, until he had seen what he had seen, and his penis that had ached for Nick, still held on for that sensation of touch and explosion. As he threw cold water into his eyes, blurring vision, he saw himself trying to break the hardness of that stony flesh that called itself Bryce.

"But why?" he asked aloud.

He wiped his face in front of the silver-framed mirror

above the sink, then threw the soft paper towels into a white bin. To delay his return he retreated to one of the toilets. They were large and the rims glistened with cleanliness as if no one had ever shitted there or sprayed their urine. While he had been with Bryce, outside in the foyer, had the poor of Paris entered, scrubbing and polishing for the few miserable euros that were offered them? Once upon a time he recalled he had read repeatedly, *The Wretched of the Earth* by Frantz Fanon. How young he had been and how the words had soaked with their blood and their tears into his brain. For a short while, memory came back with its fractured force, and there was François waiting for him and all the brilliant colours of life glowed above their heads.

He stayed in this place of cleansed defecation for nearly an hour, and sure enough, Bryce was waiting, impassively looking down at the core of his flesh that was his true source of being and the hopeful, yet hopeless accumulation of his needs and his future wealth.

They caught a taxi outside and Greg allowed Bryce to open the car door for him. An address was given near Denfert-Rochereau and the taxi sped into the night as if the trip was urgent and necessary, which it was not.

"I will pay when we arrive," Greg said.

"Yes," came the reply, and nothing more was said between them. It was not until they had gone up in a surprisingly old-fashioned lift and Bryce had opened the door of his apartment that words began to clash between them again.

"Is this where you normally do business?" Greg asked, surveying the emptiness of the room. The walls were covered in a material that looked like hessian, and when Greg inspected it, he found that it was. There were no pictures on the walls and the thick wooden floors were barren except for a large black sofa in the centre of the room. Black curtains covered the windows. But then Greg found that he had not paid attention to everything. In a corner of the large space there was a sling, complete with chains, handcuffs, and all the other extras needed for certain clients' needs.

"I do it to them," Bryce observed, noticing Greg looking, "and they do it to me. I get no sensation from my arse, and they can go as deep as they like. As for them, well, sometimes they disgust me when I withdraw from them and see their shit on my cock, and still others cry out loudly proclaiming the pleasure of the prostitute as if it was a positively biblical revelation!"

"I see," Greg said simply.

"Do you desire any of that?" came the polite request.

To Greg's ears it sounded surprisingly like a polite woman asking if she should partake of cake with her cup of tea.

"Are you sure that you feel nothing?"

"Nothing. Perhaps the vaguest of sensations as the fingers form into a fist, but then, it is like I am under an anaesthetic, or in a trance. While they satisfy their desire to see me like that, I look up at the ceiling. Have you noticed the wooden beams?"

Greg had neither looked up nor noticed.

"No, but I see them now."

"While with my customers I count them, and when I reach the last of the beams, I start again. And believe me, each second of this contemplation costs them a lot. It is the most expensive of my bodily lending."

"You have a quaint way of expressing yourself," Greg replied. "Where did you learn your English?"

"I learnt it, and I like the way I learnt it. It is one of my gifts, languages. I speak Dutch—" He pushed the sling. "*They* enjoy this the most. I also speak German and Russian, and I can just about manage in Italian and Spanish. Of all the languages Dutch is my favourite. Sexual demands in Dutch are such a simple thing. Like hearing a menu read aloud from top to bottom. It is charming. *Neuken, pijpen, fisten.* If I felt any sort of fondness, I would be fond of my Dutch clients."

"I am surprised you are free tonight. You sound as if you are extremely busy."

"Oh, it was not for pleasure that I went to that cinema. After sex with the manager, which was my objective, I watched that dreadful film, and then thanks to your collapse, I sucked him off again and gained twice as much as I usually do. He is to put it nicely, an insatiable man. I respect his greed." He then smiled at Greg and murmured, "After all, it is greed on both sides, or would you not agree?"

"Are you trying to put me off by having this—well, clinical conversation with me?"

"No, not at all, sit down, please sit down. I will join you on the sofa after I get some cognac. I am really quite civilised."

Greg laughed at this, and he wondered if this young man had ever been a child. He was so obsessed with this question that before Bryce moved to get the drinks he said, "Did you know as a child that you would do this work?"

"Such personal questions! I was a good, Catholic child. I thought only of the priesthood. I had no physical desires at all. I did not even masturbate until I began to wank at this job. *Au fond je suis plutôt monastique.* Now, let's end these personal discussions. After all, you would not like me to ask you if you were a male whore in your childhood."

"Oh, but in some ways I was," replied Greg. "I fought my homosexuality for a while, but my penis insisted on getting pleasure from other boys. I even raped."

"How opposite we are," Bryce observed, and stared at Greg quizzically. "All those years ago and you can say those things about yourself so easily?"

"Of course."

"Why of course?"

"Because my flesh has always needed another's heat."

"Not me. As a child I longed for the cold showers of my Catholic institution. How I adored the rituals. I even believed in God."

"And?"

"At this moment I believe in alcohol. I firmly believe in that. I will have a large cognac with you. This is the time of night that I start to have the longing for a good drink. Drinking goes on to dawn."

"But I came here so that—"

Bryce smiled. Some of the tightness of the smile had loosened, almost as if he was comfortable with Greg, and Greg, observing this, thought maybe he was.

"I promise we will get down to what is called work after a few drinks. Anyway, I need some rest, after my exertion with Adolphe."

"You mean the manager of the cinema?"

"Yes."

Bryce was now moving to a door that led into another room.

"I usually do not give away names. This city is so small. But I have a feeling that you will not want to return to the Bastille."

"I might," Greg replied.

"No, you are passing through. You don't really intend to make your home in Paris, do you?"

"I think I have already decided."

"Well, I don't recommend staying, certainly if you want escorts. I know about a lot of them, and they are boring. You'd have no verbal sparring with them." He paused, then added, "Can you fence?"

"I have never tried."

"It gets you really going. A client taught me. He died two months ago. He was in his late eighties."

"Was he? It's a good age to die," Greg said in a low voice.

Bryce left the room, and Greg got up and went over to look at the sling. He swayed it from side to side like a cradle and he tried to imagine Bryce in it, well lubricated and insensitive to penetration. The image made him turn away and for a moment he wanted to just walk out of the apartment, but he had done that with Nick, or rather, he had escaped from what he had seen, or thought he had seen, and that was more brutal in its possible truth than the truth of Bryce in a sling, waiting for penetration. Why was he taking so long with the cognac? Greg wanted to forget what he had witnessed with Nick. Had he really seen what he thought he had? And here, the thought broke apart as Bryce silently came up to him.

"Fascinated?" he asked, as he passed a large glass of cognac to Greg.

"I just cannot see you in it in my mind. You are too, well, what is the word? Polished."

Bryce waved his glass in the air and some of the cognac spilt onto the wooden flooring.

"I am not polished as you call it when they come for that treatment. In fact, either they or I would at this point demand for the cognac to be licked from the floor, licked until a splinter drew blood."

"But I am guessing that has as yet never happened."

"Would you like me to strip naked now; wipe away my exterior polish and become a crawling man obeying your commands? I *could* do it."

Greg moved swiftly away, back to the black sofa. He examined the leather before sitting on it.

"What about here? If I spilt some cognac here?"

"Do you want to begin?"

"Not yet."

"Then the question is not worth answering. In another room I have a cat. She likes to get drunk. As an *hors d'oeuvre* to any further acts, shall I bring her in and give her a treat? She is all white and very expensive. She bites and hisses at me. We hate each other, but she is useful for sentimental clients who like to have her nearby to make the situation seem romantic. She is intelligent and I believe she knows exactly when to purr for good effect. After all, she may hate me, but I feed her."

Greg sat down and looked up at Bryce.

"What *do* you do with your time outside of this apartment?"

Bryce sat beside him.

"Then it *has* begun."

"What?"

"Work."

"You mean there is a price to pay for information like that?"

Bryce stretched his legs as he had done in the cinema foyer.

"I give nothing of myself away without the money. Even the fact that I have a cat. Are you sure you really want to continue?"

Greg asked the price and was given it. He took out the notes that he had and counted out the required amount. Bryce silently took the money and put it into his trouser pocket.

"So, what do you want to know about me? I warn you in advance that I lie. I often answer questions about my life in situations like this when a client wants to talk. Talk can take the place of sex, and if sex is wanted afterwards, extra money must be given over."

Bryce turned and stared at Greg. His face had become a mask, and Greg knew that any real connection between them was gone. Bryce had become what Greg knew he would be, a void, a nothingness. He no longer existed, and the mask of flesh now no longer saw him. The thought of that annihilation of self brought Greg out in a sweat and the long day was taking its toll on him. He wanted to sleep, but knew he had to remain awake, and it was that which he dreaded the most, for beyond a certain point of exhaustion, the true horror of his hallucinations and terrors began. He had felt the beginnings of exhaustion in Nick's apartment but realised that was only the beginning. What else would he accidentally or by force be made to see?

"The rest of the money that you have in your pocket. I want to see that first, Greg. Some more will be needed if you stay all night. I met you in strange circumstances, and in a way that even I do not understand, I am willing to give more to you than I usually do to a client who comes strictly for the hours that are asked for."

"What generosity!" Greg replied, and he stood up. "May I walk around the room?"

"Of course."

"I don't see any books."

"This is not the only room in the apartment. I have three others."

"And one of those rooms is your bedroom? Is that where the cat is?"

"Yes."

"Do you have books in your bedroom?"

"No, in the spare room. It is my library. I read when I do not see clients. I read for at least four hours a day, and then I walk to the Seine. I always take the same route. I like to be precise in everything that I do."

Greg returned to the sling again and touched it. He knew it was not possible, but he thought he felt slime on it, the slime of abundant sperm. He saw the white on the black, and in one small blob he saw traces of blood. The smell of what he thought he saw was overwhelming.

"Do those who use this cum on this?" he asked.

He heard Bryce's cold laugh.

"Yes. Not always, but yes, most of the time."

"And you? Do you?"

"So now you want sexual talk? Are we moving away from the subject of my personal life? Do you want to concentrate on the sexual function of my experiences with clients?"

"For a while, yes."

"I do not like changing subjects. Are you sure you do not want to know anything more about my personal life, true or false, and to concentrate on the sexuality only?"

"Can't we really do both?"

"No. I am incapable of doing that. Which is it to be?"

Greg stared at the sling in silence for a while and then moved away back to the sofa. The mask was as fixed as before.

"You are wearing a mask, Bryce. I know I will not get any truth about your real life. You have disappeared in a way, and so have I."

"I think we need to drink a lot."

"Why?"

"Because, Greg, you are out of it all, totally, aren't you? There is no mask. You are seeing what is not there."

"Maybe because nothing is there."

Bryce moved uneasily on the sofa, drawing his legs inwards. To Greg's eyes he looked now like a tight, enclosed ball. A human ball encased in an armour of fear.

"I don't want to be—"

"What?" Greg asked.

"Killed."

"I am no threat to you."

Then the awful words came out.

"You are a killer, Greg. It is inside of you. Have you ever tried to kill a man?"

Greg remained silent, and turning his back on Bryce, went over to one of the walls and ran his hands over the hessian.

"This is very 1960s, this material," he said.

"You have not answered my question."

Greg lowered his hand from the material and he remembered that other time in Paris, so long ago, when he *had* nearly killed a man, or was that only a fantasy? Had it really happened? Aurélien. Memory was playing tricks on him. Underage boys in the room. His own murderous desires.

"What are you thinking?"

Greg did not want to turn to look at Bryce. He did not want to see him, with or without his mask.

"Bryce have you ever had young boys here?"

"Do you mean, am I sexually interested in them?"

"No, I am not asking that. But was there ever a client who brought one with him? Either to participate or to watch?"

"I am not answering that."

"Then there was."

Greg's anger, that former violent anger, returned, and he turned his head and looked at the body on the sofa, no longer a rounded ball in armour, but a poor, pathetic being who had blood and guts, and that could be killed.

"No, there has never been—" Bryce paused.

"The *truth*," Greg shouted.

"Alright, only once. A youth came here with his father. He was about fifteen or sixteen. He was brought to me because the father knew his son was gay. He wanted me to initiate the boy, give him his first pleasure."

"And did you give him his first pleasure?"

"Don't attack me, Greg."

"Just tell me the truth. No lies. The truth."

"Alright, the truth. I did. It was mutual masturbation. I was not attracted to him and I gave him the minimum that was needed."

"And where was his father?"

Greg moved towards the sofa and with a defensive gesture Bryce got up and backed his way towards a door behind him.

"Waiting in my study. He did not see anything."

"Was he told afterwards what had happened between you?"

"No."

"And what did the three of you do afterwards? When all three of you were in this room?"

"The man was a singer. An opera singer. He talked about the roles he had played."

Greg laughed at this.

"You are lying."

"What if I am?" Bryce cried out.

Greg looked down at the floor, and in a quiet voice asked Bryce to take off his clothes.

"But—" came the single, pleading word.

"I am too old to hurt you," Greg said, "I have not got the strength."

"I think you have."

"Then that is in your imagination. Once upon a time I could have hurt you, but not now. I just want to see you naked, and then I will go."

Greg fumbled in his pocket and withdrew several high-value notes. He bent down and placed them on the floor between them. He straightened up but did not look at Bryce, his look was directed at the money, and he considered how powerful money was.

"Aren't you going to watch?" Bryce asked.

"No, but I know *you* will see yourself. You will be alone with your naked, animal body. All superiority of clothes gone, and just your all too human flesh. You will be more ashamed to be alone with your flesh than if you were being watched. I know the shame of the human mind."

"That's perverse!"

"Is it? Get on with it. I have paid for this. You're still afraid of me, but I sense you have never had to exhibit yourself without a watcher. I'm looking down. I'm not looking. Now act!"

Greg heard the sounds of Bryce beginning to undress. He heard the buckle of the trousers being undone and could visualise in his mind the fall of them, and then the underwear, but before all that, there was the sound of his shoes. This made him realise that he was doing exactly what he had demanded of him. Very quickly he began to question.

"Did you really want to go into the church when you were young?"

"I am still young."

"I know that, but when you were a child?"

"I've already said so."

"But out of no love of Christ or the church?"

"I told you I believed in God. I had a crucifix in my bedroom. My mother had it put on a side table beside my bed. I had fantasies about torturing this naked, suffering body, and I thought of putting more blood onto the white ivory flesh of Christ. Christ was always white in the Catholic church. I played with my cock, but nothing came out. I realised then that no fantasies could really induce any sexual pleasure in me."

"Did that make you want to shut yourself away?"

"After a while, things changed. I no longer wanted to torture him. I wanted to comfort him. I knew I could, once I could ejaculate. I wanted to warm him with my hot sperm, and then after I had smeared it over his flesh I would warm him even more by licking it off. I have always been unexcited. I did not want any sexual contact with anyone, except as I said after abandoning the torture fantasies, the sexual fantasy of satisfying the statue. It was what I lived for as a child. Then, when puberty arrived, my thoughts shifted away. I felt that I had been abandoned by the statue. I had failed him both in torture and in love. I felt worthless. Then I began to think all men and their bodies were without worth. I felt no desire for them either." He paused, then said, "I am totally naked now."

"But is your body really worthless?" Greg asked.

"I know it has monetary worth. Only that. I can see its worth; I can see it now. It's sexuality that appeals and my so-called charm." Then angrily he shouted, "Why don't you look at me?"

"I may, or I may not." Greg paused, and then sighed as he asked, "Is this the only time you have spoken the truth in front of a client?"

"Why do you say that?"

"Your words are as naked as you are. That's why."

Greg now looked at the naked body in front of him. He did not look at Bryce's face, but at the body and its contours, and above all at the heavy sex that hung so still between his legs.

"I've seen enough," he said, and turned his back on Bryce.

"Don't you really want me?"

The way Bryce said this was pitiful, because Greg realised that perhaps no one had ever turned him down before.

"Nothing about your body interests me."

Greg looked around him; at the hollowness of the room; at its poverty of anything that could arouse feeling.

"Why don't you want me?"

"You are not Nick," Greg simply replied. "I will not explain further about that, other than just using his name. What *you* have is no doubt impressive to most, but there is nothing of light there. Not for me, anyway. I cannot bear the weight of it. Your thick cock and your big balls. And yet I am sure, for many, they are worth their weight in gold."

"There is no need to insult me anymore."

Bryce dressed and came back into Greg's field of vision. He stared into Greg's face, and the mask was there. If it had been gone while Greg was not looking at it, he would never know. But now, the features were completely covered. Greg knew there was nothing they could say to each other. Looking down, he saw the money he had placed on the floor.

"Don't you want to pick it up?" he asked.

"No."

"Why?"

"Because you made me an object of disgust. I was even afraid you might hurt me. I cannot accept money for an act that was so horrible to me."

Greg watched as Bryce bent down and picked up the notes, and then continued watching as he handed them back to him.

"Take them!"

"Money is worthless as well," Greg said quietly.

"The right money *is* worth it, but yours is not," Bryce replied, and then he took Greg's right hand and forcibly placed the notes between his fingers. He walked back to the sofa and sat there, not looking at Greg but staring at the wall. For a while, neither of them moved, but slowly Greg made his way to the front door of the apartment. He opened it and went out of the room, not once looking back. Outside in the street, the night air was cold.

The first thing Greg did was to go to an ATM to withdraw more money. He was overspending fast. He eventually found a shabby hotel that was open all night in the Rue de Rennes. It was near the station, in close proximity to the black mausoleum of the one truly hideous building in Paris, and the destructive ruin of the old Montparnasse. The room was functional, and not very clean. He wondered if the sheets had been changed, and he lay down fully clothed on the bed. He had no desire to check what time it was, and with a last, almost despairing look at the room he fell into a deep sleep. He dreamt of nothing that he could remember, and when he awoke, the light at the window hit him like a blow.

The hotel served breakfast in a small downstairs room. Greg felt hungry and went down to see what it consisted of. The breakfast was as mean and shabby as the rest of the place. When he sat down, there was only one woman seated at a separate table. She looked like a beaten-up version of Anouk Aimée, wearing a headscarf in exactly the same way Anouk Aimée would have worn it in the 1950s or 1960s. Greg looked at her and felt the full wretchedness of time. She returned his look and smiled. He smiled back and returned to his rock-hard croissant and the revolting black coffee that went with it. The jam on the side looked watery, clearly thinned out on purpose, and he avoided it.

"They don't give much here, do they?"

Her voice was loud and American.

"No, they don't," he laughed back. He then added, "but they also don't charge as much for their rooms as many other hotels."

He had no desire to defend the place, but his immediate thought was that the woman's expectations were too high.

"I don't have much of an appetite anyway. But I do wish the croissants were fresher. Not many people down here this morning," she added.

"No," he said, and stared at the coffee, then made a whirlpool inside the cup by stirring it fast. He wished he had bought himself a bottle of cognac the night before on his walk through Montparnasse.

"I should have asked for tea," the woman persisted.

"I don't think they have tea."

The woman interjected with a braying sound, "Oh yes, they sure do. Every hotel has tea."

"Next time," Greg said.

"No, I am going back to the States. A week here is enough. I don't speak French. I should have stayed in England. You're English, aren't you?"

"I am afraid so."

"Why afraid? It's a great country, the United Kingdom. Never been to Scotland, Wales or Ireland, but what I saw of England took my breath away. Everyone so nice and kind and polite, not like where I come from where you are constantly pushed around. Alabama. Do you know the States?"

Greg shook his head and only smiled in reply. His head was beginning to ache, and he was relieved when a young man joined them in the room. He was fresh-faced and had a backpack with him. His clothes were dirty, and he looked as if he had been walking through France on foot.

"Hello," he said politely, sitting as far away from Greg and the woman as he could. He then went over to get his coffee and the last croissant. His gestures were nervous. He sat down and jumped up again going to fetch some milk for the coffee. Greg had seen the milk. Along with the rest, it was far from fresh.

"Are you English too?" the woman shouted over at him.

The young man stared over at her and shook his head with a sigh.

"Italian," he said.

"I've never been to Italy. Which part do you come from?"

"I'm afraid my English is not—well, it is just not." He turned his head and looked down at the meagre food on his plate. Greg sensed that he did not want to communicate with older people and that he understood English very well. As youth often does with age, he had that unwritten sign on his face, don't talk to me. You are too old and should be dead. He had seen it before, that large sign, as big as a billboard. Avoiding the little that remained of his croissant and coffee, Greg stood up and said goodbye to the woman. Then without looking at the Italian, he left the room. He longed for his luggage, so that he could change into a fresh shirt. Despite a quick shower at the end of the long corridor on his floor, he felt unclean. Youth can look like this, he thought, but a man of my age can't. I too, despite my years, have a repulsion towards the dirt of the old. He went to the receptionist, who was different from the one who had checked him in the night before, and politely he thanked her for accepting late clients. She was almost as old as him and looked at him wearily.

"The owner of the hotel understands that people can find themselves stranded in the middle of the night," she said.

"I certainly could not have walked all night," he replied and smiled.

"Does Monsieur want to spend another night here?"

Greg took some money from his jacket pocket and told her he would pay for another night. He had no idea what he would choose to do, but felt this was a sort of security. She saw the money and her face looked friendlier than it had before.

"Usually people only stay one night. We're not a very attractive place for tourists, but more of a place for—how do you say it in English?—the more desperate kind of person."

"Desperate?" Greg queried.

"Yes. Men or women who do not know where to go, and have little to spend. There should be more places like ours. You have them in your country?"

Yes, Greg thought, hostels. I can see in my mind the ones I have known in Brighton. Quite a sight! Worthy of Tennessee Williams in their desperation and low cost. How much had they cost there? He vaguely recalled, a higher price than this hotel. He had once been inside one, and in the lounge he had seen the weary and the weak in spirit sitting in broken-down chairs, no doubt picked up at a local market. He had wondered then what these people's stories were and why they were there. Some were young, but most were not. Derelicts cast up on Brighton's hard stones; the *almost* homeless he called them, and lucky to be on that lower rung and not slumped in doorways.

"And what will Monsieur do with his day?" the receptionist asked.

"I will enjoy Paris," he replied, trying to sound flippant.

There is nowhere to go, Greg thought as he stared at the woman. She had her place in this hotel, and things she had to do, but he had nothing. He knew at the back of his mind that it would be hard for him to find a suitable room to live in, and yet in the forefront of his mind, he fully realised he would stay and would have to be dragged back to Brighton by force if it came to it. Who knew what the UK's eventual departure from the European Union would mean? All thought of this then retreated. He had the whole day before him, and he was tired, tired, tired, but no, he refused to go back up to that hotel room and rest for any longer, and he was hungry. The stale croissant had only tickled his stomach. He had to eat. Anything. Even the worst of food, even the worst of flesh.

"I will discover parts of Paris I never even knew existed," he added with a laugh.

"Monsieur will discover plenty. Turn the city on its back and see the creatures crawl like maggots. Monsieur will have an even louder laugh after that!"

He respected her cynicism, and he suspected she sensed his own.

Then the American woman joined them.

"Are you staying on?" the receptionist asked.

The weary tone of voice that had at first been directed at him, was now directed at the American. Greg looked sideways at the headscarf that was almost strangling her. Her face, too gaudily painted, looked pitiful in its despair, pleading in its sad way to be adored, or at the least, looked at.

"Oh no," she said. "I must go today. I told the receptionist yesterday but he must have forgotten. I'm all paid up. I have a flight this evening. So I just have time to take one last look at the place before I leave. And I must buy some postcards to send back to Alabama." She paused for a second and then added breathlessly, "Do you think I can find some nearby?"

"There's always somewhere to buy postcards, Madame."

"Call me Irene. No one has, so far. I hate all this Madame this, Madame that. I mean after all, I'm not married."

"Tell me when you want to call for a taxi," and the receptionist turned away and looked at the computer behind her.

"Also, I would like to leave my luggage for a couple of hours," Irene said.

The receptionist turned and Greg caught her look as she stared at him instead of Irene. There was a smile that almost replied, you don't have to go far for the maggots.

Greg moved away from them both. The word luggage echoed in his ears. In his flight from Nick's apartment it had not mattered, but it did now. He had enough money on him for fresh clothes and he could easily change in a café toilet and then bin what he had on.

"Is there a *grand magasin* on the Rue de Rennes?" he asked, returning to the receptionist.

"I don't know," came the reply. "I live in the suburbs, and buy everything there. What is it you need?"

He was too embarrassed to say, and Irene who was still going on about her taxi, piped up, "This city is full of shops. Perfumes, jewellery, special things." She patted her headscarf and added, "I bought this here. I just couldn't resist. I mean, in Alabama they don't know how to put them on this way and the patterns there are so awful."

"I just need a few, well, extras," Greg said.

"Clothes?" the receptionist asked.

Greg realised how astute she was. She *knew* he had nothing.

"As it happens—"

58

"I understand. Walk down the Rue de Rennes. There's bound to be somewhere, but do check the prices. Ordinary clothes in Paris cost more than they should. It all costs more than it should, and with taxes rising—" She paused, and fiddled with a couple of keyrings. "I'm not talking politics. I'm talking common sense. That Macron!" She let go of the keyrings and raised her hands in the air.

"Our President Trump doesn't like him," Irene said. Her voice was much louder than before, as if she wanted to broadcast the fact.

"What does he know?" the receptionist replied, defending her President even though she did not approve of him.

Greg left them to it and went out into the street making his way down towards the Boulevard Saint-Germain. He asked a passing stranger and she suggested Le Bon Marché on the Rue de Sèvres. She did not have to explain the way, as he instinctively turned down the Rue Saint-Placide. It was not that far, but his limbs ached. His mouth was parched and his need for food was getting more and more insistent. He had to conquer his needs, and he somehow did. To prevent a panic and possibly a fainting fit, he avoided looking around him until he got to the shop. Hurriedly he tried on a couple of suits, choosing a dark grey one and a black one. He selected a few neutral ties and several assorted shirts. The choice of underwear was confusing, and he rejected those that he thought were too young for him. He eventually found what he thought seemed suitable for his age and lots of pairs of black socks. He was about to pay and get out of the dreary place when he saw a pair of black shoes he liked. They fitted and were added to the bill. He paid with his card and left the shop. Once outside, he made his way back to the Rue de Rennes and chose a café that looked expensive, as he knew that only expensive cafés would have a suitable toilet to change in. He sat on the terrace and tried to relax, and soon the waiter came up to him.

"Monsieur?"

"Two sandwiches with lots of ham," Greg said. Suddenly he no longer wanted to speak in French. He had been tired by the constant patter of words spoken at Le Bon Marché. His tongue felt dry, his mouth thick and full, and the taste was bad. The waiter, a big man with a boxer's face, broken in, beaten up, and yet with the familiar voice of one who is there to serve, repeated what he had ordered in French, and then stared down at Greg with a look of contempt that he had ordered such basic food, or that is what Greg imagined.

"*Et à boire?*"

"Two cognacs. Large."

After he had gone, Greg stared down at the table. He picked up the menu which he had not looked at before and saw there was a far wider choice of dishes available: *steak tartare* and shellfish, even *choucroute*. This was after all a *brasserie*, and the sandwiches were indeed the cheapest things on offer. He put the menu back, face down on the table, and put his hands in his lap. His sex stirred beneath the touch, and he imagined his cock screaming at him, "What of me? what of me? I am as old as you are, but I have too much spunk left, too much, and it's frustrating me. You missed your chance last night. You could at least have let me make friends with Bryce's heavy prick and balls! What an old idiot you are. I am not as stupid as you, so don't miss your chance again, otherwise I will die on you—deliberately die on you! I want a few more shots at cumming before I burn up in the crematorium." He removed his hands, unable to bear the protesting movement in his underwear. Maybe he would try to masturbate when changing his clothes, but although silent now, he knew the frustrated penis would not be satisfied. Why should it be? Why should it be destined to a last few years of never seeing another erect cock, juice oozing from the glans, salivating like one dog greeting another? Even a tired but defiant old cock has to see the last of the day, has to be able to recollect its past triumphs.

The waiter returned with two plates, a sandwich on each,

which Greg thought was a waste of plates. He also brought two glasses of cognac. These were all neatly balanced on a platter poised high on top of his fingertips. Deftly, the waiter placed each of them on the table. His smashed in, but still vaguely attractive face stared down at Greg. The look was not one of trust and Greg politely asked if he could pay now.

"*Comme vous voulez, Monsieur.*"

No, it is as *you* wish, Greg thought, and looking down at the white bill, picked it up in silence and looked at the price. He was about to remark that he had been charged too much, when his cock came to a full erection in his trousers, clearly sensing the *beau moche* presence of the waiter and yet again protesting, but this time without the tirade. Greg put his hand into his trouser pocket to get the remainder of his notes, and through the thin material felt a wet patch—pre-cum from the tip of his inflamed penis. He placed the money on the silver platter and the waiter's hairy hand seized it.

"Keep the change," Greg said, without looking at him. The waiter moved away without a thank you, or if there was a mumbled *merci*, Greg did not hear it.

"*Il est toujours misérable,*" a voice said at a table behind Greg, and he turned to see the smiling face of an elderly man of his own generation.

"*Toujours?*" Greg questioned.

"*Toujours. Je pense que sa vie n'est pas très gaie. Je dis cela dans le sens ancien du terme.*"

Greg replied that he was tired and did the man speak English?

"Of course."

"So, why do you think his life isn't very happy?"

"I come here every day, as I live nearby, and he is always working. I don't think he has a home life, but with the face he has—and what is that delightful expression in English—like the back of a bus? I can only guess he has been rejected as a lover, many times."

"He has a powerful body," Greg replied, but felt foolish.

The comment sounded erotic, at least to him, and he had no desire to show the erotic side of his nature to this unknown man.

"Yes, but most women want a bit more charm. What do you think?"

"I think he looks like an ex-boxer who has been beaten up once too often," Greg replied. "That surely has a charm for some."

"Maybe. Women often have strange tastes. I know that from personal experience."

Greg did not want to go into this man's personal experiences and noticing that he was reading a book, and as he could not see the title, asked what it was.

"*L'Enfer. Henri Barbusse.*"

Hell, Greg thought. How appropriate.

"Have you read it?" the man asked.

"No. I remember a close friend of mine had it on his shelf. The title seemed so final, or it did at the time. That was back in the 1970s."

The man passed the book over to Greg.

"My name is Serge, by the way."

"How do you do, Serge," and Greg took the book into his hands. It was an old copy in French and had clearly been read multiple times. "What sort of hell is it?" he asked.

"The one we make for ourselves. What else? A man in a room, still young—around thirty, has a crack in his wall through which he peers into a neighbouring room. I have read it so many times, and yet I still cannot remember whether it is a hotel or his own room. He sees most of the worst of life in that room, and the hell he sees there makes him want to leave it. But as if by some osmosis, the hell attaches itself to him. His body breaks up and he loses his sight. As we all do if we look into the abyss for too long."

"You are a philosopher," Greg said, looking down at the nondescript cover.

"No, I observe. For example, our poor waiter here. He is in

a sort of hell. I am sure he wants to be wanted. The yearning looks he gives every attractive woman who sits on this terrace express that. He drools, and his wet smile only makes his face seem even more broken up. You described him well as an ex-boxer. I don't think that has been his profession, although it looks like it. I think by his own will he put himself at some time into the gangster world of Paris."

"We all have our fantasies about strangers," Greg said.

"I gave you my name. What is yours?"

"Greg."

"Gregory?"

"No, Greg."

Serge laughed. He had a rounded face, thinning blond hair and blue eyes. Greg thought how attractive he must have been. Then the words 'must have been' tolled like a bell within him. It was a death bell for his own generation. He is my contemporary, he thought, he might even be thinking the same of me, except he probably does not look at men in the same sexual way as I do.

"I think you should read the book, Greg. I imagine you are here on holiday. Or are you living here?"

"I'm not sure," Greg said, and he did not want to go into the reasons why. He did not want to say that he was now a refugee, perhaps ultimately unwanted anywhere due to the situation that England was putting itself in. Would he be allowed to live in Paris?

"Then whatever you are doing here, I give you the book."

"How do you know I can read in French?"

"You are too intelligent not to. I know when an Englishman understands our language. Call it intuition."

"That's very kind of you. I will read it."

"I have another copy at home," Serge said. "So, please do not think I am giving away any great treasure. Maybe I have read the novel too many times. Even though memory denies me the fact of whether it's a hotel or not." He waved one hand in the air, and said, "At my age, you know, you sometimes lose your memory."

"Me too," Greg replied.

Serge got up from his table and came over to where Greg was sitting. He sat down next to him and placed *L'Enfer* into Greg's hands.

"I don't know how to thank you. We are strangers and—"

"—and a stranger gives you a book. Strangers should give things to each other. I believe many people would get a benefit from that, and I repeat, I do have another in my house." Then Serge looked at Greg and added, "I think I had better say now that I am not a sad, lonely homosexual looking for a partner. I am heterosexual."

Greg laughed.

"I *am* homosexual," Greg replied.

"Looking for a partner?"

"Yes. But either he is out of my life, or I have just found him. I don't mean to sound enigmatic about this. Yesterday I believed I had found the man I lost years ago."

Serge moved his chair sideways and looked at Greg quizzically.

"Either you did, or you didn't."

"Ah, but you see, my mind imagines things. Be careful, or I might look at you and think you are one of my lost brothers from Portslade."

"Is that a place? Your English cities are so many and have the most amusing names. I remember seeing a place called Middlesborough on the map and I immediately thought of *Middlemarch* by George Eliot. Have you read it? Oh, never mind about that." He waved his hand in the air again and the waiter came hurrying over. Serge asked Greg what he would like to drink, and Greg accepted a cognac.

"*Un whisky sans glace, et un cognac.*"

"*Oui Monsieur*," and the waiter looked down at them, and Greg wondered what he was thinking. He said this to Serge.

"Oh, he's intrigued perhaps. I mean, I come here every day. It is my spot on the map as they say, and I live nearby in the Rue Saint-Sulpice. Number 11. A gloomy entrance, but the apartment inside is quite reasonable. I bought it a long time ago when it was still possible to buy at a fair price."

"I must have passed it quite a few times back in 1969."

Serge seemed not to want to probe this, but changing the subject said, "It's odd, but I have not met many homosexual men in my life. I guess I was never their type, or I simply did not notice. When I was young, I found every woman to be far too beautiful, and here I am, an old man, unmarried, and always have been." Then he paused and said softly, "But I do have one story to tell. It was in the late 80s, or was it the very early 90s? At a party given for some literary event of no importance I was introduced to a young man who admitted to being an amateur writer, and we did become friends. I was of course at the time horrified by the AIDS epidemic, and I was stupidly afraid of any man approaching me. I could see that he was homosexual, and he told me so. We talked about literature for hours. He had been a friend of Hervé Guibert and he was slightly sour about that. He asked Guibert to look at his work—he had written a sort of *récit*, and it was he implied a sort of testimony. Guibert, he said, was strangely ungenerous and said he would read it, then never contacted him again. As you know, Guibert died in 1991, so my meeting with Didier—that was his name—must have been in the late 80s. And do you know what? Didier gave me his manuscript, quite simply, at a second meeting we had in a café. We were complete strangers, and he had absolutely no other feeling for me beyond being another interesting stranger. I was, as now, a literary man myself, but unlike him, I had never attempted either a novel or a *récit*."

The cognac and the whisky arrived, and Greg wanted to pay.

"Absolutely not," Serge said, and laid the amount needed on the table.

"Thank you," Greg said.

"Now, I would like to ask *you* something."

"Anything you like," and Greg drank half of the cognac.

"Would *you* accept this manuscript?"

"What?" Greg exclaimed, surprised.

"Would you accept this manuscript?"

"But it's nothing to do with me. It's not even published."

"Didier, and that is the only name he put to the *récit*, would I'm sure be pleased to know that it had returned to someone of his own kind. He may be alive, he may be dead, but I am convinced that you probably won't want to get it published. I never knew his surname, so in practice you would have great difficulty in locating him."

"I am slightly offended when you say *someone of his own kind.* We are not exactly a tribe or a species," Greg said.

"Oh, please excuse me. I apologise. Are you in any hurry at the moment?"

"Not really, no. Except I am feeling tired from talking so much."

"I understand. You want a rest. Could I leave you here for no longer than an hour, and then return with it and give it to you?"

"But I still don't see why."

"It is a text that needs to exist for another person other than myself. I think you are that other person."

"Are you giving me yet another *L'Enfer*?" Greg replied.

"I will let you judge that for yourself." Serge said this with a lowered voice. "If I die, I do not want anybody to find it in my apartment. They will think perhaps that I have written it and given myself another name. And it's not that I am ashamed of people thinking I am homosexual, but as I am not, I don't want them to get the wrong idea." He paused, then added slowly, "It was not my fight. Deep down, I was not interested. All those deaths. I did not see it as a community concern."

"You were not alone in that," Greg replied.

"So it is not just *my* cowardice?"

"Everyone has—had—their reasons at the time."

The words came out with bitterness, and Serge noticed.

"Not many red badges of courage, eh?"

"No, there were many, but despite those many badges, there were many more who either denied AIDS, or escaped into the past; the golden past when everything was just fine, including the usual curable diseases."

"That's sad."

"Yes, I suppose it is," Greg replied and finished off the cognac.

"Will you wait?" Serge asked.

"Maybe I could walk with you to your door?" Greg suggested. "I can't drink any more. I drink too much."

"I cannot invite you in," Serge said, getting up as he said the words."

"I will wait in the entrance. I have no desire to disturb you. Quite frankly I am getting too old to converse for too long. It's as if I haven't got the time for it."

"You are offended?"

Greg was, and yet, at the same time he was relieved.

"Not at all," he said. "I am just proposing a better offer than staying on this terrace. I will fall asleep and then the waiter will definitely throw me out."

Serge agreed, but Greg noticed there was a definite note of reluctance in his voice. Both standing, they faced each other.

"Do graphic descriptions disgust you?" Greg asked bluntly. "I assume there is something in this text that most men would be revolted by—straight men, that is."

Serge was clearly silently angry at this rebuke, but replied, "I just want it out of my flat, and into other anonymous hands. I also want to tell you that this man Didier wrote it first in French, and then translated it in English on the opposite side of his manuscript pages. I have no idea why he did this. I assume he liked your language as much as I do."

Greg accepted what he said but sensed a definite coolness between them now. It was as if a shady transaction had to be done; something not altogether clean, that had to be wiped away from Serge's memory.

"Were many AIDS books published back then?" Serge asked, feigning interest.

"Maybe more were here," Greg replied, and they began walking. "My country produced books *on* the subject; the sort of consoling rubbish that usually described an AIDS death as just entering another room. All very *bring on the light* and *cast out the darkness*. There was no equivalent to Hervé Guibert, Pascal de Duve, or Cyril Collard, that is for sure, and most publishers, queer or otherwise, kept their distance."

Serge sighed, and once more changed the subject. "So, what about Brexit?"

"We will probably crash out."

"You really think so?"

"The battle between the sides has become too entrenched to agree to any deal. This has of course opened the way for the extreme right."

"There are many who want a *Frexit* here."

"Are you one of them?"

They were passing the monolith that was Saint-Sulpice church, and Greg casually looked up at the solid nature of its structure; as *beau moche* as the waiter had been. He loved not loving it and could not imagine it not being there. And yet there was no sense of lightness, and he thought of the word *légèreté* and the lack of it in its construction. How had he thought of it all those years ago? Fifty years? Could it be that long? *Tous mes jours et mes nuits devant le pissoir,* he concluded. Then the present clanged the door, cast iron in its impenetrability, on what was, and he looked at Serge who was hesitating to answer his question.

"I support neither the right nor the left, nor what is unfortunately in the middle. Macron."

"And the *Gilets Jaunes?"*

"I was not on the barricades back in '68, so I am certainly not going to join a mass of the righteous, joining up with hoodlums, to destroy the Champs-Élysées."

"But surely, there must be good people on the left? I would join them."

"Socialism has no meaning anymore," Serge said defiantly.

They had reached the dark entrance to the Rue Saint-Sulpice building, and Greg waited as Serge disappeared up the communal wooden stairs that smelled of fading polish. To pass the time he read the names of the people on the postal boxes, but they were all last names, and none signified where Serge lived. After all, they had not exchanged surnames and they had both reached that point in their stranger status where they had no desire or saw no point in doing so. Then came the hard sound of Serge's shoes on the stairs, and coming into the light, Greg saw him hold out a brown package. In silence he placed it in Greg's hands.

"Take care of yourself," Serge said briskly, now free of the burden he had been holding.

"You too," Greg replied, and they smiled at each other; the fixed smile of two people who would never meet again.

"Goodbye."

"Goodbye," Greg replied, and he left the dark house.

Once out on the street, Greg made his way to the Odéon Métro station. Barbusse was small enough to slip into his pocket and Greg put the brown package into the bag he was carrying that contained the suits, shoes and other clothes. He had not, as he had intended, changed out of the suit he was wearing. He had not gone down into the *brasserie* toilet. This is all I wish to ever carry, he thought, as he approached the steps leading down to the Métro's own heart of darkness; a hell of strangers in itself. He got his *carnet* of tickets and made his way along with the others to a destination; the only difference being that he did not have one. He only felt the brutal push of the crowd urging him forward and he clasped the bag of his new possessions closely to him as he was swept along.

He boarded the train in the direction of Porte de Clignancourt, and with trembling fingers, he brought out the brown package. He tore at the crisp, ageing paper, and revealed a tall hard-backed exercise book. The cover was printed with black lines and small squares. Opening it, he saw on the first page, the price. 25^{F}00. And then turning further, the text began. There was no title, except, at the top of the page:

Didier's Manuscript

Then there was a space and a quote from a book by Witold Gombrowicz, but the name of the book was not given. He read:

Everything depends on the first chord struck, for that is the only one we are free to choose; all those that follow flow inevitably from the first.

Greg had read many of Gombrowicz's works. Was this from his diaries? Or *Ferdydurke*? Or *Pornografia*? He guessed it was none of these, possibly *Trans-Atlantyk*, but then he shook his head. No, it was one of the others, but which? He should have known. He must have known. No, he had to stop thinking and read the manuscript. He was alone and it was as if fate decreed that he should be alone to read the text as no one else came to sit beside him. He did not look to see what time of day it was. The train was deserted, even though at Châtelet and Les Halles it usually filled up with passengers.

"I must concentrate," he said to himself, "concentrate on the text." He began to read.

Two-thirty in the afternoon waiting for the first half-dozen people to go in, standing on the corner, leaning up against the wall of a café, watching closely and counting—he is there, his eyes staring at the entrance and the words 'Interdit aux moins de 18 ans'. He must go in. He must join them. He hurries

70

across the street, not looking either way, almost hit by a car hurtling too fast, just escaping what would probably have been a fatal blow. Death. No, he must not think of that. He hands his money over and goes inside. The film has already begun. The print is worn, the image is blurred, yet despite the blurring, he sees the essential; he sees all that he needs to see. By the side of the large cinema screen, a smaller video screen catches his attention, the images less blurred, magnified, in a concentrated space. The acts are vivid, the colour brighter. A foot comes into focus, and the foot appears strange by itself, the toes thrusting forward and wriggling. It is as if the whole of sexual desire is concentrated in that foot; five toes first tightly spaced, then spreading slowly, opening like a sexual orifice; the big toe separating more than the others. A face then coming into view, joining the foot. Foot and face, close to each other, but not touching. He wants them to touch. He wants the face to lick the foot, discarding the rest of the body that is not visible on the screen. He wants to see a frantic licking tongue make the toes writhe and twist. An instant of time passes, and the head does dart forward, reptilian in its rapidity, filling the field of vision entirely. A mouth slit widening in the face, pretending a smile that is not a smile, darts as if to eat. The reptilian gesture catches the foot, or to be exact, the toe of the foot. The camera; the camera of life and hunger, has moved. The reptile mouth, futilely hoping to swallow entirely, consuming, yet not consuming, not able to tear it from the rest of the flesh, sucks. Sucks with intensity, with hopeless need, seeking a satisfaction that he, the watcher, cannot understand, nor even wish to experience. Yet his fascination for this sexual act without the penis is desperate for orgasm. He wants to see the mouth withdraw and the big toe erupt, pouring forth its own liquid. He longs to see the liquid slide down the side of the nail, the jagged toenail, rimmed with dirt. Then his longing subsides, recognising the impossible, and concentrates on the face with the mouth; concentrates on the specifics of the face to determine for himself whether it is attractive to him. The face is bland, bland pink, similar to the bland pink of the toe. He cannot decide. He watches as the smile/grimace widens as it moves to the other toes, trying to enfold all of them in one lunge. He cannot see the eyes, or what colour they are, for the eyes are closed. The face is topped by a fringe of fair to white hair; hair too long left in the sun perhaps, but his concentration on detail does not allow him to think beyond the image. He sees a bland face, a wide mouth and a foot being sucked upon. And then, when the composite image falls completely into place, he turns his head away from the screen. His eyes have become accustomed to the near-darkness around him. The reflected light from the cinema screen, that he has no interest in watching, splashes out in front of him. In the fluttering spasmodic splashes of light, changing continually in colour and intensity, he observes the details of the place itself. The cinema is, as he first perceived, a long corridor; but this simplicity of design is broken by points of entrance to other places; points of entrance in both walls. He walks down the aisle by the right wall, coming to a space for a door, without a door. He goes in and finds himself in a toilet area. A white urinal is clearly visible, and behind doors (this time there are doors) are sit-down toilets. He can see them, although the doors are closed, for there are observation holes; round circles pierced into each door. They are big enough, these holes, to see the part of the body below the waist, or a face if the body is sitting and not standing. He glances quickly, his sight invading the circle, and sees thick black pubic hair, not lessened in its blackness by the overhead pink light, but somehow made darker by it. He sees the black hair, and in it, erect, pink against pink, the penis, thrust out from the protection of its black home. The glans is large, and in the centre of the circle of the tip, seen through the circle of the pierced hole in the door, he sees drops of liquid form, but not fall, for he turns away. He has seen all this detail in one quick, rapid glance. A man has joined him, or rather is *standing near him, for the space is concentrated. The man is dressed only in a T-shirt, for the jogging shorts he is wearing are pushed down to his ankles. He stands in front of the white urinal, the white too made strangely whiter by the pink light, his body light and hairless, a penis shaved of all hair, hanging long and limp before the urinal. He watches as the man thrusts both hands forward to grasp, to excite the limp hanging object; watches as the hands pump and pull to coax it into an object of desire. Yet the object is reluctant and will not cooperate, and the man wriggles as he stands there, contracting his buttocks, thrusting and pushing, pulling and teasing. He feels tempted to go to the man, to reach out with his own hands to help, for his immediate reaction, not thought, is to help impotence. He senses, even if he does not put it into mental words, the fear of another's impotence. He watches as the wriggling becomes more acute, more desperate in movement. Then the jogging shorts are hurriedly pulled up, and the hairless object is bundled away. The man leaves the urinal and goes out into the wider region of the cinema, but he, the watcher, still continues to stand there, waiting, but not waiting, conscious of the fulfilled state of erection behind the closed toilet door, but not wanting, not needing to go towards it. He wonders how long he will wait without waiting, but this thought has no answer, for another man has entered the definition of space that he has defined for himself. This space is the space around the circle of his own body. A man, balding but young, moves quickly, grabbing at him, squeezing at the limp sex within his own trousers. His instinct of revulsion is equally rapid and brutal. He pushes the hand away, watches the instant retreat, and is surprised to see that the man without offence or visible reproach then falls to his knees before the toilet door. The top of the balding head glistens in the light, sweat pooling there in the hairless centre. As the hidden face presses closer against the pierced circle in the door, the water on the circle of the head runs into the thin hair, matting it. He watches as the man begins to bob his head up and down and realises that the penis on the other side of the door, through the space of the circle in the door, is now in the man's mouth. He, the watcher, moves himself to one side, by only an inch, to see clearer, to see the pink glans meet the pink mouth. He is reminded of the foot and the mouth on the screen and rushes from the toilet, impatient to witness what further activity is to be seen there. The cinema seats are almost full. Gazes are fixed intently on both video and cinema screen, each sharing distinct scenarios, and in a communal gesture he joins with them, watches with them. This time he ignores the video and concentrates on the large screen. A boy, for the object there can be no more than fifteen or sixteen at most, is lying back on a white bed, the young body splayed out, hips thrust forward, small sex unaroused, perhaps unable to be aroused. His face is vacant, empty, possibly drugged-out. An older man is standing over him, holding a large artificial penis. The boy appears to retreat from it, drawing back into the bed in a motion almost like dying; both sluggish and frantic, for in this futile gesture, there is the very opposite of life. The man advances towards him. He asks the boy, or rather commands the boy, to open his legs wider, to raise his legs upwards, to open the circle that is the anus. The boy obeys. On his face is a stare of blank horror at the size of the black, heavily veined penis, and yet the anus widens, the lips there opening, as pink as the mouth, as pink as the foot, and with a cry nearer to a growl, the man approaches the lips and thrusts savagely, beginning his invasion. The watcher watches as the boy watches the invasion of his own body. The head of the false object, the black-veined thing is the first to go in; with difficulty it broadens the hole, then with a scream of tearing flesh, the passage is made easier, and the long, thick machine-made object fulfils the will of the man pushing it. It is too much to bear, to watch this intrusion. He stares at the cinema screen; the people there no longer images on film, but real. Turning, he runs towards the exit, tripping on the exit step, but does not fall. He feels faint, but does not faint, balancing himself against the light of the day.*

Greg reached Porte de Clignancourt, and promptly made the return journey back in the direction of Porte d'Orléans. His hands were shaking as he held the manuscript, and a wet smear of sweat from his fingers made a stain over some of the written words. He closed the pages, for a while, then as the train gathered speed, he once again resumed reading.

The second time, the second visit, the second day at exactly the same time as before, he places his money at the entrance, and the grabbing hand of the man behind the till does not look at him. He goes into the cinema. He has returned, but instead of moving, of exploring, he sits down and remains seated, and a long time passes without him looking at the multiple sexual activities on the screen or the activities around him. He has dressed according to what he believes will suit the place best: loose hanging white trousers and a black shirt. His eyes are closed, and seen from the outside he looks as if he were dying, or already dead. The flickering light of the screen falls unshielded onto his face for he is seated in the front row. His head leans back against the rough texture of a material worn with age and use, and the heated (for they have turned the heating on in the cinema, although outside it is a warm spring day) fetid atmosphere makes his own body first hot and then sweat. Without opening his eyes, he unbuttons his shirt, displaying himself for the first time. The dead white of his face is in total contrast to the hairless pink flesh that is now revealed to the navel. At the navel, just above the top of the closed trousers, a tuft of black hair betrays his sexuality. Without thinking, he passes his right hand across his chest, wiping the sweat that is forming there; and this simple gesture must have been noticed, must have already provoked attention, for within seconds he feels the presence of another beside him. He senses the warmth of skin and the smell of sweat akin to his own. He feels neither attraction nor revulsion at its nearness. It is the same as his own: neutral. He feels nothing, remaining motionless in the seat, his head thrown back, his hands now at his sides. He looks as if he is ready, as if he has thrown off all reserve. Then he feels a hand that is not his own caress the same area of skin that he had previously touched. Without moving, he allows the unseen hand to move up from his navel to his throat, moving in one slow climb. The hand opens there, and fingers widen, clutching him, trying to throttle. He gasps for breath, and alarmed, the fingers retreat, going back quickly the way they had come, down to the tuft of pubic hair, then upwards again, arriving at the navel, revolving there an instant in a circular touch of exploration. His eyes are glued shut. He does not want to see. He is awake but in a sort of death. He feels the hand progress to the division of his chest, and now there is gentleness. It is as if the fingers speak of words of love, of eternal giving; fingers singing old songs of passion and longing, a jukebox of melodies from way back in time returning, giving back the distant tunes; fingers lulling him into submission. He accepts the seduction of the hand, allowing it, allowing himself to receive. The hand feels this acceptance and love becomes hate. He feels the fingers return to his throat, and in coma panic, his head still thrown back, he sees without seeing the murder of his own body. It would be so easy, so easy. So easy for the fingers to clutch, to press, to suffocate, to know exactly the place that extinguishes life. He cannot form the thought of acceptance. Way back somewhere in his brain, the longing to let go of the self is fighting with the longing of the self to remain alive. Then the tension of the death-threat relaxes. The hand retreats downwards, and his right nipple is touched; the sensation hardening the circle of flesh. But he does not want pleasure. He groans, not with acceptance, but with accusation and refusal. No words are necessary, for the tone of his groans bears within its sound the implicit denial, and the hand moves away. Unseen, the presence lifts itself from the adjacent seat, and his apparently receptive body is abandoned. As if his eyes were the shuttered lenses of a camera, his sight clicks open, admitting into the camera the objects that are displayed before him. And yet he feels; he feels, unlike the camera, unlike the click of exposure that coldly takes in the objects before it. He continues to groan, loudly, painfully, and the sound is so loud that the curious gather around him, not in search of pornography, but in search of something other. The rawness of the sound peels away desire, and faces, human suddenly, stare down at him. He wants to cry. He cannot cry. He stops groaning, and the human looks retreat. Everything goes back to its former state. This cinema is not a place for tears. The street, yes. All along the boulevards, in the Métro, on café terraces, the bereaved or the lonely can cry, but not here in this concentrated zone, home only to fantasy and pleasure. Only for a very few minutes, or maybe even seconds, had his groans made them human, and this human side of them had been attracted to the other that was unlike the moaning of sex, unlike the odour of sperm and urine, unlike the traces of excrement in the toilet. This smell of his distress had exuded a new if familiar attraction; familiar in its reality of the streets and closed rooms but unknown in the arena of desire's pornographic wall. Standing between him and the screen, a youth looks at him, and then silently, as if to worship, kneels down, kneeling and reaching out to open the white entrance of his trousers. The youth breaks the flow between him and the screen, blocking out the fucking and the sucking and the harsh disco backing track. He does not want the contact, and says no, loudly, breaking the silence that is not silence in this cinema. The youth crawls away, an animal retreating, and he watches him crawl and approach another perhaps more appreciative of what he has to offer. He is for a while left alone. The sweat dries on his skin, and he is cold. But this crowded solitude does not last for long. A man timidly makes his approach, standing to one side, watching him with a look of caution before sitting down beside him. The light from the screen illuminates his face, and now he, the watcher, is curious to see, and moving his head, he looks directly at the man. The man, who is elderly, who is visibly shy, speaks to him. For the first time in the cinema that day, non-formulaic words are used that tear up the conventional, oh shit I am coming, or, push it in harder, or the compulsive and insistent plea, suck my cock, take it all in. Please take it all in. This man is speaking to him, and in the sound, is the break of pain, the letting go. I heard your groans, the man says. I was watching, and unlike the youth who dropped to his knees, I remained standing, watching, until I realised that you were real. I knew I could talk to you. And you do not have to answer me, just let me talk to you. He pauses again and then continues. This morning. This morning before I woke, my own face was wet with crying. I'd had a dream. In the dream, I was in a hospital. I was told I was well enough to leave; that I was perhaps well enough never to have to think of, to feel, the disease again. But before I go, before they release me, they ask me to do them a service, to repay them for the treatment they have given me. I reply that I will do what they ask, and I am told that with another man who is ready to leave, I am to administer to a third. This third man, they say, is to be fed his cure. The cure is a thick golden liquid which is contained in a large round bowl. The bowl is made of silver and is so heavy that it needs two people, two people who are ready to leave the hospital, to lift it to the man's mouth. I join the second man, and we both carry the bowl. The sick man is lying on a white bed in the grounds of the hospital. It is a beautiful day, and there are many flowers. A spring day like today. I, and the other released man, carry the bowl to the sick body, and we just about manage to raise it to his lips. As he drinks, I weaken, feeling the force of the disease return. I realise I am not saved. I am too ill to hold the bowl. I start to shake. The bowl slips, and the man with me is not strong enough by himself to hold it. The golden liquid pours over the sick man (who cries out) and runs off his body in a stream saturating the ground. It spreads and covers the expanse of the green lawn, and the birds above us, who have been circling, seeing it as golden water, swoop down from the sky to drink it. I shout to them to stop. I scream out to them that it is poison, but there is nothing I can do to prevent it. Within seconds, the ground is a writhing, flapping mess of dying birds; their agonised bodies, burnt gold. And as I walk among them, I burn as well, realising I can save neither them nor myself. I know that I will die; that the cure in the bowl was no cure at all and never had been. I had been fooled by those who wanted my death, all our deaths, and I knew that fools like myself, and the man I was with, were just helpers in the execution of others as well as ourselves. I see all this clearly in the dream, and while I know that I am dreaming, I know too that there is no real awakening from it. I, like the others, am meant to be murdered, but first I will be offered a fake cure. The man stops speaking, and he, the watcher, watches the mouth close. He turns his head away from him and looks up at the cinema screen. The image there is of two youths in a shower. One is blond, the other dark. The dark-haired youth motions, but does not speak, for the blond youth to insert the showerhead, which is much too large for any anus, into his body. The head goes in, the water still running, and his face contorts in agony. No, the watcher thinks, this is not possible, and he turns away, but the force of the impossible image makes him return his gaze to the cruel fantasy. The head of pain and of ecstasy, and the silver head of the shower, become one. One unity. Why these boys? He asks himself, recalling the drugged boy on the bed. Will the massacre never stop? Will no one cry out, no, stop the film, stop what is happening to them and to us? His eyes persist in looking. The showerhead is pulled out, and the buttocks tighten, then relax, expelling a mock ejaculation of water. The blond youth opens his mouth wide, in an equal mockery of wonder, then puts his hands to the water, drawing it to his face and drinking it in. When he looks away from the screen, the man is gone, and now, at last, it is time for him to go, for him to temporarily leave. There is a sense of terror in these similar scenarios of penetration by objects and not flesh, as if in some perverted way this was in itself a disdain and a mockery of safer sex. He pushes the exit door that leads into the street open, and an aged woman comes towards him, her dirty hands holding coins, her mouth begging for bread and the money that will buy it. The sky has darkened (or is it his imagination?) since he has been in the cinema, and he feels naked; naked to her request as he has no more coins to give. He begins to shiver and tremble, and dreads the return of the fever he knows so well, and which the cinema, as if by magic, denies. He begins to cough, a low, wracking cough that dredges itself up from his stomach. His bowels feel loose, and he wonders whether he will make it to the Métro toilet in time or whether his thin excrement will seep from him and stain his trousers as it has before. The hot rush of the Métro, the sweet combined smells of poverty and perfume, calm the sensations of his body. He enters a toilet where sexual desire is alien, and in the freedom of at last not being watched or watching, he evacuates his bowels. In this freedom of not being watched, in the forcing of solid excrement, his own sexual excitement is activated. His rectum is sore and inflamed, for the faeces have alternated between being hard and soft, causing him discomfort and pain, yet inducing pleasure. He touches himself there; there where he has been reluctant to touch himself before; there where the shit is still hot, and he presses, presses inwards until his fingers ache and the shit glues itself to his nails. His legs are wide apart, and he sits on the cold enamel of the toilet rim, for the wooden seat has long since gone. There is a gap between door and ground, and he imagines that he is no longer alone and can be seen from outside. He looks at the door, in a state of hallucination, looking for the circular holes there had been in the cinema, sees none and finds that he is concentrating instead on the graffiti. It is mainly political, not sexual, calling for a far-right candidate to be president, equating black men with gorillas. Underneath is the crude image of male genitalia being cut from a body badly drawn with a knife. Bring back the guillotine for the homos and the blacks is the rallying cry, written, or rather scrawled in red by the same knife, and he has the impression that the tip of the knife had been dipped in blood. His eyes look further down, and he reads, send the black bastards home, make them clean our white floors with their big black cocks—obscenity joining into a climax of hatred, not desire, no not that, for this toilet is not the place. Yet a lament for love persists, like a green plant of hope fading to brown on the brown, violent wall. Looking closely, he sees a heart with an arrow through it, half scratched out, but it is there, almost obliterated, but a reminder to what is above and all around it. He also sees words close to the arrow, equally scratched at, love is a liar, and another line, no, not love, but lovers are liars. He wants to cry, but does not cry, and raising himself up, off the enamel rim, wipes himself with coarse, hard paper, then encloses his sex and anus once more in their fabric prison. His body is sweat covered. Is it the beginning of the recurring fever, or is it this time desire; the desire at last that has to be paid its due? He hurries from the toilet, up the steep flight of steps to the Métro entrance, trying to focus in the clear light of day and at the same time looking to alleviate his urgent sexual desire. He sees a kiosk, goes to it, and surveys the range of pornographic magazines; women with legs wide open and breasts exposed. He searches for the magazines containing naked images of men, and there in the corner he spots a half-hidden rack of titles. Honcho, the name with the Latin American inference, does not particularly appeal, but the image does; of a man more or less his own age, naked to the waist, clothed only in a pair of similar white trousers. The man has put his hand inside his trousers, and his mouth is open, gasping a sound that is silent on the page, will always be silent on the page, and this cried silence appeals, attracts. Fumbling in his clothes, he finds a folded note of money, damp, almost wet, and it is just enough to buy the desired object. He pays, then rolls it so that it is invisible to others. He wants to be alone with it, and he runs, yes runs, the sweat and the fever increasing, until he reaches a café, where he hurries down further steps towards the toilets. A woman is in attendance, knitting, seated on a hard upright chair in front of the cubicle door, on a stand beside her, a white, cracked plate with coins in it. She does not look up from her knitting, and as she knits, her eyes dart from needle to needle as they plunge into the wool. She takes no notice of him, seemingly oblivious in her world of created patterns, and her as yet undetermined object, nauseatingly green in colour. He locks the door of the cubicle, safe, for there is no division between door and ground, not even graffiti to distract, for this is a clean café, a place without politics or perversion. He pushes down his trousers to his ankles and leans back, sitting on the hard wooden lid for there is no necessity to lift it to uncover the bowl beneath. A hard white light glares down at him, and he notices, as if for the first time, how thick the hair is around his penis. Thick, almost black, whereas under softer lights it appears dark brown. He arouses his cock to its full length, playing with the tip, smearing the pre-cum, of which there is plenty, around the glans, feeling himself, wanting himself, yet wanting to stare at the same time. But the man, the man who resembles himself like a brother, the paper man with the silent gasp, will not come alive in his mind no matter how hard the mind tries to make him exist. The gasp on the paper refuses to lead to another gasp, and he, with his eyes, cannot make the image move, cannot imagine movement. Is the man caressing himself in his white trousers? The image is ambiguous, enticing, but he cannot be sure. Is the gasp faked for the camera? He holds the magazine awkwardly with one hand and with the other tries to maintain the will to have an orgasm. Furiously, feverishly, he flicks through the pages, but the man is not inside the magazine, only pale, flushed, rather ugly men in contorted positions that do not excite him. He *glances once more at the man, then throws the magazine down, for it is not this that will work, but perhaps the more living images recalled from the actions in the cinema. He urges memory to work for him, and the young boy on the bed with the small penis invitingly returns. He sees the man approaching (himself?) with the artificial means of stimulation. Then he is the boy, the boy in full glorious first youth, impaled on the black dildo; the cock that is not a cock, and it hurts him. Abruptly the cinema screen in his head changes reel and he is with the two youths in the shower room, and instead of the shower head an even larger imitation penis appears, but he refuses it, for now the two boys are fused into one, and he is that double-self, and he forcibly takes the heavy shower head, inserting it with force inside himself. He feels the gush of water, and this image makes him finally buckle forward and his own cock, the cock of his flesh, his real flesh in the cubicle, pisses sperm. Oh, he cries. Oh no! And then, yes! And his brain crackles, burning as the images of the mind return, burning as if the reel within had been set on fire. He cannot see. The flames blind. He rushes too quickly to his feet, pushing forward with his hands, the watery sperm falling upon the too clean floor. He hears his own cry come from far away, help, and his lungs contract as his brain has contracted, tight as a pinhead circle of pain. Help me, he cries, for the giddy, circular movement is not pleasure, not fun, not like a funfair at all, but whirling terrifyingly fast and whirling to a collapse. He is a burning fountain of fire, whirling in upon itself. Others are screaming inside him; all those in the cinema are crying out and shedding tears as the circular motion speeds into the abyss. He is approaching the pinpoint of blackness, and he is falling. He is going to faint. He is a frantic ball of help, in the infinite, and there is no release in the cry of help, and then he knows he has to push outwards. The woman cries out as he falters on the line that divides the toilet from her domain. He hears a clatter of needles and sees in a flash the gaudy green, unknown to nature, fall to the floor, as he would have fallen, as he would have collapsed, had she not held him in her strong arms. She is supporting him, his trousers still ludicrously around his ankles, and it is with great difficulty that she manages to lower him into her own chair. He looks up into her face and realises that focus is returning, for the aged lines written there, wrinkling with shock and exclamation, are all too visible. His previous cries for help are now transmitted into her mouth; a terrible, cacophonous sound. Then, circling him, curiously peering down at him, are other people, and he stares around from face to face, in shock himself at their shock. A man stoops in front of him, and roughly he feels his trousers being pulled up from around his ankles. Another man, standing behind, is hoisting him up like a marionette so the first man can finish the job of covering his lower body. While he is being manipulated, his feet get entangled in the green wool, and the woman curses and shouts at him, saying that he has destroyed a thing of beauty. He cannot speak, cannot say anything, for what is there to say in this position? But the chorus, mostly of men's voices, is getting louder, angrier. One man waves a colour printed image in his face, and he remembers the fallen magazine. Words like disgusting and abnormal are shouted at him, and a younger voice warns the group not to touch him as they might catch the disease. He senses a shrinking around him, a withdrawal caused by fear, and the woman screams loudest, as if she has indeed come too near to the plague, and it has already infected her. He gets up off the chair. He is shaking, but he knows their fear will preserve him from physical harm. He begins to run up the café stairs, and as he does so, he hears a man's voice cry out, what about the two francs? You owe two francs for the toilet. He cries then, hot, scalding tears. Once outside, his feet, his whole will, take him back to the cinema entrance. The façade is blank and dark now: the narrow entrance, a slit of red light in the obscurity. He sees the words, private club, the opening door, and without anyone noticing, he is inside. The smell welcomes him like an old friend. Here he can try to forget his sickness, for in the welcoming smell, the message is clear: all fevers have their time to rest, and the time has come to embrace collapse. On the wall, to the right, going into the cinema is a clock which he sees for the first time. The cinema closes at midnight, and he has five hours left. He goes into the flickering darkness, and once more he finds himself in the toilet area. The white porcelain fittings are bathed in red light, and he feels secure. Standing there, others join him, and the area fills with people. They come out of the cubicles, almost out of the walls themselves. He is surrounded by at least a dozen. He stands where he is, and then after a while slowly pulls down his trousers and moves backwards, so that his genitalia can be seen. He is against the wall. He has five hours, less five to ten minutes, and this is all the world to him. He is empty, white, open and cold, and this cold paradise is his for five hours. Five hours. It is as if in sympathy for what he has endured in the outside world that there is companionship here. Many of the men here, staring, looking at him, not touching, but with their presence, seem to say, we are all one here, here in the place of urinals and sex. A young man separates himself from the others, and it is as if they all make a space for him. He is dressed in a torn T-shirt and shorts. He pushes the shorts down to his knees, and now the focus of the others is on him. His cock instantly springs up. He masturbates himself slowly, carefully, considering his own pleasure, only conscious of his own pleasure. He goes to a urinal where his demands are simple: I want to be accessible and free from desire. I want my pleasure satisfied. We give pleasure to ourselves here, only really to ourselves. Each of you are like me, in isolation, but needing release. He pushes his T-shirt up above his nipples, and his right hand moves to them, tweaking each of them in turn. He gasps; not a paper gasp like the man on the magazine cover, but a gasp that echoes around the whole toilet area. Then he bends forward and opens his legs wide.*

85

With both hands he opens his arse wide and inserts two fingers. He gasps again, then widens the hole further with two more fingers, and pushes in almost his entire hand except for a forefinger which one of the crowd goes to and sucks. I am all availability, he appears to say, not with words; the limited means of the fingers speak for him. From out of the crowd, four come forward, entering into the space that surrounds his body. It is as if they have been elected, chosen by the others who now take up their roles as watchers. The four are not young. The man who kneels and sucks the youth's cock is completely bald and probably in his mid-sixties. The second who joins him is even older, his slack mouth dribbling saliva as he takes each testicle in turn and licks it with his tongue. The third is shaking with pleasure, and his hands tremble as he parts the arse which the young man has freed for them. He opens it sufficiently for the fourth, whose face is creased with lines but who still has all his hair, turned white with age. He kneels with an unsteady move to get to the floor, to put his mouth against the opening of the anus. The urinal, cold, intact, watches the ritual of pleasure. The young man bends over it, hands now pressing against the wall in front of him to steady his balance, enjoying his pleasure. He knows he is offering the gift of himself, but it is his approach to orgasm that counts. There is no rejection of age as he rotates his arse in a circular motion, accepting the tongue of the fourth man, then parting his legs even wider so that the third can join in. Two tongues meet, tongues in aged mouths that would not otherwise kiss, imitate the passion of an embrace. The youth permits this accidental embrace, and groans as their saliva dribbles down his legs. His balls contract, then fall. His penis wedges full into the bald head. The urinal and the watchers are witness to the lapping and the sucking, to the hurt of old knees upon the concrete floor. He cries out. The gasping and the moaning give way to a cry. His anus tightens as his cock releases its sperm. The first man dips his head as the youth comes, and the thick white liquid covers his baldness. All four are masturbating, but only one has come: the second man whose object had been the testicles. The youth moves away, his own pleasure satisfied, and with that satisfaction accomplished, is oblivious to the release of those who have served him. The three fall upon each other for want of anything better, uniting blindly in a circle of cries until they ejaculate and divide. The watchers lose interest as soon as the youth moves through them into the cinema. He has watched with the watchers, and watches too as the young man disappears into the flickering darkness. He goes out into the cinema, not following the youth, and the crowd in the toilet disperse as well. He looks momentarily back at the urinal; the white pillar of the urinal standing alone, abandoned, no longer a focal point of pleasure.

Greg looked up from the manuscript. He was almost at the end of Line 4, and he glanced at the Métro station where the train was stopping. The impulse to leave the manuscript was so strong that he had to inwardly fight with himself to put it back into his bag, and taking out the bag, he hurried off the train. Alésia. The place was familiar to him, and yet he could not remember it clearly. Memory brought a precise place to mind; a courtyard, and in the courtyard of a surrounding block of apartments there was a small one-room house. He had to see it again, and like a blind man guided by an invisible dog he made his way automatically to this specific house. The concierge who was once there was no longer there; she had been old and cantankerous, and he remembered how rude she had often been to him.

"Do you have to play that music so loud?" she would continually ask. "The neighbours are complaining."

He tried to recall the offending music. Yes, there was often Schubert and piano music, and it was the piano music he was especially fond of. He also had a daily impulse to play Beethoven's *Diabelli Variations*, and this especially got on her nerves.

"It is like a little girl constantly practising at the piano and only making a bad noise," she exclaimed, shaking her finger at him. "What do you think this house is? A *conservatoire* for silly little girls who should be doing other more practical things than ruining their fingers on an instrument they know nothing about?"

"It is Beethoven," he would reply, and she would shake her head in dismay. "He should have known better than to create nonsense like that. There are no tunes. It is exercise after exercise and it is terrible!" Her voice would grow louder and louder in disgust, and the wagging finger would seem to grow longer, almost touching him with its open disgust. He would retaliate that he played his music quietly, and not at a high level, but she would let out a cry and say, "You do not! It reverberates. You are telling lies and you know it."

"Do you want to come into the room and see at what sound level I play the record?"

"I would not. You would only lie and show me something different from the truth. What is it with these times, when young people lie so much? Anyway, the older people here do not like it."

This exchange would go on for a long time until he managed to release himself from it and crossing to the midway point of the courtyard, enter the white square building. Once inside, he would shut the door, make sure the blind was down at the single window, and then climb the few stairs to the mezzanine bed that was made of solid oak. There he would lie down to rest, needing quiet after the bombardment she had inflicted upon him. The ceiling was very close and a taller person than himself would have banged his or her head on it as they got up. He was saved by about two inches. Beneath the bed, and also made of oak, was a square table where he would sit and write, and while writing, often listen to the offending music. He had neither radio nor television, and wanted neither, content with his small choice of records collected over a long period of time. He had an old record player which served him well, and many of the records were old and well-loved. The *Diabelli Variations* played by Stephen Kovacevich for example. How could he live without that? And at night, coming home late he would pick up his Livre de Poche set of *À la recherche du temps perdu* and dip into it here and there, having read it twice through he chose his favourite sections and among them were the last lines of the first book, *Du côté de chez Swann* with its magnificent words, *le souvenir d'une certaine image n'est que le regret d'un certain instant; et les maisons, les routes, les avenues, sont fugitives, hélas ! comme les années.* He had learnt to read French and to write it. And in his turn, he had learnt to—but he had to stop the thought there. The house, on this April day of 2019, was present before him. The solid sides of the apartment buildings soared up around it into the sky. But the solid cube remained, and it had once been his temporary home. Alésia. But before that time; before that time of music and contemplation and work, had it not appeared before? His memory could not recall this, if it had ever been, and yet, was this not the third time he had approached it as if for the first time? How old age plays tricks, distorts and contracts and then extends. However many times he had seen this white building did not in fact matter. It still existed, was there, less white perhaps than before, grey walls now, but standing firm. He went over. The blinds were closed, the place perhaps deserted. He touched the windowpanes, and he wished he could go inside once more and write. Was the bed, the oak bed, still there? Or had the small room with its tiny kitchen area been stripped bare? No, that was impossible. Time *had* to stand still for this edifice; it had to be defiant in the face of advancing years, no matter who lived within it. No matter how many concierges had surveyed and watched over it, and yet as he withdrew his fingers from the glass, thick with grime, he imagined he saw the house façade disappear out of the space of the courtyard, become but a dot of memory in an empty space where it had once been. He ran out of the building, and it was with rapid steps that he entered the Métro once more. This was his home for the day; his home to think in, moving from one Métro line to another. This was his odyssey for the rest of the hours that remained, and on his journey, he resolved to read the manuscript he disliked; then to reflect and try to recall what was there, buried in his mind, and willing to acknowledge recall. Time regained; if only it were true, and not just a fantasy of longing, bringing out more often lies than the truth of being.

On the same Line 4, direction Porte de Clignancourt, he opened the manuscript where he had left off and began to read.

He then looks up at the screen. A youth is lying naked in the improbable grass of a studio forest feigning sleep. As he stretches in his slumber, his hand reaches down to his sex, and it is at this moment that the head of a snake appears in the far right of the screen. The snake slithers upwards, greener than the false grass, and uses the boy's right leg as a column around which to entwine itself. The circular movement is rapid, tail soon joining head in one quick convulsion around the human column of the youth. The snake's tongue darts out, tasting the light brown pubic hair in an unconscious parody of desire. The youth opens his eyes, eyes that are at first slits like the snake's, then wide open in an exclamation of horror. The tail of the snake is now around the genitals, and the body of the reptile is now slithering across that of the boy. He looks up at the screen in equal horror. His own fear of snakes is real, not faked, and he cries out, echoing the cry on the screen. The man sitting next to him laughs, and he turns to see someone he is attracted to. The boy is used to the reptile. Don't you see? It's all some mad idea of the filmmaker. He's mixing fear with porn. Never works. The man says the words aloud, watching the screen closely. He, the watcher, is still afraid and wants to hold the man to him for protection; wants to cling to the body enclosed in a coat far too hot for this cinema. The man laughs again, then turns and smiles. He is being smiled at, and the invitation beckons a response, but he cannot respond. He does not have to look at the screen to feel the poison dart of the snake's tongue despite believing no doubt as the man does that the creature has no poison in it at all. But all the same, he feels the poison in his veins, for the reality is he does have poison in his veins. He cannot deny the advancing decay within him: the lesions. In his mind, the reptile coils around his lungs. He coughs, but no cough will release the hold of the conqueror. He has been taken over, possessed by the fluid of the serpent. Once, how long ago he cannot know, in an encounter so brief, so fragmentary in its importance or relevance at the time, he had been infected. He had cried with pleasure then, or had it been a fake cry as the poison invaded his body? Then there had been no fakery like this on the screen; no pornographic illusion, but the hard impact of the thing he must call his death. In me. In me. The thing had bitten, had entered, had struck, and since then the fever had grown, following its inevitable course to annihilation. And yet he had rebelled against this death invasion; in the urge to escape, to make contact, to renew what was left of life, he had come to the cinema to watch and to make a bargain with the fantasies we call life. But seeing the snake on the screen, harmless no doubt, a gimmick, he has been recalled to his disease. He gets up and hurries away from the man, from the attraction of his thick, heavy coat, from the compulsion to be drawn into temporary protection. He hurries up the aisle, away from the man's laugh, a spark that could have lit a fire, but how cold it is inside him, white cold as his other self, the urinal, and unable to continue, he falls to his knees by the side of the exit door. It is dark here, shadowed by the darkness of all openings that lead into obscurity, and he can cradle himself, hug himself, delude himself that he is being held. The shivering and the inner shudderings increase, and warm though the cinema is, he cannot get warm. He needs the toilet and the cold urinal, but that part of himself is too far away, too distant from this part of the house of moaning orgasms that he is in. He looks down at himself, crunched up like a dirty tissue; the dirty tissue of his clothing, and beneath that, the smell that is disease. He crawls on all fours, near to howling. From that animal level, he looks up and sees that he is not, as he had first thought, alone. In the security of that most obvious of places, the cinema exit, two men are coupling. Looking up, he cannot see their faces or how old they are. He can only see their legs writhing in unison, their ankles bound by trousers, movements jerky, as if they were two creatures in the torment of hell, trying to break free. He too is a strange, unhealthy beast, looking up at their four-columned unity. Four legs, exhausted by the bond of clothes, and there in the centre, in the circle of the sexual experience itself, he sees the penetration of the penis. The thin light of the exit falls upon the circle of the act; upon the wide hole of the anus as it widens further to receive. He wants to be the dog that he resembles, must resemble to others watching; the beast who mirrors the other four legs, as a watcher, only a watcher. He wants to lap at the contained thigh, at the pumping energy of life; life that holds everything including himself together; struggling life, glue held. Hold me too in your fucking, he wants to say but cannot say; can only howl. He crawls nearer. The motions are becoming more urgent, the clothing ripped, stretched beyond endurance. He hears the words, yes, yes, take me, wishing it was himself that was uttering them, not bearing witness. His own tongue points, lengthening outwards, desiring. He braves the kick that a dog may get and reaching the leg of the man who is being fucked, makes contact. He licks. Another's body hair tangles in his mouth, and he coughs as it catches in his throat. He pushes one of his fingers down his throat, gags and brings up phlegm. He is still on all fours. His head hangs down for a moment and then rises, contemplating the glistening liquid on the leg, then staring down again at the pool by his hands. So much from his mouth; white vomit, and something else, as if there were an insect inside the pool, desperate not to drown. Was it some creature that had been captured in the hair of the other, the hair that had brought up the phlegm? Dark red, it seemed to move. He wants to watch this strange thing, but the distraction of their climax is approaching. He hears muffled screams, imagining a hand covering an over-eager mouth, preventing it from crying out its full release, and then it is done; over! The legs unjoin, the four become two. Clothes are adjusted, the rip in the cloth noticed, and what was so close, separates, and in the separation, hostility. He hears a curse, bastard, from one of them, and from his ground-level he watches as they go in opposite directions, columns of legs that had held the building, broken. Crawling, he finds the wet sperm against the wall, and on the floor where the man who had been fucked had come, and he reaches out. He does not use his hands, but bends his face towards the now cold liquid, and impulsively licks at it with his tongue. There is a longing in him that hopes the sperm will make him well, that it will give him energy and above all a cure. What a miracle that would be, if the sperm of an uninfected man could be the remedy to kill off the virus within. He licks until his tongue meets with only dry wall and dirt. He withdraws and stands upright, and as if the miracle has been granted, a renewed energy rushes through his body. His body though is drenched; drenched with sweat, and as he walks down the aisle furthest from the toilet area, he decides to sit down. The energy, sudden in its hope, has died, and as if on a mental cinema screen, he sees the virus gobble up hope, and then, like a hydra with multiple heads, rear up and rampage through his defenceless inner body. With blurred eyes, he stares at the outer screen. The images there are a fluid mess of colour; all twists and flashes of sound and movement; a distortion of a distortion in a funfair of mirrors. And yet he hears clearly; the grinding machine noises: the high electronic sounds and the low thin beats of music, alien and disturbing, emanating from this tortured screen flashing with portions of limbs, red openings and penetrations. He wants to see clearly, and with a struggle does, for only in the seeing can the chaos be reduced. His black shirt is sticking to him, and he can smell the odours of his flesh; the accumulation of the day's experience clinging to him like a second skin; the layers of differing actions and emotions that he has gone through. Then, with all the wonder that hell provides (what can heaven be without this hell?) he feels a cock press against him. He knows it is the man in the coat, that he desired and still does. He tentatively reaches out with the tips of his fingers, tracing the rough texture of the material, gently running along the rim of the cloth that covers the man's arm. The man's cock brushes his face in a gentle acknowledgement of desire, and he is conscious of its strength, its power, and the heaviness of its erect self. The man is standing before him, and still he traces the texture of the coat sleeve and of the home that is his flesh that he wants to live within. He knows this is the nearest to an act of tenderness he has achieved so far, and this blazing fire of knowing burns fear into him. He wants to get up, to move seats, to move away, to go to the furthest side of the cinema. He wants to hold the man to him, and yet run from him at the same time. His eyes want to escape to the fantasy of the screen, but he can no longer avoid looking up at the man's face. Torn inwardly between the choice of ignoring the man, or staring up at him, he stares—a pleasant face, not beautiful, almost ugly. The hair is thinning, and the flashing light from a too bright image on the screen illuminates his face. Yes, the hair on the head is thinning; the forehead is high, and there is a shine of sweat on it. How hot he must be in his heavy coat, he thinks, and some emotion, some distant relation to love, moves within him. The face itself is sharp, pointed, and the skin is drawn tightly across the bones. He can only see one eye, as the head is tilted sideways to stare at the screen, apparently oblivious to his presence. Absurdly, for it is absurd to him (what after all does the man care?) he wants to reach up and touch the taut texture of the face; wants to reach for the flesh to see if the skull is covered only by the barest tracery of skin. I—(he almost names himself, almost gives himself definition), but the single syllable retreats back into his mouth. The man, as if sensing this retreat, turns to look down at him. His eyes are blue, a searing blue, and yes, contact is made. The I of the self that he has relinquished is taken up by the man who says, I am Bruno. My name is Bruno. He glances away from the man, not able to reply, not even able to begin to explain to himself why he is unable to reply. There is no way he can give a name, either real or false to this man, and he asks himself, is the beginning of love nameless? He touches himself, touches the wet black shirt and runs his hands down the length of his thighs in a gesture that is not erotic but a gesture of assurance that he is there; that he is he, nameless, but there. He cannot look at the blue eyes and stares away at the screen. The blurring returns. The sweat on him has dried, and he is cold. On the screen, the end-titles of the film he has not been watching begin to appear. Was it the same film that had threatened him with its harmless snake, or was it another? The ludicrous, unlikely names of the actors, Brad Masters and Adam Hard, follow each other in quick succession, and for a moment he is tempted to appropriate one for himself; to take it upon himself like an invisible cloak behind which he can hide. Bruno is too plausible, too honest, too naked in its declaration. It says, I am true, I am myself. I am me; not a fantasy in this palace of fantasies, but me, a man of ordinary capacities. He wants to hide before the name, and take say Brad or Adam, or Larry Luke as one name suggests as it hurries by on the screen, but he cannot tell the truth, or even approximate the truth, and remains silent. He now wonders what the body itself is like beneath the heavy coat; wonders whether it is as heavy as the cock, or whether it is as thin and bony as the face. It is suddenly very important that he knows this, but only on condition that he does not have to give himself an identity. He tries to work out a fantasy about the man, but the name Bruno prevents this, evoking, despite the beauty of the name, all the functions of the flesh that pornographic films deny. Bruno has flesh. He is not an image on a screen that plays with the mind and directs the mind into the domain of false realities. Bruno would scream with pain if he were burnt, but the flesh on the screen would only crinkle into silence and fall as cinematic dust. Bruno is facing him. His cock stands out through his coat, and he resists touching it, for then he would need to know more, fully accept more; the knowledge for example that unlike the flat objects of desire on the screen, this cock could piss real piss and ejaculate real semen, and in accepting that obvious fact, his arse would not just be a receptacle, but a living bowel that could expel shit and could even fart while having sex. No, it was useless to create any fantasy concerning Bruno, patiently standing, head turning once more to face the screen. Another film has begun. It begins with music, accompanied by a view of what must be San Francisco Bay, for through the blurring of his vision he is able to see the form of the bridge, the cliché bridge, the bridge of all fantasies, and perhaps the transporter of his virus. It is a symbol of an era lost; a false paradise where the serpent slithered diligently through bar and backroom and sauna. Then a wave of red floods the screen, and through the red he recognises the music: Verdi; Traviata; the inevitable Traviata; the bitch goddess of all operas, of all pathetic deaths; the swansong of all those ready to die, ready to swoon into the arms of faithful lovers returned to embrace—all a lie, a musical lie, worse than the dreadful Bohème, or the sacrificial Carmen; the operatic dreams of the moronic queens who listen to it, and then dance to Donna Summer as the light fades from the sky. He mentally spits upon this heritage the homosexual has ingested to make it a part of his homosexual self, as invasive and as poisonous to the system as the virus itself. Verdi, Puccini and Bizet on the bonfire of vanities, on the waters of the infected saunas, in the dance waves of the soon to be infected writhing on the dancefloor in a pale prediction of what their bodies will endure. No, he marginalises himself from this. Does Bruno like the music? Bruno is staring at the red, which like a curtain soon parts to reveal half-naked youths, marching in parade as if their flesh is their pride and not their conscience or their hearts. Two separate themselves from the parade, and then there is a jump cut to a room, empty but for a white, naked bed. I am Bruno, the man repeats, now rubbing his leg against him. He is going to faint. He gets to his feet and stumbles his way towards the nearest aisle. He hears steps behind him and knows that the man is following. Halfway up the aisle, the man grabs him and pushes him up against the wall. The man pushes his mouth against his, and violently he tries to push him away. He uses words now, has to use words, and cries out, don't you see, don't you feel it? I am going to die. The man laughs. Bruno laughs: the same laugh he had let out at the sight of the snake. Don't be absurd, he says, this is nonsense, and now the coat is open, and the cock is impatient. The faint feeling recedes, and by the light of the screen he sees the vivid red tip. He reaches out and touches it. From where he is standing, pushed against the wall, he can see the entrance to the toilet area. Across heads and seats, and hands fumbling in the darkness to masturbate, he can see the tall, cold pillar of the urinal, abandoned, close. His vision is heightened now, clear and piercing. There is no vision loss, but a fierce taking in of all that can be seen. Another couple are fucking on the screen, and the music has mercifully stopped. Against impossibly blue skies and the crashing of waves, two men are standing on white rocks, their bodies soaked oily brown by the sun. The blond (isn't there always a blond in San Francisco?) is in the foreground. His legs are apart, and the fucking is as loud as the waves. The dark-haired one (for there must always be an opposite to enhance perfection in the perfect world of America's west) fucks the blond with practised assurance. No tottering on these stones. The pumping continues. Kiss me, kiss me. He is drawn away from the screen and his lips open to receive the saliva that is being offered. The man draws him to him. You want me, you want me. Say it. Say something to me. The man is frantic now, tearing at the watcher's black shirt, pulling it up, trussing it up above his chest; then the mouth darts down, sucking hungrily, first on one nipple, then on another. He no longer wants to push the man away, caught up finally in the motion of his own desire. He stares across at the cold, hard enamel of the urinal, then with urgency sinks his head against the man's coat, opening the coat so he can touch the flesh inside. The man draws back, looks at him and smiles. Call me Bruno, please. Just once. He gives in, he has to give in, finally resolving in his own way all contradictions to do otherwise: why? He does not know, but he has to fall against the body that could be as hard as the urinal, and maybe, just maybe, as cold. He calls the man Bruno, not once but twice, and crushes him to him, obliterating the cinema in that gesture, obliterating that final night of the world that he feels is waiting for all of them. And then the thought washes over him; how much longer is there on the face of the clock at the entrance? How long has it been already? For an instant, he needs to know, and then that is obliterated as well, and he feels the hard sex of the man in his hand. He caresses the thick tangle of hair and draws in the pungent smell of pre-cum and perhaps already a full shot of cum, now dried, but fulfilling itself in its aroma of sweat and orgasm. He falls to his knees in front of the man, rubbing his face in the now exposed groin. The coat has been opened wide; the loose trousers just loosened enough for the whole genital region to be revealed and opened to taste and touch. His face is hidden in that smell of darkness, the cock disappearing into his mouth, choking him with its length and breadth and no one can see, no watchers can watch as the coat envelopes his actions. He raises his hands and clutches at the man's buttocks, not thin or bony, but rounded with flesh, and his fingers stray to the hole of the anus, but the man edges slightly away from this intrusion. No, he whispers down, and the finger retreats, but still clings and draws the two globes of flesh inwards. He sucks the cock and the low-hanging balls, lapping at the skin there, then going upwards to the shaft and taking in once more the moist head, sucking hard, tasting the salt juice. The man groans, tells him to stop as he is about to cum, and draws him up from off his knees. His mouth tastes of that preliminary warning of ejaculation, and their mouths join. As their saliva mingles he sucks on the man's long tongue, appreciating it as much as he has the sex, drawing it inwards, then outwards, in a rhythmic spasm of longing. Then the tongue wriggles and darts in his mouth, and he cannot shut out the image of the snake. He is holding the snake's head in his mouth, and if it bites, he will bite back, and he knows that his strength is sufficient to kill it. He rejects the venom and the pain; he is going to live. He must live. Automatically, and without realising it, he bites hard on the thrashing tongue, and the man cries out, drawing away from him. I did not mean to hurt, he hears himself say. He does not want the man to leave. He does not want to return to the cold, frozen death of the urinal, and he begs, please, I did not mean to hurt. Then the man's face breaks into a smile, and he laughs and holds and hugs him. He is saved. Call me Bruno. Say it. He says the word, Bruno and the man laughs again, enjoying the repetition of having asked once more. He hears the laughter as if it is coming from a great distance and as he utters the name he loses his erection, and the warmth that he had felt now turns to ice. He stands, rigid, and frozen against the wall, holding awkwardly, unknowingly, the still urgent sex of the man in his hand. Inside himself he feels another heat; the cold heat of his disease, and his heart beats so rapidly that he feels it will break. I am dying, he says, and the man says, no, it is absurd. It is true, he repeats, I am dying. The man holds him from him, and he stares at the man in horror, knowing that he has experienced love. The man breaks open a phial of Amyl Nitrate and forces him to inhale, but this only increases the pounding heartbeat. I am a doctor, the man says, shaking him. This is all in your mind. I know. It is his turn to laugh now. When have the doctors ever known how to save, how to know? Then doctor, give me life, he whispers, and in his fragmentary mind, he sees a phantom of his self, returning to the cock, going down on knees to suck the man's cock inside him. Give me the gold liquid of life. It does not take long, perhaps only a moment before the hallucination of sperm, in full rush, pours into his mouth. He tastes it to the full before swallowing it. The liquid is thick, and life will return. He is a tawdry Traviata after all. His legs will move. The ice will not envelop his heart. The man is crying with pleasure, standing there in front of him, or is he simply crying? The ice is gathering force now, murdering the saving gold, and he hears himself cry, I am dying. He shouts again, one last time. Can't you all see that I am dying? The light is going out in my head—HELP!—

Paris, March 1988

Greg felt the gold of memory in his mind. The manuscript slipped from his hand, and he watched it fall, and a woman beside him asked, "Are you alright? You look ill." He replied in French that he was not ill and bent down to pick up the manuscript. The memory of the book is the memory of writing it; he was in Paris in March 1988 and he had seen what *he* had written, fearing that he too had caught the virus and that he was going to die. *Didier's Manuscript!* He never gave it a title. Only *Didier's Manuscript*, as if this name, plucked out of nowhere *meant* something. It hadn't.

It was Nick who had taught him to write, to read and write, and hadn't a book of his short stories been published back then? And another, only last year, in 2018? But this; no, this dreadful testament had not been published. The train stopped at a station. How long had he been on this one line, going backwards and forwards as he read the words from his own text? He recalled now vividly, how he had written on the cover, the title that was not a title, and how during his stay back then he had met Hervé Guibert, and the author had read the manuscript, almost throwing it back in his face at a party. After that, he had hated the text and wanted it lost. Guibert had hated it, calling it vulgar, bad, bad. How could he like it after that? Serge had been at the party and had taken hold of the text, and he had allowed the man to keep it. But Serge, like him, was old now, and neither of them had recognised the other, or remembered that year so many decades past when old age was in the far distance, and any mention of ageing to the point of unrecognition could never have entered their thoughts or words. How could they even have begun to imagine that they would meet in 2019 by accident and not know each other? Back then in the years of 1988 and 1989, they lived. And there, in those years in Paris, they could not see around them, through the peacock's fan, their lives in the cruelty of time.

Had Serge taken him to the party? Or had he gone alone, knowing that Hervé Guibert's judgement awaited him? Had there been a sexual relationship between him and Serge? If so, he had forgotten and certainly Serge had forgotten, and this very afternoon, Serge had forgotten his bisexuality, or was it, the whole thing between them, an invention of Greg's mind? All he was absolutely clear about was that he had known Serge. The crumbling mausoleum of the years was overwhelming, and feeling an intense claustrophobia, he decided to get off at Barbès–Rochechouart. He thrust the manuscript back into his bag as the train drew into the station, and when he got up, the woman next to him looked at him and asked again, "Are you alright?" He smiled down at her and assured her that he was feeling well, and with unsteady steps made his way to the door and with the same unsteady steps he made his exit onto the street, and going towards the main boulevard, glanced at Tati on the corner, still with materials outside to buy, and still on the street, the same hawkers and men approaching him with various offers;

various services. He took the pieces of paper they offered and going up the Boulevard Barbès, saw that the colours in the street were less vivid, less attractive than they had been before. Nothing had really changed, and yet all had changed in that slow but sure way that places do; there was, he felt, a loss of community, or more to the point, a loss of the intensity of community. He saw many more white faces; people who clearly looked as if they lived there, and he realised as in all Paris, that money and the rise in sales of apartments, had drawn in those who could not afford to live in more central, more desirable parts. The place smelt cleaner as well, but then it would have to, to satisfy this insidious invasion. He saw a gay couple hand in hand, which was a sight that would never have been tolerated before. The indigenous population did not give them a look, and yes, tolerance was good and he valued it, but the traditions of old were fading, and in that again there was a loss of colour. As he reached the Métro Château Rouge, he saw a bright new hotel not far from the station. His mouth was parched, and he needed to drink, and out of curiosity and a certain puzzlement he went towards it. It was a hotel more suited to the 4th *arrondissement*, but here it was out of place, falsely bright and glistening, and in the glass windows he saw bright yellow chairs, chairs that welcomed with a rich, sunny smile, and looking inside an equally bright young man was standing behind a very fashionable counter. He entered through a glass door and sat down on one of the chairs along with his shopping bag, feeling absurdly well off as he saw the various and still relatively poor population pass by. The young man came over to him, giving him that expert waiter greeting that is only offered in the best of hotels.

"*Monsieur, vous désirez?*"

"*Un tilleul-menthe,*" he replied with the customary "*s'il-vous-plaît.*"

"*Vous voudriez manger quelque chose?*"

"*Non, merci, simplement à boire.*"

Then the young man broke into English. His English was

not the best, but he threw himself into the language with gusto.

"We love English customers here," he gushed. "I thought you were English because of your small accent. We are new, you see, and we want to offer the best in this district. From my experience, which is not so much, I have seen a lot of people from your country roam these streets looking I think for a decent place to stay, and now, here it is! We have the most comfortable rooms and our prices are—how shall I say? Reasonable."

After this pompous declaration of worth, Greg asked, "Are you from here?"

"From Paris?"

"No, I mean, *here*. This *quartier*."

The young man looked a little defensive at this question and rather nervously began to pass the tray he was carrying from hand to hand.

"I know it very well, but I have an apartment in the 13th *arrondissement*. My wife and I came here often in the past and we noticed how much a *good* hotel was needed."

"No bedbugs or passing trade in the night?" Greg queried with a clear tone of mockery in his voice.

"Monsieur has the wrong idea. I never meant the other hotels were like that here. But a hotel of class, certainly was needed."

"Yes, the décor is beautiful and so are the yellow chairs."

"Thank you, Monsieur," and the young man hurried away and when he came back with the *tilleul-menthe*, Greg feeling suddenly hungry asked if there were any cakes available.

"I will bring you a choice." The smile had gone, and the voice sounded snobbish and proud.

"Is there a washroom nearby?" Greg asked.

"First on your right," came the brisk reply.

Greg sipped at his tea and then slowly got up and went in the suggested direction. As he made his way to the impeccably clean toilet and washroom he saw an imposing staircase leading to an upper level. Clearly the young man and his wife had a lot of ambition and money to spend on this enclave of glamour near Château Rouge Métro station. Very grand, Greg thought. Very Kemp Town, with its chandeliers hanging from high ceilings. He wondered how long the hotel would last and whether the English would still come once the Brexit doors had been locked? Or at any rate, once they had been made less easy to open? He relieved himself in the toilet as elderly men do, with a painful slowness, and during that time he noticed how much silver and gold had been lavished on this essential room. Curious, he glanced inside the cubicles. The Ritz itself could not have done better, he thought. The air was perfumed, and the toilet rolls looked as if they had been made by hand. When had these toilet rolls been last used, he wondered. He had a vision of the young man immediately leaving his post to clean up and restore the bowls to their rightful purity after every use.

Returning to his table and yellow chair he saw a choice of cakes on a cake stand that would have put the whole of Great Britain to shame. He chose an *éclair au chocolat*, followed by a *tarte aux pommes*. His appetite or need for food was not great that day, and he hoped that this artificial energy would fuel his system. The young man was nowhere in sight. From this vantage point Greg was able to watch the crowd go by, Black women, Asian women, tired men, traipsed past and not one of them stared in through the glass to see this aged man gorge himself on luxuries.

"I am an imposter here," he whispered to himself. "What would François think if he saw me now? Would he think I had bought one of the new renovated apartments at their new and highly renovated prices?"

The young man returned to his post and had heard the whispering. Quickly he came over, and looking down at the table and not at Greg, asked if he wanted something else.

"Just the bill," Greg replied, wiping his mouth with a serviette, conscious perhaps that a smear of chocolate was at the corner of his mouth.

"I will bring it at once."

And at once it came, and Greg put down the sum that was specified on the bill, and then got up and faced the young man.

"I hope this hotel goes well for you," he said politely.

"We will do our best." And then from his pocket he withdrew a card and said, now with a forced smile, "Perhaps Monsieur will tell his friends about his visit here, and maybe he could recommend us."

"Of course," Greg said, then he smiled his best smile and walked out of the glass door. Back on the street he felt more at one with the people around him. The late afternoon was advancing, and many were clearly eager to reach their homes. The hawkers had gone, and reaching Château Rouge station he saw various rough sleepers. This, even way back, he had not seen before. Light fell on their abandoned bodies, and some were very young and looked scared and vulnerable. Perhaps he was giving the years he had lived in Paris too much gloss, but he could not recall such downright poverty even in this district that was well known for its less well-off. A degradation had happened, at the same time that the well-to-do had risen. The population who could no longer afford, had slipped through the system to lie out in filthy clothes, showing to an indifferent or an overworked crowd, their sores and society's ruin. He gave an old man what was left of his change, and then catching the eye of a young Arab with outstretched hand, he placed a twenty Euro note in it. The youth clutched it as if it had fallen from the sky, and with a mouth almost devoid of teeth, grinned up at Greg. Judge us, Greg thought, we are all guilty.

Then, deciding what he had to do, what he had decided to do when he had left Barbès station, Greg turned into the Rue Doudeauville and went towards the house he had known so well. He passed new buildings; buildings that had no doubt been raised up to a higher standard (or a morally lower one, depending on one's political thinking), and then reached the familiar door. He looked for François' name, but it was no longer there. Where it had once been, he rang the bell. He waited, his heart beating fast and eventually through the speaker he heard a woman's questioning voice.

"*Qui cherchez-vous?*"

"François—" he replied loudly for the voice seemed to come from a great distance.

"*Il n'est plus ici.*"

"*Je suis un ancien ami. Je viens de loin.*"

The door clicked open and he went up the familiar stairs unchanged by time. He expected the black woman François had arguments with to come out of her apartment, but the door was firmly closed. Behind it, he heard the sounds of a chorus of children. She was not young then, he thought, and now in all probability she is dead. So does the river flow! He reached the door he had gone through so often, and there was no bell so he knocked gently on the wood. An elderly woman opened the door just wide enough to see who was on the other side. She did not look particularly alarmed or surprised.

"*Monsieur?*" she asked.

"*Je suis un ancien ami de François,*" Greg said.

"You have an English accent. I speak English. Would that be better?"

"It is less tiring for me," Greg replied. "I am not as young as I used to be."

She laughed at this and withdrew the chain and opened the door fully to let him in.

"We are both of us not as young as we used to be. Come in. I have not met an old friend of François for so long."

He entered the room, but it was not as he remembered. The colour was now muted where once it had been so vibrant. The furniture was sparse but heavy. The wardrobe took up almost a whole wall, and a sofa covered in a frayed, brown material faced it against the opposite wall. The vivid red curtains provided the only real colour. In another corner was a bookcase full of books, and in the centre of the room stood a long wooden table with chairs. The immediate thought was of a rural country house. Everything was spotlessly clean and the table polished. It had been done perhaps that very day and Greg could smell the wax. He looked at the room closely, trying to remember how it had been. Intrigued that he was not looking at her, the elderly woman faced him. He saw clearly the questioning look of her curiosity.

"My name is Hannah," she said, and then he looked at her. Her face was dark, and her black hair was flecked with white. A white shawl covered the long black dress that hid her body, and tiny black slippers peeked out from beneath the cloth. She was beautiful in her bearing and in her features; her face carved with time and a sculptor's skill. Brown eyes and a rich, firm mouth completed the picture. Or to be more exact, the carving that nature had bestowed on her.

"So, tell me about yourself, and please sit down."

"My name is Greg," and he went to sit on one of the chairs at the table. Following him she sat down first, and he chose the chair facing her.

"I will make us some tea," she said, "but first I want to know why you have come looking for him." She paused, then added, "You do know he is dead, don't you?"

"No," he replied, and lowered his head. All the brilliant colours that he remembered died as well in that moment.

"Is it such a shock?" she asked and stretched out a hand across the table. Her fingers then gently touched the candlestick that was between them: a menorah with nine candle holders.

"There are no candles," he said quietly.

"Why should there be?" she replied. "I'm no longer a believer, but I keep it. Just to recall what I was. François never saw it. He did not respect the things I had hidden away concerning my lost faith." Then getting up, she said that she would make some tea. "I will make it the English way. You see, in my time, I lived in England for a year. Am I right in believing that the English are not too friendly to the Jews at the moment? I do not have a television or read the news, but I hear things."

"The English have always had a certain Fascism in them," Greg replied, "hidden behind politeness, but there. Israel has given many people a reason for the old hatreds to return. I imagine you have heard that the world is returning to a renewed form of fascism."

"Yes. Jews. Homosexuals too, in places. None of us outsiders are safe," and she laughed. "But I am in France. The French were once great collaborators. My mother was French. I was a baby when she was sent east to the camps. She died there. An aunt kept me hidden here, and here I suppose is my real home. My father was Polish. He too died in the camps. At least England was not tested to that degree."

"It would have failed the test," Greg said.

"I believe you are right, but excuse me while I go to the kitchen. Look at the books." She paused and then added directly, "Are you the young English man who was François' lover?"

"Yes."

"Be welcome here. I understand."

She left the room, and in silence Greg went over to a collection of mainly paperbacks. He found a whole row of Isaac Bashevis Singer's books and took out a Penguin of his Collected Stories. It was the only one in English. As he turned the pages, Hannah returned with two cups of tea on a tray and a collection of biscuits. She placed the tray on the table.

"You may have that," she said, "I think it is right it should find its home in English hands. My favourite work of his is a slim book called *The Penitent*. I lost it. Years ago. It too was in English. Now, come and sit down."

He sat again facing her and placed the book in his bag along with the manuscript.

"Are you surprised that he talked to me of you?"

"A little," Greg replied.

"He told me everything. I knew when I met him that he was essentially homosexual."

She handed the cup of tea to Greg and then offered him the plate of biscuits. He took one and placed it by his cup.

"How did you know?" he asked.

"First let me explain a few details. I lived in this house for many years, in a smaller flat than this. Five years after his wife died we began talking. While his wife was alive we only passed each other on the stairs. I took in sewing to make a living, and there was no reason for us to talk. I had my faith then, and he was an Arab. Prejudices run deep." She paused and sighed. "There are many different animals in the world, and we humans are sadly the worst."

"Do you *really* believe that?" he asked.

"No God that I can accept, could have created us like this," she answered, and for the first time there was bitterness in her voice. Then she continued talking. "Yes, he talked about you. I think you were the only person he truly loved. As for his wife—no, it was not love. It was his sacrifice to his parents and to their Catholic beliefs. As for me, I was a friend he made love to, and yes, he looked after me. I say made love to with caution, as there was only friendship in his passion. I loved him as a lover, but it was not reciprocated."

"I am sorry," Greg said.

"Come now, no sympathy. Drink your tea, and please eat some of these biscuits. I do not eat them. I keep them for guests, but I have seldom guests. I opened a box of them just for you. Don't worry, they are fresh. And may I say, you look hungry."

Greg ate two of the biscuits and drank the tea. He dropped a few crumbs on the table and apologised for doing so.

"It is so clean here," he said.

"*Too* clean," she replied, laughing her soft laugh.

He stared at her face again and sensed that she had more to say about François. He could see it in her look, in the moist sadness of her eyes. He did not want to rush her.

"You have been very honest with me," he said.

"Have I? No, not quite. There is more, but I am afraid."

"Afraid?"

"Yes."

She got up, and going over to the sofa, sat down upon it. It was as if she did not want to be seen.

"I sensed that there was more," Greg said. "Is it true, or is it a myth that the old have more intuition?"

"It is a myth. I know."

He heard the words, but from where he was sitting he could barely see her. Gently he asked if he could come and join her.

"I would rather you stayed where you are. The things I need to say—who else was there? Who else has there ever been to tell these things to? I have no family or genuine friends. I speak with neighbours, and sometimes they come in, but briefly. A new generation has moved into this house and the rents are much higher and some of the flats are for sale. On the ground floor there is a couple who used to live in Auteuil. Can you believe it? They rented there, but they could not afford to buy there."

"What is it that makes you afraid?" Greg asked gently. He wanted to see her face, he wanted to remove the candelabra and the height of the table that hid her from him. He saw the top of her hair and the slippers on her feet and even then he had to bend down to the floor, pretending to pick up something that had fallen to be able to do so. Also his vision was not as good as it used to be.

"Did *you* love François?" she asked. Her tone of voice was incisive and clear.

"At first, yes," Greg said slowly. "It was in England that things really fell apart, and anyway, he was already questioning the need to get married. I am sorry, but it all seems, *is,* so long ago. Precise details fade. He left England. He disliked, if I remember clearly, what he saw of homosexuality there. Brighton, where we were, was a rather vulgar town in his eyes. And now it has become a city, everything has become somewhat diffused. What is called gay life has dissipated itself, become fragmented. The community comes together in yearly Pride events. But even then—well, I am distant from it. I cannot judge what the new generation wants."

"Are you a true homosexual?" she asked, and the question shocked him. He could not see her, and she could not see him. It was like being in a Catholic confessional.

"I fought my homosexuality when I was very young—but yes, I am. However, I consider myself marginal to many of the gay community's concerns. That is why I like France. To be marginal here is still possible."

"You have many illusions about France," she said slowly. "There is much fragmentation here too, and in the provinces it is not easy to be different. In some places I would not want to be openly Jewish. Whether under Fascism or Socialism, Jews and homosexuals will always be persecuted. It is on the rise again, almost reaching the surface of our lives right now, both in France and England. We do not have to go as far as Eastern Europe, or to Russia where it is already terrible."

"That is why I am marginal," Greg said. "I want to watch, as it were, from the gutter. I do not want to join the fragmented movements that remain. I am perhaps a coward, but the fight must now go on without me. I have seen the gay world up close, and being on the margins, I criticise my own kind. I want the right to do that."

"Even if they go under?" she asked.

"I will weep for the wasted years. That is all I can do."

"No, Greg, you will raise yourself up. I would not hide from the enemy if they knocked on my door. I would spit in their faces."

Greg was silent. He was ashamed of what he had just said to her, but he was thinking of Renaud and what he had witnessed with him. But then his mind insisted, no, not now. You must think of François. This is why you knocked on this door.

"I would like to talk about François," he said.

"Alright. Time is passing. You must have things to do, but I like you, Greg. I think you are deeply conflicted and need healing. Profound healing. The problem of homosexuality has, I think, eaten up most of your life—and yet I feel you had so much else you needed to discover."

Greg liked the way she said his name. He felt that this was a true encounter and that if he remained in Paris he would return to her. Her honesty of tone, and her voice, opened up memory, and he felt a sort of love that could not be named, but even the best of love cannot be named, even more so by the word itself.

"François," she said slowly, "was a good but cruel man. That last description is hard to say, but he did dreadful things while I lived with him. Even now I cannot sleep in the bedroom. I sleep in here. I roll down a sleeping mat and can only rest in this room. The bedroom was the exact place of cruelty," and here she paused.

"Please go on."

She rose then from the sofa and stood in the light. Her face was wet with tears, and she was not ashamed to show them. She sat again at the table.

"Hannah," he said her name softly, "please tell me only what you can."

"No, *all*," she replied, and drank a little of the cold cup of tea in front of her.

"Then, what happened in that bedroom?"

"Although we were still sleeping together, sex had died between us. After breakfast he would leave me alone and go for long walks. I have no idea where, or in what part of Paris, although I guessed it was not often outside this area. He hated much of Paris."

"Yes, I know," Greg said.

"Then around three in the afternoon one day, he brought a young Arab boy back, and without a word he took him into that bedroom and closed the door. The boy was sixteen, perhaps seventeen, and I heard the crying coming from that room, and screams. I do not know if it was pleasure or pain, but it was I sensed a violation. I remember that first time so vividly. I sat as I am sitting now at the table and I could not move the shock was so great. Then, an hour or so later they both came out and he asked me, yes, he asked *me* to make them both tea, and to give the youth something to eat. I remember looking at the Arab boy's face. I know the look of shame, and it was there, and also I sensed a pain that the boy dared not say. I saw he was totally under the control of François."

"How old was François then?"

"It was around the turn of the century. Late middle age. He was fat. He did not age well. In my mind I see his body—yes, I see it as if it was now—heavy with years of overeating and self-hatred and sexual repression of his true nature, and that day—that afternoon—he had released all that pent up rage of sexuality upon this youth."

"How could he have done it with you—here?"

Greg felt sweat break out on his skin. He asked for a glass of water and Hannah fetched him one. He drank it down quickly.

"Eventually this youth left, and I was alone with François. I felt so much pain for myself, for him, and the boy, that I said slowly to him, 'Please do not do that again in my presence. I heard everything,' and he replied, 'I had to. I had to do it for myself. I had to break free.'"

"Freedom?" Greg exclaimed.

"Yes. It was for him. His freedom to break the chains of both of us women—the wife who was dead and in his memory, and I who was no longer his physical lover. It was said in such a way, with such a plea in his voice, that I knew it was an act beyond his control. He had to avoid my existence. And yes, you no doubt think that is terrible. It was. Another woman would have left him, but I stayed."

"Why?" Greg asked.

"First I must explain a little of my own psychology. I have never understood people. In my youth they were all strangers and remained so—all the people I knew; the people I had relationships with. As a very young woman I only understood the people who killed my family in the concentration camps and those who marshalled them into the gas chambers, or worse. I could not love people. But when I met François I sensed he was an outsider like myself. As I fell in love with him I felt fear. I understood that fear often breeds love. Fear that he would go, or betray me; betray my feelings—and he did. That afternoon he did, and I realised it was inevitable. It was cold fear that let me understand the awful act he had committed."

"Hannah, no."

It was all Greg could say. He buried his face in his hands.

"I also let it continue. He would go out quite regularly, and around two in the afternoon I would go out. I wandered the streets or sat in a café, knowing that he had probably, almost certainly, brought someone back. At night I smelt it on the sheets. I changed the sheets every day, and he was silent. We stayed here in silence, and I read a lot then. Singer and André Schwarz-Bart. I would buy old books. Sometimes I read a book all night and did not sleep, not wanting to join him in that—" and here she pointed to the bedroom door, "—that room. I was my own prisoner. Don't ask me how long this lasted."

"What ended it?" Greg asked, letting his hands fall to the table.

"Call it fate. One day he brought back a white boy. A rough type. He had brought him back earlier than usual, and I had not yet gone out. And when the bedroom door closed I put on my shawl and hurried into the street. I don't know if I sensed something was wrong, but I stayed nearly all afternoon in a café in the Rue Polonceau. When I returned in the early evening, the apartment was wrecked, and the bedroom door was wide open. Naked, François was on the bed. He had knife wounds and he was alive, but not conscious. I called the police and an ambulance. I lied to the police, saying there had been a break-in and that jewellery had been stolen. I am sure some people in the house must have seen some of the boys he brought back, but no one contradicted what I told the police. None of us here are very friendly with the police."

"Is that when he died?"

"No. His death hit him two years later. A heart attack. Quite suddenly, here in this room, and the silence between us became eternal." Hannah looked at Greg and whispered, "I'm tired. I'm tired of remembering."

"Would you like me to leave?"

"Only if—if you want to and would like to come back."

"I am searching for a small apartment here. When I have moved in I will return. I like you, Hannah."

"Do you?" she asked, and her tired face stared at him.

"Yes."

"Do you believe I did the right thing? I should have thought more of the boys and the damage done to them. I was wrong in that, but it was as if I was in chains. I cannot explain."

"I am not a judge," Greg replied. "I feel you are a very good woman and I would like to become a friend."

"Yes—we will see," she said, and as Greg got up from the table, she did the same. She held out her hand. "Just think of one thing, Greg."

"What is that?"

"François was destroyed by forces he could not fight. Catholicism. His family. His own weakness. What he did was a crime of the heart, but who of us are not guilty of such crimes? Crimes in the mind and the heart we commit unseen. He came out into the open."

"I will try to remember him as he was," Greg said, "and the brilliant colours he showed me and the emotions that he shared with me. He was partly responsible for those terrible acts, but he was also responsible for the good acts in his life."

Hannah kissed Greg on both cheeks.

"The whole of our society is responsible," she said, then patted his cheek gently and told him to go. He closed the door quietly and looked again at the unchanged door. His mind was blank as he made his way down the stairs to the street.

Part Two:
The Métro Stations

Greg felt tired, brutally tired. He needed sleep, he needed food, and the sky was so pale above him that its paleness seemed to reflect his own fragility. His shopping bag, containing the suits, book, manuscript, shirts and shoes, clung to him as if a part of him; these, his only belongings, the others left in Renaud's apartment. No, he could not think of Renaud now, but knew the memories would come despite him not wanting them to. Renaud, the mask, the great deceiver. He saw the name in bright lights, floating in his head. Renaud, the magician, the sleight of hand and the immaculate clothes as if constantly ready for a gala. No, he could not think of Renaud now.

At Barbès Métro station he bought a dubious-looking hamburger from a stand. A swarthy Arab face leered at him, and no, it was not desire (how could it be?) but hatred. Is hatred abstract? Could it be? Variations of hatred, like all variations of love, all jogging together in the circular kaleidoscope of life—who knows what the next permutation can be—a kiss or a knife? It is all the same as the kaleidoscope revolves, revealing its colours. He hurriedly ate at the kiosk and he was joined by several more Arabs. They too looked at him and it seemed to him that their look was as full of hate as the other man. He bit into the burger, and it tasted like horsemeat. This revolted him but he did not care because he had to eat. He bought a Coke and found that his pockets were full of cash. He could not understand it. How had the money appeared? Yes, he had been to a cash machine. He had withdrawn money. He had bought a copy of *Libération* and now he had bought a burger, but why did he have this quantity of small coins in his pocket? Irrationally, he felt like a beggar; a beggar who had succeeded in gathering enough money for the pitiful food he was now eating. He felt sweat break out beneath his clothes, a horrible clinging sweat. He threw the rest of the burger into a bin and hurried into the station.

Back on the same line, he felt sleepy, and huddled himself into a corner, and there was a free seat beside him and, despite the fullness of the train, yet again no one sat next to him. He rested his head against the glass partition beside him, conscious only of darkness. His eyes closed. Jagged nightmares jumped and haunted him—nonsense nightmares, but frightening. He dreamt of numbers, of a five followed by a two leaping at him, skimming across his sleeping consciousness, then falling houses and a smell of burning. He was in a womb and heard bombs dropping. He was not safe in the womb and he struggled free, but into what freedom? The gaze of life fell ferociously upon him. Birth was a terrible thing. Then came disconnected images, one after another; a cascade of them all unrelated to each other. What was it within him that was casting this absurd jigsaw puzzle of un-meaning? And God was there with a white beard and a grin as wide as a devouring beast's mouth. "I do not believe in you," he cried in his dream, and heard a sob as if someone, somewhere was crying. He had refused God, and the sobbing pulsed in his dreams; a beating blood heart of sorrow sounding through image after image. He scared himself awake, and no one noticed him. The seat beside him was still empty and his hands were still clutching his bag. What harsh text was it that he had with him? The thought almost voiced itself. Then he realised, and remembered out of his old memory, his own words; the words in the manuscript written by him so long ago, his words, repetitive, soaked in sex as sweat soaks the body. That old handwritten manuscript, held in the bag, like an aborted child; never to be born, to remain a half-formed thing. Repetition is the key to everything, he thought. It is the only thing; the clock within the self, the clock with its hands, and on walls, even in cell phones and emails written, the constant repetition of life as it unrolls, wrapped in words to cover the fact that every birth is a crime. But a crime against who? Against the clock of repetition, against the need for time that drives the pain of every living thing to annihilation. He put his hand shakily into the bag and felt the manuscript with its ancient encounters and its grinding of sex against sex, all there in a repetitive litany of words that ultimately reached no one, and which if they had, would have drowned in an orgasm. Drowned against the sound of the clock that is the constant repetition of the sexual act.

He was coming into a station and saw that it was Saint-Germain-des-Prés (oh, lost fields!) and he got up, shaking himself like an animal in need of a full awakening and got off the train. He perched himself as well as he could on a bench, brown in colour, that was meant more to be leant against than sat upon. The discomfort of this irritated him. A young man perched next to him, close enough for Greg to hear one of his favourite tracks of music, *Not Dark Yet* by Bob Dylan. As he heard the words of the song, faint but strong enough to hear the darkness, it hit him again. A love song. Or was it? Was it love that hits hard? He closed his eyes, and in a waking dream, felt himself being pulled downwards, sinking to aquarian depths. From those depths of liquid force, a monster emerged, no face, no form, but monstrous in its enfolding, invisible presence. Then he felt it to be himself: a child, crying, "I want a brother to love, to make love to, a twin to me, both torn from the same womb." This, all in a moment, a fraction of a moment, and then joining him, another monster, an antagonist. It is Renaud; again Renaud, and in this waking sleep, absurdly perched on the uncomfortable bench, the blow fell. His body was hit, and he felt pain in his stomach.

"Puis-je vous aider? Vous vous sentez malade?"

In a shaken voice, he replied that he was not ill, and the words came out in English, and then absurdly he knew that he was telling the young man how much he liked Bob Dylan. The young man's stare was one of withdrawal, and a train hurtled into the station. The young man had disappeared, and Greg had not followed him. He remained on the now-empty platform, his bag still in his hands. He shook it and the force made it fall to the ground. Stretching down, he picked up the contents of the bag which had spilt out onto the concrete. This whole process had exhausted him, and longing for a real seat to sit on, he walked the length of the platform, and waited for the next train which he knew would lead him again to Alésia, and there perhaps he would get off again.

"I must try not to think."

The words echoed around him as if they had not come out of his body. But he did think, and while pacing slowly up and down the Saint-Germain-des-Prés platform a whole scene from the past came to mind. Did it really exist? It came complete, and he looked at it, gazing into the mirror of this past where his former self was clearly visible. Conjointly with this scene, another scene, of him as a four or five-year-old competed for attention. The child for a moment won. He was in a room with his father and the kaleidoscope in his mind turned.

"I want a brother. To touch me there. To touch me below the tummy. To be together."

A coin spun in the air, and Nick's voice said, "*We* are the same coin. You are the same coin as me, but the other side."

"The one with the heads or the one with the tails?" Greg asked, and Nick laughed.

The kaleidoscope stopped moving. The scene disappeared. A longer one followed.

"Do not impose your own philosophy of what it means to be homosexual."

The kitchen area of the Islingword Street house. Nathan was with them, and he was there, Greg, his former self as Greg, and this Greg was angry.

"You have turned your Gay Liberation into something else."

"What?" Nathan asked.

120

"Into the mainstream. The mainstream of so-called gay culture."

"That's rubbish and you know it."

Nathan in his strong and defiant way pushed past both Nick and Greg and went into the garden. But Greg was relentless and followed him.

"Listen to me," he cried out.

"Why should I?" Nathan replied.

"Because what I have to say is true."

"Your truth, not mine."

"I agree," Greg said. "We have to defend ourselves against straight persecution, but is that done by retreating into mainly straight-run discos and dancing to *It's Raining Men*?"

"I really, really do not like you anymore, Greg." And there in the garden, with several neighbours peering out of windows from the house opposite, the argument continued. Nick came between them, and in his usual conciliatory voice, said, "You are having a stupid discussion. Who cares about all those doctrines and what we must do or what we must not do?"

"Shut up, Nick." Nathan replied.

"He has every right to give his opinion, Nathan. You are a fucking fascist. It is all about you as leader, isn't it? The leader of a parade that has long since left the streets."

"Okay, okay. Maybe the clubs have taken over. But there are still a lot of us left who are militant. And anyway, so what if we have liberated men to be able to have sex with multiple men in one night? At least they don't stay together in one house and fuck each other up mentally."

"Nathan," Nick said firmly. "Go home! Go home to Karel. Take it out on him. And what you said just now was—"

"—sickening," Greg interjected.

"Karel has arguments with me as well—and anyway, I *was* in this house, remember? It was not Gay Liberation as I saw it. I just took the place of Bart, who left your *ménage à quatre* and then Karel and I—"

"—loved each other one to one," Greg added again, a sour note of sarcasm in his voice. "I had a one-to-one with him too, and yes, it was love—a variation of love that played itself out as most love does."

Nick stared at Greg and asked, "But surely you believe some love does last?"

Greg knew he had been wrong in saying what he had just said and silently nodded his head, giving no verbal reply, and quite unexpectedly, not understanding it himself, he got up, went over to Nathan and kissed him on the mouth. Nathan pushed him away.

"You want to dislike me," Greg said, "and my opinions. Especially the opinion that all real lovers are outside of society completely; that sex and love are marginal and should be attracted to no political, and above all, to no sexually political movements."

"We are marginal *in* society," Nathan shouted.

Greg mocked him then, and said, "Then get out of society. Be really marginal. Ignore the fuckers and live on the outside of things—to the side of life as it were!"

"Is this man mad?" Nathan asked, turning to Nick.

"Yes, I am mad," Greg replied.

"You are both fools," Nick said quietly, "and believe it or not, our neighbours could elaborate on this and call it obscene. To them, two men kissing *is* obscene."

"I wanted to show Nathan that his dislike of me at the moment really boils down to him liking me too much. You really, really do desire me, don't you, Nathan?"

Nathan began to jump forward, looking as if he was going to attack, and Nick held them apart.

"I am Jewish. Karel is Jewish. Isn't that marginal enough?" Nathan cried out.

"You are not exactly forming an Israel for two, are you?" Greg replied, and Nathan, disregarding Nick, hit Greg in the face. It was not a hard blow, and Greg just rubbed at his skin. Nick did not move, and Nathan looked down at his shoes.

"Hot-blooded beautiful man," Greg said, "I forgive the blow. Put simply, I do not believe in the collectivity of Jews any more than I believe in the collectivity of homosexuals, or should I say, gay community? I am alone and join up with others at my will, and theirs of course. That is not a community. I never exceed, or would want to exceed, the number of four in my life."

Nathan mockingly applauded.

"How do you see old age, Greg? A loner can become very much alone."

"I know."

"Look, this is enough," Nick said.

Greg went into the house, and as he did so he heard Nathan say, "Now, why don't you make us all a nice cup of tea? And if they call the police—those people hanging out of their windows—I will take full responsibility. I will tell them and the police I am a riot in myself and that it is all my fault."

There was silence and Greg poured water into the kettle. He paused, then sat at the long wooden table, and Nathan, returning inside, joined him.

"Still friends?" he asked, as he sat down beside Greg.

"Of course."

"Will you kiss me again?"

"Are you trying to be provocative?"

"I admit I like it from you."

"Admit you love me."

Nathan shook his head.

"Greg, we would tear each other apart like wolves."

"Wolves also cuddle each other," Greg said.

"What is this about wolves?" Nick asked as he joined them.

"Nathan thinks I would tear him apart if we were lovers."

"Karel *is* his lover," Nick replied. "Not you."

"Yes, Nick, but don't let's get puritanical all of a sudden. We shared each other before. I would just like to win Nathan's heart, that's all."

Nathan laughed but looked awkward. "Why do you play around with people, Greg?" he asked. "I saw you as a magician, one night, binding us together. And we were bound for a while. But the magic failed, or don't you remember?"

"Not for me," Nick said.

Nathan turned to Nick. "But you and he are one, aren't you? Nothing will break you apart."

"How about loss of memory or death?" Nick replied, and then leaving them, went to make the tea.

"The neighbours have gone inside, no doubt a little disappointed. I exaggerated about the police. None of them would like to get that involved with us," Nathan said.

"Then let the three of us take off our clothes and have sex in the garden," Greg suggested, laughing.

"Horny?" Nathan asked him.

"Why do you ask that?"

"I know you."

"Not enough, Nathan, but I can tell you something. If we were together, you and I, the terrific fights would excite you, and we would take turns in wearing the boots and also take turns in fucking each other."

"Is this after my death?" Nick asked, placing mugs of tea in front of them."

"No, you are there—somewhere," Greg replied, and then the dark shadow of the future fell across his vision. He felt that he was in a vortex of his own making.

"I saw it all. I saw it all," Greg said, as he watched one passing train after another. He then made up his mind to give up on Alésia and to make his way to the platform opposite. He decided that he would change lines at Châtelet, his mind empty except for the words of Bob Dylan's song, *Not Dark Yet*.

On Line 1, he had almost walked into the glass barriers that separated the platform from the tracks, and it had been difficult to get a seat. A woman, not much younger than him, gave up her seat for him and he felt embarrassed taking it. I must look dreadful, and this suit I am wearing is clearly showing a great deal of wear and tear. It looks probably as creased and tired as I am, and then he patted the carrier bag, knowing that there were two suits inside that would save him in an emergency. He regretted not having changed into one while he was at the *brasserie* on the Rue de Rennes. The train was swift and wore its arrogant number 1 status with typical French pride. He laughed to himself as he passed the stations of Tuileries and then Concorde, prime places in a prime city, one noted for its homosexual cruising (or had that ceased thanks to AIDS and Grindr?) and the other for disposing of the aristocracy by depriving them of their heads. Yes, Métro Line 1 must be proud of these stops, and even more so of Franklin D. Roosevelt and Georges V. American bastions both, glowing with mercantile power and highly priced hotels. Hadn't Olivia da Havilland had lived in one of them? To think, she was in *Gone with the Wind*, before he had been born. The thought rejuvenated him enormously. His mind began to frolic in the cool pastures of the past and he was young once more, ejaculating with strength as he wanked himself off. No more dribbling semen, but the full spurt like that fountain in the Tuileries gardens. He was tempted to get off and have a glimpse of the Champs-Élysées, but then he thought of possible *Gilets Jaunes* protests and changed his mind. As the train moved towards Argentine, he remembered that the ritual car burnings on the Champs-Élysées took place on Saturdays, and this was not a Saturday. Did he care that the *Gilets Jaunes* were doing that? Not in the least. Did he care if Macron massacred the lot of them? Not in the least. He was tired: tired of society and its wretched change of clothes; a change of clothes that meant quite simply, power. Greg had no need for power now that he was the age he was. He had sneered at society in his late to middle years, but now he just let society do what it did. The wheels of persecution always turning somewhere, and soon he would be off the wheel, safely he hoped in the arms of whatever followed the distress of death. Had Nick been Nick in that café and that room, only yesterday, but seemingly aeons ago? Had he truly found him? And then his mind switched off. Unconsciousness hit him like the knockout blow of an over-keen boxer, and here was another scene, complete before him.

Greg murmured, "There doesn't seem to be a plot to our lives, just incidents and people, passing, returning, passing again. Incidents happen, then fade away, and we remember so little and suffer like—"

"—animals," the youth in his bed replied. Greg had come to his house in a small street near to the Old Vic theatre. It was in the early 1990s. The youth's name was Charles. He was eighteen, rich and from a good family. He had left his education and the prospect of going to Oxford as his parents had wanted, but all the same, they had bought him this small house in this small street, and then left him to himself, ashamed of him as he had declared his homosexuality. He had elder brothers who were straight and had straight friends and did not want to be embarrassed by a queer (their words) brother. Charles liked the arrangement and did not even have to work as a yearly income came with the house. He also liked mature men; rough men; and Greg could play that role easily. Charles liked to call him bear, as he liked teddy bears and had read *Brideshead Revisited*. Greg enjoyed being taken out to expensive restaurants and didn't mind not paying.

"Couldn't they have bought you a bigger house?" he had asked Charles.

"Not a bit of it. I like most people to think I am on the poorish side. I want to be an actor."

"Poor you!" Greg had replied with more than an edge of sarcasm.

It wasn't love. No, it certainly was not love. It was as Greg called it, the call of one animal to another, and in his own way, Charles too had a contempt for society.

"I want to play the working-class man. Only those roles. I want to pretend I have come from way up North or somewhere and am fighting it out against the posh actors of the day."

"With your accent? Dream on."

What had really brought him to this youth's bed? He was now in his fifties, which to him was simply the prelude to old age. He had lived a long time, and already the emotional compass of his past was piling up behind him; not death, except for Anna succumbing to cancer in the Orkneys, but the smell of death was in the air; the smoke of many crematoria in the gay community had suffocated him, and he could no longer breathe as he had once breathed. He had tried Paris in the late 1980s and now it was London, again, the second time that he had tried it since he had lived there in the 1960s. The kaleidoscope was moving very fast now, and the overspill of shapes and colours made him giddy. Each shifting shape and colour *was* him; it was *his* kaleidoscope, and he was at the heart of its relentless movement.

"I want it to stop," he said to Charles one day. They were in a café off the Charing Cross Road and the surge of people passing beyond the café window brought on a feeling of panic.

"Stop what?" Charles asked, fork poised with a rather large piece of chocolate cake on it.

"This—this life!"

"Don't be silly. Eat the cake in front of you. You've barely eaten all day, and I know how hunger brings on a tantrum."

"A tantrum?" Greg laughed and stared down at the plate.

"I know it's partly a lack of food, and also the news I had today."

"Oh, yes," Greg said, and looked at Charles.

"Well, it has upset you, hasn't it?"

Greg's mind had already forgotten the so-called news and he looked once more at the crowds as they paraded themselves, as they stared into shops, as they laughed and followed each other in a never-ending flow.

"I apologise, Charles," he said. "Call it simply my fear that the years are advancing too fast."

"You are in the ripest decade of all. Full maturity. I love it."

"Love it? Or me?" Greg asked.

"I don't mind being a child bride."

"Don't be camp."

"Sorry, it must be the chocolate cake. It brings out a sort of Madame de Pompadour mood in me. I will return to my normal self and lower my voice to its butchest pitch. Like I had to do for the audition."

"The audition?"

Greg's mind was confused. What was Charles talking about?

"The one I had a short while back—and the reply, the news I had today, which I really do suspect upset you. Me going on tour and all that. Leaving you for a while."

Oh, yes, Greg thought. Charles has got himself a role. Then he had a harsh vision of the future; there would be other actors. The play in a way was just beginning.

Irritated by Greg's silence, Charles replied, "Well, has it upset you?"

"What's the name of the play?" Greg asked.

"Oh for God's sake, Greg, you are not that old yet. Senility has not set in—or has it?"

"There are so many dramas, tragedies, comedies, and further on down the line, vulgar farces."

"But I told you today—"

"Yes, I know. They have given you the part." He paused. "Well?"

"Well, it only happens to be Cliff in *Look Back in Anger.* That's all. A touring company. Brighton, Leeds, York, the list goes on."

Greg's mind cleared. He saw Charles as being a far too pretty Cliff. Passive to whoever was going to play Jimmy Porter. He will probably be the youngest Cliff ever seen in the play, he mentally concluded. "It's a good role."

"It's a bloody good start," Charles replied.

"And the lead? Is he good?"

"We won't get on," Charles said petulantly, and finished off the chocolate cake. He then started staring at the uneaten cake on Greg's plate. "May I—as you are not?" he asked.

Greg pushed his plate towards him. One day this eighteen-year-old will be very fat. How many times had they eaten a box of chocolates in bed while watching a film, with Charles demolishing the contents?

"You'll need to watch your figure," he said, disdain in his voice. Greg did not like plump people.

"I'm not exactly a male Rubens. I have a six-pack and my arse is firm. There in all its vulgarity is my splendour."

"Which cannot, and never has, lasted for anyone."

"You're not fat! Why shouldn't I be like you *eventually*?"

"Let's change the subject," Greg said.

The play was not a success. The young lead was too posh and Charles imitating a working-class voice and background was embarrassing. Only a young actress as Alison saved the tour from total disaster. The actress who played the other female role was as bad as Charles. After it was over, Greg at last commented on it.

"You want me to say that you were good, don't you?"

"Not if you don't want to," Charles replied sulkily.

"This was your first role, and you were terrible."

Angrily, Charles replied that his agent didn't think so, and that he had a part lined up for him in a tour of a Restoration comedy.

"Now *that*, you will succeed in!"

"What exactly was wrong with my acting as Cliff?"

"Your agent should have told you that you have to *be* the part on stage, not just act it as best as you can."

"Method rubbish! That may have been good for your generation, but in a touring company in the 1990s it really is no longer the point. I know I am not in the Brando league, but what I did was good enough for the provinces."

"Wouldn't you have liked a West End transfer?"

"I am training for that. And so what if I was on the, well, juvenile side for this part? The girls in the audience loved me."

Greg knew that there had to be an end to his relationship with Charles, and quietly he told him so. Charles burst into tears and Greg thought it was the best acting from him he had seen so far.

"That's good," he said.

"What?"

"What you're doing now. You're almost making me believe that you will really miss me."

"I love you," Charles said, and for a moment Greg wanted to believe him."

"Then I am sorry if I have to hurt you."

Charles shrugged his shoulders.

"But what's the use of loving you, if you don't love me back?"

"Maybe I am tired of all those boring towns and cities I watched you play in," Greg said. "I travelled to every one of them. Do you think those audiences really cared a toss about England in the 1950s?"

"It had contemporary relevance."

"*Look Back in Anger* is about the 1950s, and yet the director and the designer tried to make it look as if it were set now. The absurd clothes for a start, and the haircuts."

"Can we talk about *us* now please? *Look Back in Anger* is over."

"I know," Greg said, and that was the last he saw of Charles.

Delirium. He was in a hospital. A Paris hospital tied to a bed. The ultimate sadistic act of male nurses all dressed in white.

The kaleidoscope had another shaking and another pattern, but it was similar to the one that had gone before.

London. Another young man. His name was Chris, and he

had met him at the publishers who were working on his book of short stories. Chris was compact, sexy and dark-haired. Greg took him to the Salisbury for a drink and after half an hour they were holding hands in the pub.

"I've read your stories," Chris said, "and there was nothing to edit or correct."

Greg smiled. "I'm not that good."

"Don't underestimate yourself."

"It's not that. Maybe I can express myself, but what am I capturing there on the paper? What, in the great scheme of things, does it matter?"

"It matters."

"Maybe and maybe not. If it hadn't been for a man called Nick and his passion for books, which fucking got on my nerves back then, I would never have put pen to paper. I wrote them. He typed them up."

Chris looked at him with his deep, dark eyes, and Greg longed to see his body.

"You excite me," Greg said, pressing Chris's hand tightly.

"Your work excites me."

"Only that?"

"No," Chris smiled back. "I like your solid body, and you are taller than me. But perhaps we are going too fast—"

"A train can speed," Greg said. The words came to him as though his life depended on this fact. "Carry me far," and the words in his mind sped along the tracks of an unknown line.

Looking up, Greg saw that he had crossed onto another line: number 6. And he was crossing the Seine at Passy, stopping at Bir-Hakeim. He was tempted to get out and walk by the Seine, but he did not have the time. He was in a hurry to recall as much as he could and there was nothing to make him remember anything at Bir-Hakeim. He closed his eyes, and the shape of Chris reappeared, and that day in the Salisbury.

"I want you," Greg said, and the pressure of Chris's hand in his grew stronger. Underneath the table, hidden by the crowded laughter and high-pitched words, Chris moved Greg's hand onto his thigh, and then slowly moved it upwards until Greg felt the bulge and the solid mass of Chris's erection. Then they looked at each other. Greg fell in love with the darkness in those eyes.

"I want to know about your background," he said.

Chris laughed, and pressed Greg's hand ever more fiercely against his sex.

"I went to Cambridge. I met many interesting people. I studied the so-called Magic Realist writers."

"The South American writers?"

"Not only them, but in the main yes. You have read Márquez?"

"No," Greg replied.

"I will read him to you. It is beautiful to read aloud after making love and travel to those impossible places of the imagination where Márquez created his images."

"No wait! I have read him. You are talking about *One Hundred Days of Solitude*."

"That's the book. Now I only want to talk about us. I don't want to know about other lovers, even if they were—are—special to you."

"Jealous?" Greg teased and began to rub at Chris's erection. He saw Chris's eyes close, and a look of concentration appeared on his face as if the force of sensation and desire had now totally possessed him. Greg stopped the sliding pressure of his hand and waited for Chris's dark eyes to enchant him again.

"Why did you stop?" Chris asked, and the dark eyes looked angry.

"I was afraid I was getting you too near."

"No, I can hold off for a long time. My cock can be wet for hours before climax. I have trained myself. People are always greedy when they see the size of it. They eat too quickly, so I have learnt to hold them off from satisfying their greed."

Greg took away his hand.

"Why do that? I like the warmth, the assurance of it."

"Don't tease me," Greg said, and then looked at the people around them. A smattering of gay men, but more women than he had seen here before, in the past, not that he minded their presence, but the so-called collective he had once experienced in this place had thinned out. Death? No, not death, just a loss of interest. He had to believe that. With Chris beside him the virus did not exist. The exterminating God of torture, blindness and ultimate annihilation had been drawn back into the vortex of itself.

"Why so far away?"

"I am just looking, Chris, at the others. I do not see many lovers here."

Chris reached out with his hands and forced Greg to look at him.

"We were talking about my background. My grandfather came from South America, which accounts no doubt for my love of Latin American literature." Then he paused and added, "To be exact, he was from Cuba. Have you been to Cuba?"

"No," Greg said, and he saw a large city of broken buildings and palaces in his mind; the edge of the world, once given over to voracious American tourists.

"I must let you read my copy of *Paradiso*. José Lezama Lima. A great writer. Those who know, call it a gay book, but I am not sure I agree with the limitation of that category."

"I've never read the book."

"I will lend it to you."

Chris stood up, close to Greg and Greg could see the contours of the erection in his trousers. He wanted to kiss the outline of the shaft.

"You want to come back with me?" Chris asked.

"Where?"

"Earl's Court."

"Why there? Is it for the bars?"

Chris looked serious, and briefly sat down again next to Greg.

"To hell with those places. I may be very sexual, but I do not give to those men. I pleasure myself, not them."

"But you said about the men you went with—how you hold off—"

"And you believed me? I was lying. Bravado. Showing off. No, I am scared of the virus, and I am not someone who likes variety. I want just one man. I have in fact been with relatively few men, and if you don't believe what I am saying we will say goodbye." He looked down at his hands, and for some reason that Greg could not understand, Chris hit his thighs with them. The sound was loud, and several people looked.

"Don't," Greg said.

"Better not to know me," Chris murmured.

"I want to go with you."

"And then? Will you stay? I don't want you if you won't stay."

Greg was doing nothing with his life. He knew that it was not too late to hope for something resembling a future.

The Métro station at Chevaleret. He got off there and left the station, walking down the Rue du Chevaleret, glancing at the once poor houses, and found a café where he could relieve his bowels and have something to eat. A clock ticked loudly on the wall. The hours were moving swiftly. He got up, paid, and returned to the station and got on the same line where he would change trains at Nation. He wanted to return in memory to Chris.

"Did you know that Christopher Columbus was supposed to have landed in Holguín Province? I like to think that is why I was given the name Christopher."

Greg was in Chris's arms at his home in Earl's Court as Chris said this. Relaxing after sex, he watched as Chris rubbed gently against his body, and he felt that large sex grow larger, as the inexhaustible desire returned.

"I want you to do something," Chris said.

"What?" Greg asked, reaching down and touching the tip

134

of the glans. He was obsessed by the purple and the constantly wet slit. The shaft itself was very dark, a dark brown colour that he had sucked on so many times and wanted again. "To take you in my mouth? I am ready—"

"No, not that. I want to lie on my stomach and for you to hit me."

"Hit—?" Greg asked.

"Yes. On my buttocks. Hard."

"But you have never—"

"We've been together for two months now, and I was too ashamed to ask. I like pain. Physical pain. Then, and it will be the first time, I want you inside me, and I trust you, so, no need for a condom."

Greg sat up in the bed. "I can't fuck you without one," he replied.

"I want the—"

"—danger of it? Does the adventurer in you want that? Well, I can't do it."

Chris did not reply to this, but turned over onto his stomach, and said quietly, "Then just hit me. Make the flesh red. You have heavy hands. I love your hands. Then lay as many blows as you can higher up on my back. Imagine I am a slave. If you care for me, please do this for me. I have wanted it for years. I have never asked anyone before."

Staring down at the body he desired so much, Greg felt at first confused, then the anger he felt towards Chris made him act. Without feeling, he made the buttocks red with his blows. He slapped and he beat against them, and Chris raised himself higher and then he was kneeling, and Greg saw the length of the sex and the hanging balls which he hit as well. Chris screamed, either in pain or in pleasure. The balls swung defiantly, side to side, and alternating with the buttocks, he attacked them.

"Now my back," Chris cried out.

Kneeling over Chris, Greg now sexually excited, hit his back with heavy slaps before his hands turned into fists and began to beat hard. Chris screamed that he was about to come, and Greg, stopping, asked him to lie on his back.

"The pain—I can't."

"Do it. Lie on your back."

Chris lay on his back, and his face was covered in sweat. The sweat dribbled into his eyes and his black hair was matted. Greg stared at the ugly beauty of what he had done to this man, and then, lowering his head, sucked on the erect penis. Within seconds his mouth was full of sperm.

"I love you," Chris said, and Greg stood up and walked naked to the bathroom. He looked at his lined face in the mirror, staring at what he thought was the darkness there. He stepped under the shower and within minutes Chris joined him. It seemed to Greg like a last act of submission as Chris soaped his back, smearing the lather tenderly over the flesh. Greg felt as Chris reached for his buttocks and washed them and then going between his legs caressed his balls and penis with soap.

"Thank you," Greg said coldly, and reaching for a towel, stepped out and wiped himself dry. He then left the bathroom and walked back into the bedroom. Avoiding the turmoil of the bed he made his way into the living room. The walls were black, and this set off the Art Deco objects that Chris had collected over the years. He poured himself a cognac and sat down on the sofa, elegantly grey, and slight in frame. As he sipped the cognac he had only one thought, and the thought was terrible for him. I have ruined my life, he thought. I have ruined my life. Then Chris came in, dressed as he usually was, impeccably as if he had to be in tune with his surroundings. He poured himself a glass of gin and then looked down at Greg.

"What should I say?" he asked.

"Nothing," Greg replied.

Nothing. Greg was no longer in the room, but memory, as it can, shifted into dream. He was in a city that resembled Paris but could have been any other beautiful city in Europe.

It was European, because the train station that the dream started in had the times of trains departing for the East: Warsaw, Moscow, and also for the south, Madrid, Lisbon. Lisbon was a city he had often wanted to visit, and as he stared at the board with the names and numbers of different lines, he thought, that is the last of improbable cities. Lisbon is the jutting out point of our Western consciousness, and the thought gave him vertigo. He was on the brink of falling, and then, as dreams do, he was in the centre of a city and around him were fine houses, many vacant with open windows, curtains flapping in the mild wind, and beyond the curtains, vast tall rooms with no furniture. House after fine house was the same, and when he had left that area he entered a park and there was a lake surrounded by statues and in the middle of the lake a mansion of great elegance and beauty; the sort of grandeur to be seen on the Italian lakes, and it was in the process of being demolished. As he wandered around the park, he saw people walking by oblivious to the destruction of this magnificent building. And at some points on this desolate walk, statues were falling apart, not by any natural causes, but toppled by the hands of men. He found himself in a maze of destruction. The park had villas hidden in the trees, villas broken into, looted, and some even half burnt out. Furniture, mainly chairs and tables from the 18th century were scattered among the trees, and the feeling he had suddenly was, this is France, and zig-zagging his way through the debris and the thin yet densely packed trees, he found the lake again, and behind him was a dark soaring tower, black with tightly closed black windows facing out over the destroyed park. "Monsieur looks troubled." Turning, he looked into the face of a woman standing next to him. Her attire suggested she held some official capacity, but he could not define it, and her voice was quietly considerate. "Yes," he replied. "What are they doing to this park—and to the mansions in the city? Why are all those empty rooms and vacant places half-destroyed?" She sighed and looked down at the ground. "It is to make the city better," she said at last. "It is to improve on what was. Do you remember how it was?" And she looked up and he saw tears in her eyes. "I was here," he said. "Then the change must be a shock to you." After she said this she walked over to a scarred statue of a youth by the side of the lake, and reaching out with her hands, touched the ruined marble. A piece of the statue fell away as she did so. "Apollo," she said. "He is not known any more. I was once a guardian of these gardens, but now I am only here to see that the work of destruction is completed. It has been a frightening cycle in my lifetime to watch the turning away from enlightened beauty to the prospect of more skyscrapers, more architects raising monuments of icy steel and glass. The beauty of the future, they tell me, but it is the forgetting of all aesthetics, of all memory of the past." Greg, dismayed, went and touched the statue as well. The fine features of the face were pitted as if shot at by bullets. "Apollo by the lake," he said softly, "and the poetry? What of that? What of the books and the paintings? Are all the mansions empty?" "Yes, and the palaces as well. New government buildings will be built, and here, in the centre of the lake, where that fine building still partly remains, will be a new cathedral. Ice and white, they promise us. The coldness of their new God. The Catholics and other denominations have joined together, and it is their belief that God should have better; a better monument than before." "And the leader of this country?" "Monsieur, even the leader has been fragmented into many leaders. The leaders of the suburbs have joined with the leaders of the centre of the city, and as a group they rule. The people are happy, because they have been promised the riches of the rich, and their banners of protest will no longer be necessary. The skyscrapers will protect them, and the supermarkets will be full. They know all this and see it as a new paradise, and that is why the ice and the steel of the new cathedral is necessary. The lakes of the city will be drained of water, and concrete will be laid down for all to walk upon." A man joined them. A man with a face as pitted as the statue, and Greg could see the woman was in fear of him. Suddenly she changed her voice and looking at Greg said, "Monsieur is happy, *non*?" Bowing his head, Greg moved away, and from the dream he stepped onto another train.

He was at Nation Métro station and had boarded a train on Line 2. He sat without dream or memory and saw the station of the dead pass by, Père-Lachaise, and his mind once more began to recall Chris.

"I have bought this for us to read," Chris said and handed Greg a fat volume of gay theory. It was a brightly coloured volume, rainbows intertwining on its front and back covers.

Greg was seated in the Art Deco room, this time at a table, and there were manuscripts to be edited and read piled up in front of him.

"What would I want with *that*?" he replied.

"I was so interested in it that I put little bookmarks in to show you the pages you should read," Chris said. "It is full of things we need to know about ourselves as gay men."

"But I am not a gay man," Greg said. "Not as those books define it."

"Greg, there are pages of special importance here. For us. As a couple. A new century is only a year away. Do you realise we have the full responsibility of that century before us?"

"At my age?"

Greg got up from the table and paced the room.

"Those who are growing old should know as much as the young. Look at these pages about the disappearance of us as a community. The elderly will be separated off from the young; pushed to one side. They will have no more need for us."

"Who are *they*?" and Greg knew that he had to reject this book.

"Aren't you concerned that the clubs and bars where young and old used to mix together will be emptied out, shut down? That all the community centres will be closed?"

"Not particularly."

"Greg, remember the past and what it was like. Do you want all that to disappear?"

Greg paused in his pacing and went over to an art deco table lamp: a golden bowl of light mounted on a slab of marble beside the figure of a faun. He touched it with his fingers. He had grown fond of this object over the years—a full seven years since he had met Chris.

"The past is a fiction," he replied. "This book is for the noble in mind, not the truthful. Nobility of theory is the worst lie of all about the homosexual. The idealisation; the mock heroics, like Don Quixote attacking the windmills."

"Rubbish!" Chris said.

"I am sure it is," Greg replied sarcastically, caressing again the cold flesh of the faun.

"We cannot, cannot shut ourselves away into selfish cubicles, little boxes that we will be forgotten in."

This made Greg really angry, and he shouted, "So, how was it exactly in these mythical bars? The young chose the young, as they always have and always will, and the elderly chose the young as well. I suppose you are thinking, what of the daddies? What of the ageing bodies in leather or jeans or conventionally dressed? Well, they were alone, Chris, as the elderly have and always will be. Alone, waiting for the occasional youthful crumb to be thrown at them. Sitting or standing in corners, either in groups of aloneness or very seriously alone lonely."

"And the happy ones?" Chris shouted back. "People of a certain age together, and very often with a younger partner, yes, all together in the same—"

"—boat!" Greg finishing the sentence for him.

"So, you want us to be holed up in isolation?"

"I am not in isolation. Neither are you. We have not been to a bar for years because we do not need those places. Or maybe you think that a drunken couple, both addicted to alcohol and feeding the pubs and clubs with money is a good thing? Or whole groups of drunks—on getting there—putting money into straight hands—which is so often the case—is just fine and dandy?"

"That's an Americanism. Delete it from the text."

Greg burst out laughing, and going over to the table, picked up a random manuscript and without looking, marked a page with a red pen.

"Don't do that!"

Chris knocked into Greg, and Greg slapped him across the face, still laughing, but now Chris was serious, and fell to his knees and taking out his cock began to wank. "I need this," he said, as he pleadingly looked up at Greg. "Hit me harder." Greg did so, repeatedly and after Chris had splashed his cum all over the carpet, Greg walked into the kitchen and drank a glass of water. How many blows had he given over the past years? How many welts and even the drawing of blood? On one occasion he had knocked Chris out with the ferocity of his hands. It was a day that had appalled him, but still he stayed on. Chris joined him in the kitchen.

"Did you clean the carpet?" Greg asked, faking dominance. He was not in the mood.

"The white disappeared into a light part of the carpet. It is dry."

"Not good enough," Greg said.

"I tried to get it all off. It was not thin cum, it was globules, easily lifted off—most of them."

Sitting on a chair, a bright light overhead, Greg put his head in his hands.

"Are you ill?"

"No, Chris, I am not ill. I am tired, yes. While you were out working, I was trying to catch up on work you left here."

"I'm grateful."

"Doesn't your publisher friend publish any books that are not about wars in far-off galaxies or robots on heat?"

"That is the firm's speciality. We are waiting for the next great science fiction novel."

"The twenty-first century," Greg said, and lowered his hands. He stared blankly up at the white overhead light. He saw nothing and wanted to see nothing. The parade of the future was too far into the distance.

He looked out of the window at the Métro station. Blanche. He had walked all over Paris, many, many years ago and could not recall the outside of this station, but before he could leave the train, the doors closed, and wearily he sat in another seat, this time facing the doors. A noisy child sat next to him. A girl. She was too young to be alone. No more than seven or eight and Greg was worried about her. There was no parent in sight and leaning towards the girl he asked her name.

"*Hélène.*"

"*C'est un joli nom, ça!*"

"*Tu trouves?*"

She stared up at him, then laughed and put out her tongue.

"*Et tes parents?*"

"*Je ne sais pas. Là-bas. Loin de nous,*" and she pointed down the carriage where a young couple were embracing each other.

"*Ces gens là?*" Greg asked.

"*Oui. Maman et papa.*"

Greg walked down the carriage, and the man had his hand up the woman's skirt. There was practically no one else in that part of the carriage, and anyway, if there had been would anyone have cared? He tapped the man on the shoulder. A thick-set face turned and looked at Greg angrily.

"*Quoi, encore?*"

Greg asked if the little girl was theirs, and the woman shrugged and the man said yes, then he asked Greg if it was any of his business. Greg said he was frightened for her and the man laughed, and then resumed the embrace. Greg giving up, walked back to the girl who was watching him with curiosity. He sat down, smiled at her and there was silence between them. The girl hummed a tune, and Greg tried to pretend that she was not there, that she was not abandoned, but safe with the couple who were, as the girl had described, far from her. When they reached the Métro Monceau, the couple came to fetch her, and with a sneer on his face, the man looked down at Greg.

"*Vieux con!*" he said, and they pulled the child away and got off the train just in time.

Old bastard, Greg thought. Not so far off, I will be eighty soon. That's what I am, an old bastard to all of them now. It is of no importance. I have aged in one day. He glanced at the advertisements in front of him and was nauseated by the era he was in. "Savage days," he whispered to himself, and for a moment he wanted to die, to throw himself under one of the Métro trains. Then he laughed aloud at the melodramatic thought. That is for the drama queens, he thought—the diva lovers, the opera buffs who want to go out with the maximum of attention. I am not gay enough for that. I am not gay in their terms full stop. Not gay in their tribal terms at all. I will not, cannot fit into their world, maybe not into any world anymore. I had sex with men for decades, loved one above all, Nick, and Karel next, but I have never been gay in the terms imposed upon me by either gays or straights. He closed his eyes, and the carriage seemed to slow down as if it was gliding, gliding softly over a track covered by a film of thin water.

"The lake. I am crossing the lake," he murmured silently as he went back, back to the room with the faun and the golden light.

"It is better to talk to a cup of coffee than it is with you."

Chris was staring down at him, taunting him.

"Go to hell," Greg replied.

"I am already in it. With you."

Greg got up out of the chair, out of the Métro seat, out of time itself, and hit him hard across the face. Chris hit him back. The blows between them now were mutual. The year was 2001 and Greg had been with him for so long, so very long. Yet distant. Distant as the parents of the child in the

Métro carriage, only worse; he was not vulnerable, and he could have left. How soft the laziness of life becomes the older you get. He thought that often, but it did not make him move. He was passively aggressive with Chris until Chris turned the tables on him and became the master (as he called it). He was heavy in his violence and in his now physical ugliness.

Chris went into the bedroom and the pattern of Greg's life weaved again the same old routine, the same old story. He quickly and quietly put on a jacket, collected a few manuscripts of his own in the room, and finding a satchel; a schoolboy's satchel that had once been Chris's, and putting the manuscripts inside, he was ready to leave. He went to the bedroom door which was ajar. Chris was on the bed, asleep and snoring. He closed the bedroom door, and after selecting a few books from a bookshelf, went out of the front door, taking the keys of the flat from his pocket, he slipped them through a gap that should not have been there beneath the door and walked out into the street. A vagabond stranger.

Greg looked at the twenty-two-year-old male escort who called himself Luke.

"Can I use a dildo on you?" the young man asked. He had a bag with him, a little black bag that made him look like a doctor.

"Shall we sit down?" Greg asked and waved a glass of cognac at him.

"You sure you want the full two hours? I mean I can get it over with in an hour."

This was not what he wanted from a doctor. And what else did Luke have in the black bag? A scalpel?

"No, I like the operation to be done well," he replied.

"It's your money," and Luke took the cognac and sniffed it. "Expensive," he said.

"Are you a connoisseur?" Greg was in the mood for games. After all, this was to be the last of them. He had promised that to himself.

"You having a laugh?" and down went the cognac, down the broad lusty throat. Greg watched the youth's Adam's apple rise and fall.

"I like your throat," Greg said.

Luke placed the empty glass on the small living room table.

"I can take the biggest," he murmured, then blushed as if he had never made that amazing revelation before.

"How extraordinary!" Greg replied.

"Now you *are* having a laugh."

Then, both he and Luke did the strangest of things. They made what can only be described as a dance around each other. In a decreasing circle they went, legs raising slightly as if in some courtly ritual, and this movement of strange tenderness went on for quite some time.

"We should have music," Greg said.

Luke looked at him, and his dark eyes and his dark face glowed red as if he was on fire within.

"Never could stand still," he said. "At my infant school they always thought I needed the toilet. I was constantly hopping on one leg, and then the other."

"How confusing for you," Greg said.

"I liked teasing them."

"Do you like teasing me?"

"Not particularly."

"You know I am not going to have sex with you, don't you?"

All movement stopped, and Luke stared at Greg in amazement, then opening his jeans, brought out his erect penis.

"But what about this?" he asked.

"Thank you for showing it. I will keep the memory. The last one perhaps—or at least with someone so young."

Putting the object of so many desires away, Luke blushed again. He hid the erection with his hands as it still showed in his jeans.

"I have never had to do that before," he said.

"Don't take it seriously. I am sure many clients want very little when it comes down to the—well, the reality of it."

"Most want too bloody much. I am a bottom. People think it is easy being a bottom, just lying there and taking it, but some of these old blokes have such whoppers. They expect me to take it all, and my boyfriend doesn't like me having a gaping arse afterwards."

Greg wondered if these graphic details were meant to turn him on, but Luke looked too straightforward for that; in fact straight was exactly how Greg would have described him. His dark eyes seemed to plead to Greg for understanding.

"Don't you ever penetrate?" Greg asked.

"You mean am I versatile? No, I like to receive. But if I really have to with a client I will, but I hate seeing their old arses."

"Then aren't you glad I am not asking anything more of you?"

"I'd take your cock."

"No, Luke. The desire is simply not there. But I wanted one last time to be with—" he paused and made them both a cup of coffee. He didn't want alcohol to blur his decision.

When he placed the coffee in front of Luke the youth said, "What did you mean by *the last time*? Are you dying or something?"

"Something, yes. I do not think I am dying. Who can ever be sure. A tumour somewhere, just waiting."

"For fuck's sake, I don't want to talk of tumours, not with a client. It's the final private thing, isn't it?"

Sensing a contradiction, Greg asked, "But you wanted to know if I was dying. Be consistent."

"Sorry," Luke sounded like a child. "My nan died of a brain tumour. I was there at the death bed, in the hospital. It was fucking bad of my parents to have taken me there. I was only ten. You remember things when you are ten."

"Yes," Greg said, recalling his own early years. Ten was

about right for the memories to collect; before it is all fragments and blurred images, like tearing the flesh on his thumb in a lawnmower. How he had screamed, and looking down, he saw the childhood scar still there. He was seven, in a garden in Portslade and had fallen forward in the grass just as the cutting knives approached. He had screamed, but the rest of the memory was gone; all swallowed up in the reservoir of the brain, perhaps one day to return in a nightmare. He rubbed his eyes as for some inexplicable reason, tears were about to fall. He did not want to make an old-age spectacle of himself.

They sat in silence for a long time. Luke just looked around the room, and Greg looked at Luke, at his face, not beautiful, but mushy in its fresh blushing cheeks, overblown somehow as if youth had too rapidly given him its gifts. His mouth was rich, and Greg wondered how his kiss would be, imagining too much saliva and too much sucking on the tongue of the other who was sharing it. His body was well built, not in a gym-trained way, but in that casual way that nature produces, compact and strong, but needing to be taken care of. Too soon the flab would begin, and the sagging of buttock and breast would become all too apparent.

"I have to go," Luke said, and stood up.

"Yes," Greg replied and took the appropriate amount of money from his pocket. He was not used to get-down-to-work escorts and he was concerned about tipping. How much would please Luke's ego? He had not done his research. He erred on the side of caution and brought out perhaps too many notes from his pocket.

"This is a little something to go towards a gift for your lover."

Luke blushed again, and with a sense of the ridiculous Greg felt like a grandfather clumsily showing the right sort of affection which he assumed in the straight world was money.

"I didn't earn all this, did I?" Luke said, the blush increasing, and Greg's sudden amusing fantasy was of a nineteenth-century farmer's boy.

"Goodnight Luke. Take care of yourself."

After fumbling with the front door, Luke was gone, and leaving the door ajar Greg listened to his heavy steps as they descended into that lost domain of his world.

"Good night."

He woke up. Porte Dauphine. The train had stopped, the carriage was empty. He went out onto the platform and stretched his legs, then decided to sit for a while and look around him. He was bored by what he saw, and he desperately needed a cognac. He was also hungry again. The flesh demanded these satisfactions, and he knew he needed to go to the toilet. All the signs of being old, of having crunched the body, over the years, into this abject state of need. The train slowly left the station, and he waited for another one. He decided to make his way back the same way that he had come. When the train arrived, he got onto it and soon he was rapidly passing many stations and there were few people now getting on. At Métro Blanche he decided to get off at the next stop, Pigalle, and when he exited he made his way to the fountain, the fountain of his first youthful visit to Paris. Many of the former invitations to pleasure had gone, and the lights promising the most daring nudes in the world, had perhaps long since disappeared. During which decade had this happened and where was the hotel he had stayed in? He did not want to look for it but made his way to the nearest bar. He asked for a sandwich, but all the bread was gone. He drank two cognacs, and then went and found another bar where he got the food that was needed, and then made his way back to the fountain. He called out, "Bart," and stared into the darkness within that overwhelms.

"Bart," he called, and instead of Bart, there was Nick looking at him in dismay.

"It's late," Nick said, "and you have been dreaming."

The television was on in the basement room overlooking the garden. The big red clock on the wall showed the time as being almost ten o'clock at night.

"I dreamt of Bart," Greg said. "I am dreaming of you."

"How is he in that Orkney house?" Nick replied, and laughing, went to make some tea.

"I was on a train," Greg added, I've no idea where I was going, or if I was returning."

"That really is a dream about *life*, Greg."

"Yes," and Greg got up off the too comfortable, too old sofa, and yawned. He looked up at the ceiling and there was a dark water stain on it. "How did that happen?" he asked, pointing.

"You had a bath, Greg, and it overflowed, for God's sake, are you losing your memory or something? If you are, let me bring you up to date with a few news bulletins. Bart is in Anna's house in the Orkneys. Karel has gone to live with Nathan as we predicted he would, and there is just you and I."

"I know," Greg said.

"All of us slowly drifting towards middle age."

Nick came towards Greg who took him in his arms. They kissed for a long while, and then Nick released himself.

"Come on, let's go to bed," he said.

In the bed, Nick intimately sniffed at Greg's body. He sniffed at his armpits, then burrowing down under the sheet, sniffed at his groin, then he smelled his way in a line up past the belly button, the neck, and ultimately the face.

"What did you do that for?" Greg asked.

"Just testing."

"Testing what?"

"When you last had a bath. You're groin smells of urine, and the rest."

"So what?" Greg said.

"It means you are depressed and that you are not taking care of yourself. I could smell you downstairs, but I thought it best to challenge you here where it matters."

"Do you want me to sleep in the other room?"

"Of course not. I would just like—not to insist, but would

like it if you started taking baths once more."

"I'll have a French wash tomorrow."

"You mean your cock and your arse, and maybe, if they are lucky, your armpits."

Greg got out of bed and went downstairs. He ran the water, and as he was about to step into it, Nick joined him. Naked they stepped into the bath together, and Nick at once started to wash Greg's chest and neck.

"Like a child," Greg murmured.

"Is that our fantasy for tonight?"

"Silly fucker," Greg replied.

"Now stand up."

Greg stood up and his erection embarrassed him. As if taking no notice of it Nick washed around it, and flannel in hand, washed between his legs and then approaching the anus, asked Greg to open his legs wider. Using the flannel, Nick cleaned the hole thoroughly and laughingly told Greg that he was and always would be that filthy boy from Portslade. Without answering, Greg deliberately splashed back down, making a large wave of water.

"Oh, no you don't." Nick said and pulled out the plug. "No more overflows."

"That's what dirty boys do," Greg replied, then pushed Nick's head underwater. They struggled for a while and after this game was over they lay in the remaining water, plug put back and gazed at each other.

"I love you," Nick said.

"Don't be sentimental."

"Why not?"

Greg reached forward, and with lips tasting of soap, kissed Nick and forced his mouth open. "Now I will wash your mouth out with a kiss," he murmured, and their tongues met and battled in tenderness.

"Wank me off in the water," Greg asked, and then resumed kissing Nick. Nick reached over for his penis, and Greg felt him grip it hard. "Don't hurt the slimy submarine," he said, and they looked at each other as Nick brought him to orgasm.

"Now stand up," Greg said.

Nick stood up and showed that he too needed the same relief. Greg obliged him with his mouth, and then with Nick's sperm still on his lips, he kissed Nick passionately.

"That's what I call love," Greg said, and clung to Nick in the water.

"Do you miss any of the others?" Nick asked.

The question disturbed Greg as he often for some reason thought of Bart. He missed the heaviness of his big body and the bearlike embraces. Nick he loved, but it was Bart that he needed, not out of deep feeling but for sensual pleasure. Karel's beauty was lost to him and was now with Nathan, but Bart he sensed was alone.

"It was great while it all lasted," he said, and getting out of the bath, wiped his body dry.

"There must be one—"

"Don't insist, Nick. It is of no importance."

"It is for me."

"Why?"

"Just because."

"I brought us all back here, Nick, didn't I, under my magic cloak that night in St Ann's Well Gardens? I brought us all back except for one of us."

"Bart?"

"There, you have your answer. He was lost to us, Nick. Nathan was no substitute. I thought he was at the time, but he was not Bart, and now, Bart is grieving, and we never go to him."

Nick stepped out, and without drying himself, put on a dressing gown. He sat or rather perched on the bath's white rim.

"Tell me the truth, Greg. What did you like most about him?"

"The way he fucked me," Greg said, and without looking at Nick's reaction, went back upstairs to the bedroom. After a while Nick joined him and they lay awake together. There was a full moon, and the room was lit by it.

"Anna died, and I asked you if you wanted to go to the funeral," Nick said.

"I hate funerals."

"Out of respect."

"She had gone. Respect meant nothing to her. She was no more. Nothing."

"She had her faith. Out of respect for that we should have gone, and Bart was alone with it."

"I'm sure there were others who were there. Friends we know nothing of."

After a long silence, Nick whispered, "It's not only funerals you hate, is it?"

"I don't know what you mean."

"*It*," Nick said simply.

He did not want to utter the four letters that Greg avoided. Greg knew that, and said in reply, "It is a closed book for me. I don't want it to take over our lives."

"Supposing one of us—"

"Stop it, Nick. I won't talk about it. Talk to others, but not me. The whole thing is so—I can't express it."

"You hate them for it, don't you?"

"What?"

"You hate them for putting themselves at risk. I can read your mind, Greg."

"Better than I can," Greg replied.

"Well, don't you?"

"They didn't know it was around. The demon in the darkness. The something in the corner of their desires. They did not know it was there until the first cases appeared—and even then, what did they do? They still carried on, or rather they still *now* carry on. What night is this?"

"Friday."

"The starting point of a weekend's fucking. How many will go back to where they came from, those who come down here for a weekend visit? And how many will go back with *it* inside them?"

"Don't hate, Greg."

"Let's go to sleep."

"What if I—"

"You won't."

"What if I should?"

"I said, you won't. I would rather never see you again." He paused. "You forced that out of me."

"But if I developed another illness? If I got pneumonia, simply because it was just pneumonia? Would you not want me then?"

"That's different. You would be watched over, even in hospital I would always be there. I would never want you to go."

Nick was silent for a while.

"I hope you never lose me, Greg," he said eventually.

Greg pretended to be asleep, but he was not. He was staring into an abyss that he did not understand. Above all, he did not understand the abyss was within himself.

The following morning, Nick was up first, and Greg found him sitting on the doorstep that led into the garden. He was writing in a thick notebook.

"Busy?"

"No, Greg, I have just finished something. A poem."

"May I see it?"

Nick closed the notebook and standing up, moved into the kitchen area. He made breakfast, and at the table Greg stared at him and silently refused to eat. Nick had made the usual Saturday morning fry-up which consisted of bacon, eggs and mushrooms. It was Greg who had started this weekly ritual when the others left, and he called it *La Grande Bouffe de Portslade*. At the time he had joked and said, "we could die of *this*, but who cares?"

"Aren't you hungry?" Nick eventually asked seeing the grease from the eggs and bacon congeal on the plate.

"No."

"I forgot the toast today," Nick said.

"Toast was never on the menu. In my childhood it was just white bread and butter on the side. We never ate toast with it."

Irritated by this reply, Nick pushed his half-eaten plate to one side. Greg watched the gesture coldly.

"Why *did* you forget we never eat toast with this meal?"

"Oh, for Christ's sake, just eat, Greg."

"It's cold."

"I can refry the bacon and the eggs will be hard but edible."

"I don't want the fucking meal."

Nick got up from the table and stared out of the window.

"What's wrong?" he asked.

"I call it depression."

"I think it is about last night, isn't it? Not the sex, but what we were talking about."

"Think what you like."

Greg then picked up the plate and smashed it, and the food splattered all over the floor.

"In Portslade they could never, ever have afforded the fucking mushrooms!" he shouted.

Nick stood over the mess, then fetching a cloth, and a dustpan and brush, began to clean up.

"Stop that! I did it. I will clean it up."

"It's almost done."

Angrily, Greg knelt down and pushed Nick away so fiercely that he fell back and hit his head against a cupboard door."

"Oh, no!" Greg cried out and rushed to him.

"Go away Greg. Take a walk."

"I didn't mean—"

"I know. Just go."

"No. I love you. No. I remembered them in Portslade. It was that. They were always mean. Of course we could have afforded mushrooms."

"Greg, I really don't care if you were deprived of fried rats! Now please leave me and this mess alone."

Running up the stairs, Greg went to the front door, and still running, made his way to Queens Park and stood by the tennis court where he saw two men playing very badly. They were dressed to kill, but neither of them knew what to do with a racket. Greg, despite a warning from inside him, cried out loudly, "Is it your first bloody lesson?"

One of the men stopped playing and turned to face him.

"It is new to us!"

"Like your outfits!" he shouted back.

"Are you trying to cause trouble?" the other joined in, and in a solid block they stood together on the court and pointed their rackets at Greg as if they were guns.

"What if I am?"

Greg felt Nick beside him, and quietly he heard Nick tell him to move away and take a walk in the park with him. All anger suddenly gone, Greg complied, and a sob escaped from his mouth.

"Boyfriend got his boyfriend?" one of the players jeered.

"Take no notice," Nick said.

They walked towards the Kemp Town exit and finding a bench far from the court, sat down. Greg pointed to the open-air theatre nearby.

"I guess better drama goes on there," he said.

"No," Nick replied, "just badly acted Shakespeare."

"I'm sorry," Greg said.

"About the acting?"

"Don't be daft. Me. The mess that is me. Can you clean me up, Nick?"

"No, but I think *you* can, given time." Nick paused, then added quietly, "These deaths are really getting to you, aren't they?"

"How many will die at the final count, Nick? How many will fucking die because of a fuck? And can they be right in hating us? All these nice people who live close to us and fear they will get it from drinking out of a cup, or sitting on the wrong toilet?"

"Of course they are not right."

"But that woman—what's her name?—Harriet? She used to come round, and you would help correct the mistakes in her stories, like you do with mine. Why has she constantly got flu now and never comes?"

"I don't know."

"You talked to her for a long time on the phone last week. I overheard a part of it. About her husband."

Nick looked at Greg, and he nodded his head. Then he looked over at the theatre.

"What is it with her husband?" Greg asked.

"Fear. Naked, awful fear. He does not want to put his wife at what he calls *a possible risk*. There!"

"It is all around us, isn't it, Nick? Their fear. Our fear. But you never show yours. Are you hiding it?"

"I genuinely don't feel it," Nick replied.

"What if—what if you *did* get it?"

"You'd leave me. You said so. I'm more afraid of that."

Greg said nothing, but then as a cloud crossed over the sun he placed his hand over Nick's hand. He was filled with a sense of shame, but at the same time he knew that he would not be able to bear that illness in Nick. The disfiguration of the body, the loss of sight, the skeletal form. In Nick? *It* in Nick, eating at him, devouring his body from within until he was nothing more than a pale stretch of flesh on bone. And what of me, he thought, if I had it? I would run, run as fast as my energy lasted and die far away. Die far away from the rest of mankind. He hated his black romanticism as much as he hated the disease. He would fall, and be picked up, and die, suffocating in life like the rest, in a hospital. The drips and the tubes, and the useless, useless drugs. Unlike Nick, fear was destroying him.

"Do you think those guys have finished their game of tennis?" Nick asked. The sun came out as he said the words.

"Let's go back the long way round," Greg replied, and by the Kemp Town exit, they left the park.

The dream over, the madness in sleep, Greg murmured, "It never happened. It never happened like that."

Greg started playing with the water in the fountain. It felt cold and he shivered, but still he played on. He wanted to talk to someone, anyone, to get out of the prison of these unreal memories, but as yet there was no exit from them. Won't the ghosts ever go away, he thought, and then he saw in his mind, the man in the room who he believed was Nick. What he had seen wasn't so terrible after all, was it? Then the image began to cloud over. Nick was scarred and old. That was all it was. He was not the death mask in a green light. It was all in Greg's imagination. The cloud around the image thickened further. Then, as if by a miracle, thinned out. A youthful old Nick was there, beckoning like a guide.

"I am not ready," he said aloud, and moved away from the fountain. He had to go into the Métro; a crazy spider making a crazy web of places to pause at, perhaps see, but always to move on. He had so little time left. His long recalls, his long visits to his past actions took but moments in actual time, in Métro time. And yet in those visions, those fugitive visions, it was days, hours and even years. What do any of us know of the reality of all this? He cried and brushed the tears away. It was a waste of water, his tears; any tears only made the bitter illusions and the clear truths even more obscure than they were. Then as he was about to re-enter Pigalle Métro station he turned, and his mind blank, he went back to the fountain. His heart was beating fast, and he felt giddy with a dread that he did not understand. "I cannot remember, I cannot remember," he said as he sat on the rim and sitting there, looked around him at the long, straight road, at the signs of cafés and of people walking with a purpose, and if they did not have a purpose, then just with that simple pleasure of being there. He could not think why *he* was there; click, and all memory gone.

"My name," he said, and let his right hand trail in the water. "My name. My name is—"

A man stopped near to him.

"My name is—"

The man came forward and stood over him. He was very tall.

"My name is—what?"

"English. You are English, *non*?"

"I am—"

"Have you drunk too much? Too much wine in the cafés? Is that the problem?"

"I have no name."

"Of course you have a name. How can you go back to your hotel or wherever it is where you are staying and not have a name? Poor old man. You are out too late and Pigalle is not good. If you have money you could lose it."

"Money?" and his voice was frail as he looked up at the man's face, a black hole where the features should have been; black as night and he was afraid. He. Who was he? Who was the man? And who was he?

"Your name," he stammered.

"Michel."

"Michel, I cannot remember a Michel in my life."

"I will call for help. You want me to call for help?"

"No."

"You speak French?"

"I cannot remember."

"*Tu parles français? Tu comprends ça?*"

He heard the sounds—the echoing sounds in his brain. He was mentally in a labyrinth, and he had to get out of it. If he did not get out of it he was lost. He did not want to be lost. He touched his face with his hands, and his face felt rough and cracked, like a building badly in need of repair. The word *mirror* entered his mind. If I have a mirror I will know. I will be able to see who I am.

"Mirror," he said.

"Mirror? *Miroir?* Is that the word?"

"Yes. Mirror."

"Old man, you are crazy. You want me to get you a mirror? Will you see yourself better if you have a mirror?"

He nodded his head at the man.

"Yes," he said.

The man moved away, and he watched as the man accosted two women. One of them was angry and shouted, but the other opened her bag and brought out a mirror. She handed it to the man. Michel! I remember his name. Michel! He watched as Michel returned.

"Stand up."

The words were barked at him.

He got up and stepped away from the fountain. The man led him by the arm to a nearby lamp and handed the mirror to him.

"Now, look at yourself."

"Yes," he said, and he held the mirror up. He saw a face staring back at him; only the mouth and nose, and two empty-looking eyes. The eyes had no voice, and just as he was about to give in to total despair, his mind said the name, Nick.

"Nick," he said.

"Your name is Nick?"

The two women joined the man.

"*Tu as fini avec mon miroir?*" one of the women asked.

He understood the words. Memory was gathering itself together, like the old man that he was, awakening from a long sleep.

"Nick," he said, and handed the mirror to the woman.

She took it, and the woman beside her who appeared kinder, asked him in English if he was alone in the city.

"I am not sure," Greg replied, and he shrank back, out of the pool of light.

"*Il est fou,*" the man said to the woman.

"*Non, il est malade.*"

Malade? That meant ill. He was ill. He knew it. He wanted

to hide himself away, far away from this spectacle he was making. Then the word spectacle resonated in his mind, and he recalled another name. Renaud. He was an actor. He knew that.

"Renaud," he said.

"Is he your friend?" the kinder woman asked. "Have you lost him? Is he in one of the cafés along the boulevard?"

"Actor," he said, as if he was a child learning speech. Then the full name came to mind, and he said it aloud. The women laughed, and the man, giving up, moved away. His vocabulary was getting richer now and he was angry at the women for laughing at him. "Why?" he shouted after them.

"Why what?" and one of the women turned.

"Why are you laughing?"

"That man Renaud is famous. You cannot know him. He is a cinema actor. He used to be very popular. My mother loved going to see his films."

Her voice was loud and clear, and he began to put the jigsaw puzzle together. The mad haphazard pieces that had invisibly fallen from his brain began to assemble themselves.

"I am not Nick," he said, and the name Greg hit him with full force. "Greg. I am losing my memory," he said to the retreating woman. "What is your name?" he cried out. The other woman with the mirror looked impatient but said nothing.

"Claire," the other woman replied.

"A nice name," Greg said, and all the while in his mind, he was longing to get away. He was collecting himself, and he had to be alone with the process.

"I am well now," he shouted.

The women, strangely confident that he had an identity at last, moved back towards him. Claire smiled at him, then patted his arm; an act of reassurance that made him feel nervous. He had fallen apart; he had collapsed, and memory had fallen into itself. This most private of invisible acts had been made visible to strangers and Greg felt ashamed.

"The Métro," he said, pointing.

"Are you sure?"

"Yes, very sure. Thank you. I was distressed. That's all. I must go."

He smiled as he said this, and it was a strain that pained him for he treasured his real smile more than anything, and he was not capable of giving it to them. He watched as they walked into the distance along the boulevard. The fountain drew him back to itself. He sat again on the rim and closed his eyes. Slowly, bit by bit he recalled.

A bathroom conversation. Nick was naked in the bath and washing his face and then his neck. He laid down the flannel and stared at Greg who was watching him.

"You shut yourself away, Greg. You do not know what help there is for people in this town who have *it,* as you call it. You have no idea how good people are, sacrificing their time, facing hostility from the public, the straights—"

"That's excellent, just fine! But keep me out of it."

"I just don't like the way you are so derisive. Every time I mention the subject you have something bad to say."

"Then let's not mention it."

"We can't *not* mention it."

Greg washed his hands at the sink, and with a sense of dark irony he saw an image of Pontius Pilate doing the same thing.

"Do you want me to leave the house?" he asked.

"Of course not."

Nick stood up and as he got out of the bath he brushed against Greg. Ordinarily, Greg would have reached out for him, but this time he kept still. Nick put on his clothes in silence and left the room. Greg looked at his face in the mirror. He felt alone, staring at himself in the bathroom mirror, he noticed a grey hair and pulled it out. He watched as this sign of ageing flushed itself away down the sink. This is the beginning, he thought. He was not thinking of the grey hair, but of the emotional and sexual landscape around him. I will be an old, old man before *it* goes away, before *it* fades with its full retinue of horrors. With this thought he joined Nick in the kitchen.

"I have a meeting," Nick said. "I am one of the humble volunteers who has his shift on the phones."

"Yes," Greg said, and sat at the table.

"I will see you later," and Nick went back, up the stairs to get himself ready. Greg heard him move around and then slam the front door as he left. This was an ordinary afternoon when the sun was not shining.

What else about his life? What else to bring out from the water of the fountain, from the waters of his mind? He had seen Lauren Bacall act badly on stage in Tennessee Williams' *Sweet Bird of Youth*. She was not at ease in the role, or maybe it was a first night. He recalled the month. June. The stalls were full of gay men, and they applauded with the devotion usually afforded to a goddess. Who had played Chance? Obviously the actor had done well for the audience, because the applause continued for a long while, but for the first time, he thought that acting equated to the worst of lies and he was one of the first to leave the theatre.

He walked along the seafront towards the West Pier, Brighton's lost pier, and descended the steps to be close to the sea. Standing at the water's edge he gazed into the darkness. No light from the town fell on the waves, and he barely perceived the shift and the swell. It was while standing there that he thought of the white town behind him, in all its elegance, in all its polite cruelty; a place of intolerance, masked as tolerance, a place now of sexual fear and collective catastrophe. He too was full of the fear, and he could not live with this emotion. As he looked out to the seeming nothingness upon which no one could walk; that wet path that no one ever had walked upon, he thought of the New Testament. He did not consider himself religious, and the heights of belief escaped him, but he did have a belief in the depths. Hell is in that place behind me, he thought. And all the great actors, all the laughing parade of its history, could not evade that fact. What is built on pleasure, is destroyed by pleasure. He picked up a stone and cast it into an incoming wave. He heard the draw and the indrawn sigh that the sea often makes, and he felt suicidal. What if I just end it now, he thought. Walk in up to the waist, get used to the cold and carry on walking until a dip comes and I go under? Am I not under now? Hasn't my vision of life gone? And once more he thought of the phoney set on the Theatre Royal stage and the cramped atmosphere of the production. Lauren Bacall. What sacred monster is she to draw in the elite of Brighton and Hove and perhaps even further afield? Her voice, her distinctive voice, faded before the text of Tennessee Williams, and her strength on stage became a weakness. This was not a woman who could portray a film star in need of second-rate male prostitutes. He did not believe a word of her delivery of the lines she had to say, or the presence of a male, so weak that she was obsessed by him. But the cluster of male couples did, fanning themselves with programmes, whispering in each other's ears at certain moments, wanting, desperately wanting and needing to believe. This is what it means to be gay, they intoned to each other. Silent words, but audible to Greg. This was yet another altar upon which to sacrifice their lives and their feelings. The woman who clings and pleads, and who finally holds the card that wins by walking out of the door, even then offering the man a possibility of going with her. What a majestic shrug to exit by when Chance said no, and how the audience relaxed; the end of the approaching play and its catharsis, not involving the goddess, but left to a final monologue of handing oneself over to death's hands. Chance would die of it. The sexual man would die of it, and there was no care in the front row stalls over that fact. Why weep for him? A weakened male. What use is he to us? And with castration and possibly worse, the curtain fell. Greg had wanted just one thing. He had wanted the sea, and now standing by it he wanted his own ending, his own annihilation; not to wait in a house or a hospital, but to finish it all, here in the dark night of natural waters.

But he could not. He went to the brink and could not. Was it some saving hand; some mystical guide who held him back? Or was it the worst action of all on the stage of life, cowardice? He kicked the shingle, and words came to his mind, loud words as if the sea itself had brought them to him: the sickness is not with the sick, but with the rest of us. It was at that moment he accepted the words *Acquired Immune Deficiency Syndrome*; the words which when abbreviated in publications and newspapers began with a large wide-spreading 'A', as if symbolising an evil that would encompass them all. But now he knew that he was sick, had been sick, sick because he was well. He made his way back to the promenade. Christ *had* walked upon the waters, and in half-belief he closed his mind over that thought.

He met a youth standing in the shadows of the Palace Pier. He was in his late teens, and he smiled at Greg as he went past. Intrigued, Greg made his way back and approached him.

"Dark, isn't it? No moon."

The young man is poetic, Greg thought, and yet he noticed in the voice, an echo of loneliness.

"Yes," he said in reply, and the youth offered him a cigarette. Greg declined it.

"Given it up?"

"No, just not in the mood," Greg lied.

"Do you mind if I do?"

"It's your cigarette," Greg said, and the youth laughed, and after lighting one, said, "My name is Patrick. Can't you tell by the accent? Irish."

"Which part?"

"Dublin."

"I've never been to Ireland," Greg said, moving closer.

"It's a closet case country. No abortion, no gays. What a way to live. Worse than being poor here, believe me. Shall we walk a bit?"

164

Greg nodded his head and now with a companion Greg walked again upon the shingle, walking underneath the solid structure of the pier, then, leaning up against one of the pillars, the all too solid pillars that led into the sea, Patrick unzipped his jeans and let them fall to his knees.

"I'd take them right off," he said, "but who knows when those bastards are going to show up?"

"Who?" Greg asked, knowing.

"Queer bashers, police, you know."

No more words were spoken between them, and there in the almost total obscurity and meanness of light, Greg fucked the youth. He had no condoms on him and he acted on impulse. He took his first conscious risk. This may be *it*, he thought, returning to his former expression for the virus as he shot his seed into the youth's rectum. Then Patrick masturbated himself and walked alone, away from Greg, along the shingle. Greg returned to the waves and kneeling, pulled his trousers down; just enough to wash his genitals with the saltwater. It stung, and he was glad of that. If it was suicide, if it was murder, so be it.

Greg asked Nick if he had promise as a writer.

"I can't answer that."

"Why?"

"Because I am not sure. I am not sure you are capable of being objective enough to be intellectually ruthless."

"Explain."

It was a bright afternoon.

"This is how I see it," Nick said. "The ruthless, or to put it another way, the clearly ambitious, have their sights on the ladder upwards. Once you are on the ladder and get accepted by *The Guardian* etc. you have failures that are forgiven and successes that are overrated. And eventually, if you are very lucky, and luck has a lot to do with it, and a certain conformity, you will receive a gift of recognition and letters after your name bestowed on you by royalty. This is what I call the calculated track. The less lucky have a moment of recognition, then die like a firework on New Year's Eve. That's how I see it."

"I see," replied Greg, looking up into the sky. "Well, I don't think I will make it then."

Nick laughed.

"In the end, Greg, everyone ends up in the same vaults or whatever they have in the British Library."

"You've had success with certain volumes of your poetry."

"No, not really. I am considered as being just that little bit old fashioned. David Gascoyne, George Barker etc. A once middling-to-famous poet told me that. He knew *his* place and he had a good idea of mine. Clearly at birth I was reincarnated from one of the ones who died in the war."

"You don't believe in reincarnation."

"Anything is possible," then Nick turned to Greg and said, "but you, dearest Greg, are a marginal. You have been infected by certain French authors, and the English will never forgive you for that."

The scene shifted. Greg gave Nick a short story he had written about a fourteen-year-old who was given permission by his mother to have a relationship with a man in his thirties.

"You might find a gay publisher to publish it in a compendium of short stories," Nick said briskly.

"What do you think?"

"It needs tidying up, but it is clear, precise, classical, but with an edge that might disturb a lot of people."

"No publisher would take it except for a gay one. Is that what you mean?"

"Too much propaganda. Write about women with close gay friends. That will appeal to the traditionalists who want to appear liberal. Nothing like the women's market, for selling books with nice friendly not-rocking-the-boat gay characters."

Greg tore the short manuscript into two. Nick stared at him in silence, then went upstairs to his bedroom. Later he came back down to the kitchen to find Greg getting slowly drunk.

"That's a melodramatic gesture," he said.

"Fuck off, Nick."

"But it is. It's silly. Childish. You will write the same story again."

Greg shook his head.

"What if I write about aids—not with a capital 'A' like in the newspapers, the worthy pamphlets and books, but with a small 'a' like what it feels like to put yourself at risk?"

"Have you?" Nick asked.

"Yes."

"Deliberately?"

"You've heard enough."

"Then you should—"

"No, I don't want to know. Don't ask why. I think I could take the hit of a positive result, but then again I might just—well, go under, before *it* gets me."

Greg looked at Nick and saw that he looked shaken by this admission. In silence, Greg gave him a glass of brandy.

"You look as if you need it as much as I do."

That night, Greg went to Duke's Mound and allowed himself to be fucked by a young man who said he came from Worthing. Greg had no desire to talk and told the man to shut up.

Greg did not know which line he was on. He had changed arbitrarily from one train to another at any station that had a connection. He had read *Didier's Manuscript* twice, and he wanted to destroy it; destroy it in the same way as he had torn the pages that afternoon with Nick, but somehow he could not do it. He was the manuscript, and the manuscript was like a big invisible badge of A for AIDS on his inner self. Tearing it up would not get rid of it.

"*The Scarlet Letter*," he whispered to himself, then added, "Who the fuck reads Nathaniel Hawthorne?"

Serge. After the humiliation with Hervé Guibert, and then giving the manuscript away to Serge, forgotten Serge, with a face that no longer had any resemblance to his former face, had returned it to him. He saw the café where they had met again, and then recalled how shabby he looked, and dirty, despite having bought two new suits and other clothes. He looked into the shopping bag, now soiled with the kilometres of Métro travel and saw the suits. Would he ever wear them? He recalled the first time he had met Serge. Then, he had worn a grey suit, and they had been to the premiere of some film that was not worth recalling, and afterwards, a group he was with, joined up with another group. They went to a party (or was there another version of this in his mind? It did not matter. It did not matter at all the exact circumstances, the whereabouts of the party or who he was with; this was his final version of that encounter with Serge). He had already written his *récit* as he liked pretentiously to call it, and he had written it in English and French. It had been an exercise in how to write in French, more than anything else. He had used a dictionary and a grammar book, and as if it would bring him luck, Flaubert's *L'Éducation sentimentale* and *Madame Bovary* were with him as well. He also tried to push the long sentences of Proust as far away as he could, but mostly failed. Reading it on the Métro he had seen how much he had failed.

"So, you are a writer?" Serge had asked him, and Greg watched as the good-looking man looked first at Greg's face and then at his suit. He seemed to approve.

"I would like to stay in France and become a French writer," Greg had replied.

Greg stared around him at the few people in the Métro carriage. They were mostly badly dressed; a group out for the night, reeking of bad perfumes and the stale odour of drink. The men howled at each other, jackals in the night, and the women responded in kind. Perhaps it was the aftermath of a wedding party? Some of the women had confetti in their hair, or maybe it was a celebration in a newly opened club. They were all young and Greg, despite his aversion to them, envied them their youth. He had not been young when he met Serge; younger than his years in looks, but he was middle-aged, and so was the handsome Serge.

"So, what have you written recently," Serge asked.

"A very short work. I need to learn so much about form."

"Read Gide," came the prompt reply.

"It is set in a sex cinema."

Serge twisted his good looks into a parody of ugliness as he replied, "From experience?" From mock gargoyle to prince, Serge restored himself. "I mean, everyone goes to those places sometimes. In the early 1970s we all went to see explicit films in the Rue du Dragon and other places. They were films then, with stories—now, well it's background, isn't it?"

"I don't know." Greg was suddenly floundering.

"Alright, so I know. As an observer. How could anyone write a description of a sex cinema if they did not know?" Serge was sarcastically elegant; learned from so many such parties where a put-down had to be said with finesse, and yes, a certain charm. "My dear friend—may I call you that?—it really is of no concern of mine, how you went about exploring. Keyholes, I always say, are the best places to watch, and observe and make notes. But then, I may be thinking in terms of another century, another mindset. Oh, for a gay Laclos back then! How exciting that would be to read now. The mental desire is so much the best."

Greg wanted to finish the conversation, but Serge had caught his prey.

"May I read it?"

"Well—"

"I could assess whether it is well written enough to have a chance with a small publisher. A slim volume can be just twenty pages in France today, and *voilà*, a book!"

That night he went home with Serge to an apartment near the Rue de Rennes. It was spacious and sparsely furnished with period furniture of the finest blue. The long windows had neither blinds nor curtains. In the bedroom, where their bodies collided more than joined in any harmony, the bed appeared to Greg to look neutrally upon them. I have never seen passion here, the too beautiful headrest and the too beautiful white sheets seemed to say, and when it was all over, Serge smiled and commented, once more with that delicacy of sarcasm, "You know what you are doing, don't you? Are your written words objectively perfect?"

They went into another room which was a library holding the finest collection of bound books. All the Pléiade editions were there, and other lesser writers, bound in grey bindings. Serge took down a volume of Colette's *Le Blé en herbe*. He gave it to Greg.

"This *is* perfection," he said. "I'm not sure we will repeat tonight's excellent performance, but I want to give it to you in return for seeing your ambitious little project of a book. To write in both French and English! You are the first Englishman I have met to do that. Discounting Julien Green, but then, we have adopted him as one of our own, and he writes almost exclusively in our language. If only he would translate his own books."

Greg hurriedly left and read Colette in one go. He had no affinity with her work at all. The fussiness of style: such blasphemy, but that is how he found it. It was as if he was reading through the most delicate of lace curtains. It suffocated him. But he did send his manuscript to Serge, and this was followed by several meetings, and Greg met Hervé Guibert. He thought of Aurélien all those years back in 1969; Guibert had the same beauty, but with an added electricity of presence and attraction. How was that possible? It was, and he took an immediate dislike to him. The deadly thrust when it came from Guibert was swift and to the point.

"I read it in French. I hope the English was better."

As if he had said something kind, Guibert bowed slightly and saying goodnight to Serge, walked away from them. Greg was not sure he had seen Serge again, or his manuscript. Not until today. This long day that felt like twenty days, like a hundred days. He touched the manuscript in his vagrant bag. It needed to be destroyed, and yet he was its prisoner. All things we create put us in a prison of the mind, he thought. He looked out of the carriage window as the train stopped. Les Gobelins. What was he doing on Line 7? At Place d'Italie he changed to Line 6, direction Charles de Gaulle-Étoile. He would drink his last cognac of the day there, and maybe, just maybe, walk back down the Champs-Élysées.

The Paris days. The mystery of those years, dying out inside him. He had lost a great deal of confidence with that Guibert blow, but then he knew nothing of the man's work, nor his illness, nor of the other writers such as Yves Navarre and Bernard-Marie Koltès. So many, many writers then, far superior to anything he could put down on paper, a cluster of feelings, of minds, of experience. And his offering was so feeble and yes, now he could admit it, not fit to be seen by them. Years later he read *Cargo Vie* by Pascal de Duve, who died so young. He liked this book because of its supreme simplicity; the greatest pearl of all so-called AIDS literature.

He reached Charles de Gaulle-Étoile and there he stood for a long time facing the cascade of people and cars going down the Champs-Élysées. He did not walk far. He was too tired, and he went to the nearest café and asked for his usual cognac. He sat on a terrace, and the figures passing by were blurred. He knew the cataracts in his eyes were slowly advancing, and he feared blindness. Then there was a sudden focus, and asking for a glass of water, he dipped a napkin into the glass and wiped his eyes. The windows were temporarily clean. An old man, even older than himself came up to the terrace. He had a placard hanging around his neck, explaining how poorly Macron's government had treated him and how much he was in need of money. Greg gave him what he could, and after the man had gone he smelt burning in the air as if a catastrophe had happened or was about to happen.

"*Le feu*," he said aloud to himself, and then beckoning for the waiter, requested two more cognacs and then he asked him if he too could smell the burning. The waiter sniffed the air and said that he could, but then, there was always a vague scent of burning on the Champs-Élysées now. After saying that, he walked away. Greg wanted to go to sleep, and yet there was so much to wade through, like thick mud in his mind, and below the mud, where the true demons lie and hide themselves, he knew many memories awaited him.

No more Métro rides. He would walk. However tired he was, he would walk. He thought, once again, I have nowhere to go, and he clutched his bag and paid the waiter, and then he walked.

Part Three:
Pompes Funèbres

Greg looked through the railings of the Tuileries Gardens. Were the skeletons of the homosexual dead dancing? Did they join in a chain of bones, and pirouette through and outside the buildings? He imagined the flesh joining to the bones, and the surprised cries of joy as just once more (or was it nightly? The dead forget) they were allowed to return. No blood in them; nothing but skin and bone, and despite the loss of blood, a desire forever remaining to have sex. But that was impossible. He imagined their frustration and their cries of remembrance: a great piercing like the call of a species of unknown bird in the night. He gripped the bars, trying to discern the thinned-out shadows, but if they were there they hid themselves from view. Would he become part of their company? Not so far off now, the coming of death and that passing across to emptiness. Would his own bones revolt at that, and if he died in Paris, would he go to these gardens where men faked and sometimes believed in the gestures of love? He had gripped so hard that his fingers burned as he tore them away. It was past midnight. He looked along the street and peered at the shadows of the Louvre. He wanted to visit the pyramid; that creative fantasy, built to recall the lost glory of a president, but he decided to walk in a straight line; that walking line that stretches for miles and encompasses so much of Paris. Would his force endure? Would his legs survive such a walk? He knew that he had to try and although he knew his ultimate destination, he did not want to name it.

Memory, that knife that made its way to the heart lied so often. What had he recalled that was true? Of Nick; of the circumstances of his middle age and the years when AIDS had been at its most ferocious; what of any of that was true? He had imagined the dead in the gardens. What else had he imagined out of the long trail of years that he could say—yes, that is how it was! That is how it happened. He needed a witness to verify all this, and there were none. Even Nick, if he was the Nick of former days, had cast a veil across his former self. And there was so much else. He crossed the road to Galignani's, still there, still more or less as it had been before. It could have been a witness if it could speak, but all buildings, all stones, contain and hide their knowledge. All of one's memories are subsumed in them. He pressed his face against the darkened window and tried to make out the new authors advertising their fictions, their memoirs and their theories. They were looking out in unison at him, blinded by their enclosed words and only the cover titles told something of what was inside. The memoir that fabricated, the novel that could not tell the truth and the many theories of whatever beliefs that were held. He gazed at their white covers, because this was France, and the French had not succumbed completely to the vulgarity of decoration and images on these sepulchres of imagined truths. But no, he was wrong. There were more than he had thought who had fallen to the gods of simplistic demand and blurred figures or scenes of abstract banality jarred against the white continent of the rest. He thought of Renaud. Renaud had a book written about him, but he had not read it; had refused to read the exploits of the false Casanova of the silver screen. And anyway, it was written too early to write of the possible crime committed.

Greg shrank from the glass. He leant against one of the pillars of the stone arcade that sheltered the *flaneur* from the rain, and he gazed across again to the railings of the gardens. His heart beat fast. Had it all been a fiction, that crime, invented like some cheap narrative, fabricated in the subconscious self? Yes, he had invented it. He was sure for a while that that was the version he had to believe. If he did not believe in it, he would die; fall dead before the pastures of sexual cruising and the indifferent statues. He tried to walk. No one was walking near to him, and the solitude of this was a comfort. Paris was in fantasy entirely his and here he was in love with it, alone with it, and he stopped and kissed a wall. The gesture was ridiculous. He knew it. The boy, the youth, the young man, the middle-aged man, and now the old man, jeered at the spectacle. All his selves rose up and laughed, convulsed by the mockery of silent laughter.

He stayed on the Galignani side of the Rue de Rivoli and he moved very, very slowly. He did not look up at the streets that he passed, except once—the space that led off to the Palais Royal and the long route up to the outdated, opulent, opera house. He had seen Birgit Nilsson there. As ridiculous as it was, she had descended a flight of stairs, the flow of Puccini's sentimental music, contrasting with the strength of her voice in *Turandot*. A lie? No. It had happened. The ancient opera house had shuddered with pleasure, and he too, young as he was, had fallen into the trap of the all-encompassing diva, embracing her with his cheers as the others did, and now, old as he was, he felt appalled at that youthful response. But why appalled? "I should have known," he said aloud. "I should have known that the magic was but a seizure of manufactured madness, an obscenity of opulence and a lie to life itself." I bought into it then, he thought. During that evening, the date forgotten, I had drowned into the ritual of those who need to believe in the golden calf of sentimentality, and how that sentimentality enriched them all, just for a while, just for a few hours of life suspension and its needs. He was with a temporary companion at the time, one of those passengers who spray us with their paint of sexual beauty and then scrape off the paint at dawn. Greg laughed. He laughed the vision of it away. Or was it a dream? Another story?

"But let us get on with the lies," he said, as if to another companion beside him, and he wants to talk about England, about a last visit that he had.

It was the previous year in the month of July. He was at his lowest in spirit, and the loneliness of his life in Brighton was at its most intense. Just for the company and the presence of others he had gone to the pubs and found many other solitary older people in them. Loneliness is the scourge of most elderly and solitary men and women, but to Greg there was a different kind of sadness in the presence of men who used to be attractive to each other. He realised the depths of homosexual solitude in those pubs, but still he went, and very occasionally he would have a conversation with a stranger. In any ordinary pub, this would have no other connotation but camaraderie, talking of the weather, or football, or the wife who was either living or who had died. It would have an amicable solidarity, but here in this environment, where men saw each other as sexual objects or possible partners, a test of nerve was needed. How to open a conversation? A glance? A smile? That was how it used to be in youth and middle age, but in old age it had the most pitiful element of all; a hungry reaching out with both mouth and gesture that had nothing to offer but pleading words. And yet, sometimes need responded to need, but it was in Greg's experience always cautious. If the man was younger, he was wary, and usually walked away after a few sentences, and if it was an old man like himself, there was a saddening acknowledgement of only final loss or talk referring to the young in the room. Isn't he good-looking over there? Do you think he will see forty again? Nice thighs though! The *young* in those pubs were usually over forty, with a very few young men (in their twenties or thirties) scattered around the premises, aware of their advantage of years and their market value. So Greg would occasionally open a conversation with a man around his own age. It passed the time, but there was no spark, no tenderness in the voice as if both Greg and the other person knew; would always know, that the old do not meet up again with the old. The cruel irony, and this was clear to Greg, and in a dreadful way he accepted it, that both parties preferred solitude to the pittance of speech that was on offer. The dribble of words seeped from one to the other, spreading like an invisible stain over heart and battered soul. The bowl was empty, and Greg knew they both knew it. The old not in each other's arms. The terminal definition of obscenity.

"Hope we talk again."

"Yes."

"The name's Ted, by the way. Not often here though."

"No, neither am I."

"See you around in St James's Street?"

"Yes," and a hollow laugh.

Who said this dialogue? Who opened with, "Hope we talk again?" It did not matter; it was random speech that was not relevant to either of them. And because of this, Greg stayed away. He gave up. He thought of Paris and the slender hope that in a different language there would be a significant contact he could not have here. And in his fragmenting mind, he knew only too well, that there was very little generosity to give away once passed the biblical date of seventy. He thought, not only of himself, but of all those invisible in their rooms or even in their vast houses or apartments; solitude is not a snob; it invades both rich and old, and yes, some of the rich choose to buy a few hours of lies, but the serious among them realise the futility. As for the poor, they have no choice whatsoever.

We have had our lives.

How many times that cry in an empty place, sitting in an empty room, or resting a tired body in a bath. No self-pity, but a clarity that burnt hard like the scorching flame that it was.

Just before the doorbell rang, Greg was thinking, no I am wrong. There are the old with the old. They have been together for years; forty, fifty years of relationship, either celibate or still sexual. I cannot believe in pessimism. I must not. The homosexual is the same as any other human being, and he brushed aside the *Beckettian* image of Winnie piled up to her neck in sand, calling out to a man below her who seldom responded, but despite that, she had her umbrella. She held it up high, and yet there was no rain and there was no sun. *Happy Days* when the soul is held by an umbrella thread to the body.

The doorbell was constantly ringing. He went to the door and opened it.

"Do you recognise me?"

A smile. A look in the eye that was familiar. Bart, standing there, face blurred by time.

"It was hard to find you."

"How did you?" Greg asked and moved to one side to let Bart in. There was no answer. Flustered by Bart's presence, he led him into the main room.

"It's quite empty here," Bart commented, looking around.

"I have, how shall I put it, thinned out a bit, but I have some cognac. And sit down. Please."

Greg pointed to the nearest chair. Bart sat, perched on the edge as if he only meant to stay for a few minutes.

"So long, so long it has been," Greg said as he handed Bart the glass. Then he turned away, and with vivid recall, he knew, had to know that Bart was dead.

"Bart, you are—"

The chair was empty. He looked around him and Bart was at the window, staring at the wall outside which was the only view that Greg had.

"You can afford better than this," Bart said.

"I know, I know, but it is not important. Bart, you are—" and he could not use the word.

"The Orkney islands are beautiful at this time of the year," Bart murmured. "The straight lines and the ancient stones, bearing witness to those who have gone. It is a shame you have not come to visit us."

"But Anna?"

"She is buried near St Magnus. The place she loved the most at the end, and that she often painted. I would have liked to have brought one of her paintings for you, her vision of that cathedral, but there was no way I could do that. They are such strong works, in colours as vivid as the landscapes and as rich in mystery. It is a paradise, the Orkneys. I could make a place there for you, if you wanted it."

Greg felt chilled. He turned on the heating. He excused himself for doing so, as after all, it was a summer's day.

"So, will you accept my offer? Near to Anna? She talks so much, even now. Her food of thought is just as nourishing. The bread of my dreams I call it."

Greg watched as Bart returned to the chair. He sat again on the edge.

"You look uncomfortable," Greg said.

"Ah, no! I sit on stones and look at the sea."

There was a long silence, and the room slowly warmed Greg. He had time now to look at Bart's final face. It was furrowed like the soil and hard as the rocks that faced the waves. Bart held the glass, but he did not drink. Bart who had once been a poet; a poet equal to Nick was now formed by poetry itself. Greg could see that, and as if it was a confession, he told Bart that he too had written stories, and that he had begun a longer work. Bart made no comment to this, and it was as if awake, he was asleep, woven into the *Orcadian* tapestry of dreams.

"Why *have* you come to me?" Greg eventually asked.

"You are alone, and there is a place waiting for you. With us. On the islands it is peaceful. The storms make no impact on Anna now, and I—well, I can appreciate the roar and the tumult; the anger of nature which in the end is ultimately kind. There is a kindness on the islands, Greg. Believe me, the caresses of the wind and the words the old people sing, are precious. It is not like here, where everything is petrified by the fear of extinction. We live on there. Truly we do."

"I believe you," Greg replied.

"Then bring yourself to us. It is only a step. Make that step."

"How, Bart?"

"Let go," came the reply.

Greg felt the force of life, still strong in his limbs and he shook his head. "My place is not the Orkneys, but I love you both for thinking of me. I have to leave Brighton. I know that."

"How could you not, with this emptiness around you?"

"I must go to Paris."

Bart sighed; a long sigh as if he was remembering those long-gone days. He got up from the chair and murmured softly, "Were those days *kind* there, Greg? Did they promise you peace?"

"Not then, no."

"Not ever."

"You don't know that, Bart."

"I was there—like a shudder in a nightmare. I *was* there."

"It was not your place," Greg said. "You came there because of me—"

"—and I come here now, because of you. I am offering you a rest from all this. All this inevitable death in life that is Brighton."

"I've never been to the Orkneys. Please understand. Tell Anna that it was not for me—it was not for me when she left—it was not for me when you left."

"I tried," Bart said, and the voice was a whisper. He got up from the chair and went to the door, raised his hand in a gesture of farewell, and then he was gone.

Greg screamed at the silence for giving him this illusion. Then he was quiet, desperately quiet. He stared at the chair where Bart had sat and reaching out, touched it, and he felt a flow of energy enter his body. Bart had brought him a gift; the energy to leave, and he made his plans.

As he reached the Tour Saint-Jacques, Greg sat on a bench. The gardens there were quiet. It could not have been Bart, he thought. He could not have travelled so far. And then, as he stood up, he saw a shooting star, or was it a light at the top of the Tour Saint-Jacques? It lightened the whole garden around him, and he was taken back to another day; a day the previous year which had been a day of light, a brilliant light within himself because he had returned to Paris.

Renaud. It was time to think of, to remember Renaud. Greg imagined him asleep in his house. It was a large house near the Métro Saint-Paul. It was almost as grand as the house in the Place des Vosges, which he, Greg, had imagined for Aurélien all those years ago. The house was situated in the Rue du Roi-de-Sicile and was tall and grey. It looked like an austere apartment building, and was, except that every floor belonged to Renaud. Towards the top of the house, he had his bedroom and it was there Greg imagined him asleep, and Renaud slept well. Only less than twenty-four hours before he was there, and it was there that his journey to the Gare du Nord began.

Renaud the mask, the twin masks of comedy and tragedy on one face. He could change from one to the other in an instant, and there was only one other actor he could think of, Isabelle Huppert, who could do the same, in quite the same way. He was older than Huppert by several years, yet his facial massages and all the other treatments and facilities that wealth permits had made him much younger in appearance. Even the mask of tragedy (which he wore quite often) could not make him look his age. There were no cracks, no fissures in which the real face of the man could be seen.

August 2018. It was very hot in Paris and on arrival, Greg had found himself a cool hotel room which had a view of the opera house at the Bastille. It was his second night there. He was bored and wanted to test out his French and a woman called Cécile—who rather took to him—recommended a play at the Théâtre du Palais-Royal.

"Such a charming walk through the gardens," she had said. "It is only a stone's throw from the Louvre itself."

Cécile was from Chartres, on a short stay in Paris and she had eyed Greg up the first evening that he had gone to eat in the hotel restaurant. They had made conversation, and Greg was complimented on his French, and being flirtatious by nature he gave the woman the impression that he was interested in her. Greg was playing disgracefully, but he was out of Brighton now, and he was flattered that anyone should notice him at all. He was wearing good casual clothes, and his hair had been cut well and he looked his ageing best. The fact itself of being back in Paris had inwardly rejuvenated him, and Cécile, widowed, was about ten years younger than him. He lied and told her about his fictitious house in Kemp Town. She had been to Brighton once in her teens and she recalled those white buildings facing the sea.

"Have you seen the play?" he asked in French.

"Not yet."

There was a hint in this that Greg should invite her along with him, but he looked away and ordered another bottle of wine from the bored hotel waiter. The moment had passed, and he made a mental note, not to return to the subject. He pleaded a headache and went to bed early. The following morning, he did not see Cécile at breakfast.

"*Où est Madame Laurent ce matin?*" he asked the woman who ran the hotel.

"*Elle se promène. Je crois qu'elle vous a laissé un message.*"

In a delicate hand, on delicate notepaper, Cécile had said she would be at the hotel around 16h00 that afternoon if he would like to have some English tea with her. The word *tea* was underlined and written in English. Greg was not charmed by the note. He said thank you to the woman, added that he would be back at the hotel late that night. She nodded her head in silence, looked at the purple notepaper in his hand and gave him a sharp look. With the insight of all women who own hotels, she intuitively knew that Mme Cécile Laurent was *interested* in him, and that by telling her he would be late, he was in some way turning her down when he had clearly encouraged her.

He wandered around the Bastille area for a while, and bored by it, made his way down towards Saint-Paul. This was more his territory, and he sensed that something should happen. Wish fulfilment can often lead to a wish come true, but he did not know that at the time. By mid-afternoon he was at the Théâtre du Palais-Royal and by chance was offered a ticket for the play, *Edmond* (a fictionalised account of Edmond Rostand's writing of *Cyrano de Bergerac*. It cost him €20.

A light dinner, and he was at the theatre a good half-hour before the starting time. In the foyer he lingered, looking at the programme. The play promised to be visually exciting, fast-moving and also promised to stimulate the mind. As he was reading the cast list, a man, younger than him, came up to him.

"I heard you speak in English just now when you asked for the programme." He had a few touches of grey in his hair, and he was handsome. He also *knew* that he was handsome.

"I would like to talk in English with you for a while. May I?"

"Of course," Greg replied, flattered—the second person who had taken an interest in him in two days! He was overwhelmed. The man interested him, and Greg felt his penis respond. As he had grown older, Greg liked more and more the heaviness, the sheer weight of another older man, but that was not to say that he did not prefer the young if given the chance, but the chance had not been forthcoming in Brighton. And yet, that night at the Théâtre du Palais-Royal, Renaud had brought out the lost and almost forgotten sexuality in him, and this was because, in the subtlest of ways, Renaud made sure that every glance, every movement of his body, spelt out desire. "I am not dead," his body had said. "I respond. I give."

"Shall we after the play?" and then Renaud had given him his full name. For a split second, Greg saw a look that implied, don't you recognise it? It was fleeting, and then the charm returned. The comic mask was at full play. "I will meet you at the end of the play, just here. Will you wait for me?"

Renaud disappeared into the gathering crowd. Greg entered the theatre and gasped at the sight of it. This was an opera house, not a theatre, and proudly displayed in the centre of the curtains were the letters P. R. and the date 1783. He sat down and looked at the boxes on either side. He thought he caught a glimpse of Renaud in one of them, with company, but he could not be sure. The lights were bright, his eyesight poor for distance. Three beats, and the play began.

After the performance, walking through the gardens of the Palais Royal, Renaud asked what he thought of it.

"I was at a bit of a disadvantage, as I have never seen *Cyrano de Bergerac*," Greg said.

"I once played him. I was terrible. The nose really did not suit me, and the critics were unkind. I brought the audience in all the same." Renaud paused and smiled. "I much preferred watching this."

"It was imaginative," Greg said, "and a good beginning for my stay."

"Staying long?"

"I have booked in at a hotel for ten days."

"Where?"

"Bastille."

"Why don't you—?" and in the half-light of the gardens, Renaud bent his head forward and kissed Greg on the mouth.

All Greg could say was, "But my age. I am—old."

"I started life having relationships with older men than me. Why shouldn't I finish life the same way? Young men for trust and kindness are best for the early and middle years. Or do you prefer young men and not men of my age?"

Greg put his arms around Renaud, and the moment of relief made him light inside. He was happy, and he in his turn kissed Renaud, their tongues meeting.

"Come back with me," Renaud said.

"But the hotel?"

"We will fetch your things tomorrow."

"They won't refund."

"To hell with that, I will be very persuasive with them. I will sign a photo for the hotel. It is a woman who runs it?"

184

"How did you know?"

"I know all the hotels in that area. I even guessed which one," and he named it.

The following day, the woman refunded him, and in return she was kissed by Renaud and received a framed photo.

"I saw you in—" and she gave a list of films that astonished Greg.

"I was younger then," Renaud said, the mask of light comedy firmly in place. He looked at her with indifferent eyes, and Greg saw for the first time, how distant he could be, pretending to be near.

They arrived back at the Rue du Roi-de-Sicile, and Greg felt comfortable for the first time in a long while. The main living room was expansive and full of soft furnishings. The place itself, showed no sign of excessive wealth, and yet everywhere there was riotous colour, old theatre programmes and books on the cinema. The walls were covered in framed film and theatre posters with Renaud's name always prominent. The only painting on the walls was a fake: a copy of the German Expressionist Christian Rohlfs' *Red Amaryllis on Blue*. The wooden frame itself was of the darkest blue and Greg was drawn to it. He was impressed, and yet at the same time, felt that it was a work that he would not want to own himself. The heads of the three flowers, painted in the full flowering of that hour or day before decay, depressed him. Intensely red, two of the six-petaled flowers had a centre of black; the black was thin in texture and yet at the same time represented to him a void. Only the vase held out a hope of life; the water in it white and translucent, but above this object of hope, the third flower faced away from the viewer, its head held high, and Greg imagined it screaming. A blood-red scream afraid of the depths of blue night surrounding it. If there was one thing in the room he would have taken down, it was this fake.

"Someone very special to me painted it," Renaud said, joining Greg. "It is a copy of course. Do you like it?"

"I am sorry, I don't."

"Then we must take it down."

"Of course you mustn't. It is precious to you."

"Dear Greg, it is, as I said, a copy. It was painted as I also said, by a friend, but it has no value. We live after all in a world saturated with copies. Nothing much outside of museums can call itself original anymore, except for the minor, very minor painters and no one really wants them."

"But haven't you had it for a long time?"

"For years!" Renaud exclaimed, and then added, "Help me take it down. I will, with your help, take it up to the most remote room on the top floor. For as long as you stay you will not have to see it."

"I don't want you to."

"It is too early in our friendship for you to be petulant. You dislike it—but tell me first, why do you dislike it so much?"

"They are dying," Greg said.

"Are they?" Renaud replied, stepping back and looking at the picture. "I would say in full bloom, but then Rohlfs was an expressionist, so it probably does depict some terror. It has to by definition of the movement, doesn't it? All that wildness and harsh brush strokes. Personally, I like a little over the top melodrama—God knows I've been in enough of them. Rohlfs was I believe hated by the Nazis. That is why my friend painted it for me." He then smiled and reached out with his arm in a gesture that was purely theatrical. "Anyone who was hated by Hitler is a friend of mine." Then the arm dropped, as if it was a sign for the theatre curtain to fall.

"But you were born—"

"Yes, after Hitler's death, but he was responsible for my grandparents' deaths on my mother's side. My grandmother, you see, was suspected of being a spy in occupied Paris. Here in this house, in fact. They, she and my grandfather were taken out and shot."

"I am sorry," Greg replied.

"I have hated the Germans ever since. I won't perform in

Germany. I can't help my films being shown there. Now of course they get a brief airing on television, and some mediocre actor dubs me. That really is the limit!"

"I insist, really insist, Renaud, that you keep the painting on the wall."

Renaud patted Greg's face. "Really?"

"You make me see the flowers in a different way now."

"How?"

"As a requiem in paint for them. Rohlfs himself, I am sure, would understand what I mean."

"You mean as *funeral* flowers?"

Greg walked away and without replying, looked at the film posters.

"How many films were you in?" he asked, changing the subject.

"Too many, Greg. I was only fifteen when I started. My parents were very ambitious for me and took me along to see some producer they knew. It was my looks and not my talent that got me that first role. I was a young boy seduced by an older woman. All very risqué as I had to show my naked bottom, but that in itself gave me an enormous following among people of our kind and of course women."

Greg turned to a theatre poster.

"But on stage, you seem to have been more of a classical actor," he said.

Renaud came over and looked at the poster of *Le Cid*.

"Yes, I have the art of exaggeration. I can bring out the emotion of even the driest old play. It's all a question of holding a stage, and I did. My finest hours were in Racine's plays. All tight concentration, and a great claustrophobia that needed large gestures. I made less money on the stage than in those bad films, but it was on stage that I felt the best, by being close to an audience. We homosexuals do like to face the applause, don't we? And talking of applause, do I get some from you for last night? Did I satisfy you with my theatrical kiss?"

"Were you acting that too?" Greg asked with a smile.

"A love scene always brings out the best in me, but no more sentiment please. I had enough of that during my Italian period. After the age of thirty, the French got a bit tired of me. I was in the same league as Belmondo and Delon, but I was not acknowledged as such. My public came, but the critics started carping at what they called my superficial interpretations. They never blamed it on the directors as they should have done. It was as if I was responsible for what I was told to do. In revolt I took up Italian offers and made very bad films there. It became my trademark and the Italians adored me. I learned their language and I was never dubbed. Even Cardinale herself congratulated me. Lollobrigida and Loren were less kind and as for Elsa Martinelli—well, the less said about her the better." He paused, a little breathless after this long, and to Greg, not very interesting monologue. He is overplaying himself with clichés, Greg thought.

"Other than Cardinale, was there any other actress you got on with?"

"Mangano. She was the best of all of them. I prayed to be in a film with her, but it never happened. We met socially, and even spent a weekend together in Venice. Her boorish husband was not pleased. I am not sure the De Laurentiis family are that gay-oriented, and Mangano's love for Visconti and Pasolini must have displeased them. I was at the premiere of *Death in Venice* with her and a relative of the family had the nerve to say that she did not like films about old men with boys. This, to Mangano! She survived the philistine remark with great tact." Greg laughed, and Renaud opened a bottle of wine. "Just a glass before lunch," he said. "I will take you to a favourite restaurant in the Marais, then we can have a look around Les Mots à la Bouche. Could you choose some good gay novels for me? Preferably English ones in translation?"

"But surely you read in English?"

"I can, but I don't. I am not happy with the English at present, except you of course. All this leaving Europe nonsense. What do the English think they are—an island?"

The meal was good, and the visit to the bookshop not so good. Greg saw how arrogant Renaud could be and how astonished he was when no one behind the counter recognised him.

"They are gay, and they didn't recognise me! I need a drink after that," he said as they made their way towards Beaubourg.

"Now *she* knows something about theatre," Renaud said, pointing out the Niki de Saint Phalle objects in the Stravinsky Fountain, jazzing it up quite shamelessly in the sunshine. Renaud stared at them and Greg thought, the mask is slipping. The force of comedy is bringing the real Renaud to the surface. Then quite surprisingly as Renaud was staring at the sculptures, he asked Greg, "Would you consider coming to live with me? I am a bit of an old Cleopatra, and you are an aged Anthony, but Shakespeare made some wonderful music out of their dialogue. The darkness holds many old sins, and my bedroom can be the best of all theatres."

"I would like that," Greg said. He was not in love or anywhere near to love, but the colour of the fun objects, the pleasure on Renaud's face, all added to that one accepting word, "Yes."

The following few days were a roundabout of fun. Renaud talked mainly of himself and as those pleasant few days passed, Greg realised how lonely Renaud actually was. Yes, the phone rang often in the house (Renaud refused a mobile phone) and he clearly knew a lot of people, but Greg saw beyond that, and what he saw was a desert with little water in it, and Renaud, despite the jokes and the laughter, knew it. Amid the mad clutter of former glory as represented by all of the memorabilia, there was sadness.

"I feel as if I have known you for years," Renaud said one night in bed. "I wonder what we would have made of each other in our youth."

"You must have had many lovers back then," Greg replied.

"No, actually I didn't. Certainly not in the profession. I had an unrequited passion for Gérard Blain, but he was—well, he was not really on our wavelength. His feelings towards homosexuals were to say the least ambiguous. Despite that silly film *Les Amis* and the camp of Chabrol's *Les Cousins*, even if he had been so inclined to love another man, it would have been a disaster. I played a truly dreadful Hamlet while that unrequited love ran its course." He paused and sighed. "Gérard should have played in some good comedies. I balanced my diet, and he didn't. As you can see, I am alive."

Greg kissed Renaud and held him close.

"I was a bit of a fucked-up bastard myself," Greg said.

"I hope you never went too far. Be cruel to enemies and strangers is my motto, but never to those whom you choose or who choose you."

"We are all cruel," Greg said.

There was a long silence in the darkness. A pale light from a streetlamp seemed to dance on the ceiling.

"Can we get up?" Greg asked.

"Not tired enough for sleep?"

"No, just a premonition, I might have a nightmare. Perhaps you have something I can take."

"Hot chocolate and a Valium. That is all you need. I have taken Valium for years."

They went down to the kitchen, and as he approached the door, Greg saw the light was on.

"I thought you had turned it off," he said to Renaud.

Renaud looked at him and smiled. Greg did not like the smile but could not exactly say why. When he was alone the next day he identified it as being Renaud's smile of lies.

"It must be Antoine," Renaud said casually, and Greg asked if Antoine worked for him in the house. It was the only thing he could think of to say.

Pushing the door open, Renaud went in first and Greg remained on the threshold. He looked beyond Renaud's back to see a man in his thirties, seated at the kitchen table. He had blond hair and a fair skin. He was muscular and handsome. Antoine looked at them both, and Greg also saw that he was looking particularly hard at him.

"Greg, you must meet my very own Baron de Charlus. That is what I call you, isn't it, Antoine? It is our private joke, although he is a little young for the role. I want Antoine to know that you are now a part of the household."

Antoine languidly got up from the chair, and despite his strength and seemingly clean-cut masculinity, he moved with the slow sureness of a snake. He bypassed Renaud with a smirk and grasped Greg's hand and shook it. The grip was fierce, and the hand felt cold.

"Have you read Proust?" Antoine asked Greg, and Renaud, turning, doubled over with laughter.

"Yes."

Greg's reply was brief. He did not like Antoine.

"I have no idea, Renaud, why you create this fiction that I am a young Baron de Charlus," Antoine said returning slowly to the table.

"Because it suits you to be a fiction of a fiction, Antoine. Let's all sit at the table," Renaud said, and beckoned to Greg to join them.

"So, who *is* your friend?" Antoine asked.

"His name is Greg. He is English, and he is to be respected."

"Ah, that absconding little island. Your politics make ours seem positively simple. What a Byzantine mess you have found yourselves in. I am not sure after you have left Europe whether our dear Macron will want any of you here anymore."

"I always thought you were a Le Pen voter," Renaud commented. "She does draw in the aristocrats."

"I am not that kind of person."

"And what kind of person are you, Antoine? Please tell my friend Greg here a little about yourself. You do, like Charlus, come from a background far superior to mine. I am in awe of it." Renaud then turned to Greg and said, "Our aristocracy is still alive and well here. On their toes at the moment, with the ruckus going on around Macron, but still they hold strong. And you *do* hold strong, Antoine. The grip of a once gorgeous bully, straight out of an elite school like the ones Cocteau and Gide adored."

Greg sat back and his stomach began to ache. Was it hunger? Was it the call of old age? Or both?

"Could I eat something?" he asked.

"There is a *baguette*, and some Camembert. Will that do?" Antoine asked and went over to the fridge.

"Also a fine paté," Renaud added. "Give him some of that with that especially good toast."

Antoine did as he was asked, and Greg faced a portion of paté and two dry pieces of toast. There was silence in the room as he smeared some of the paté onto the toast, and only when he had swallowed a small mouthful, was the silence broken.

"So, is Greg going to live with us here?" Antoine asked, staring blankly at Renaud.

"It's all to be properly negotiated," Renaud replied.

"Do *you* live here, Antoine?" Greg asked, sickened by the grease of the paté. His stomach churned, and he had the feeling that his guts were being twisted by an iron hand.

"He has a key," Renaud said, speaking for him.

"I came here tonight, because I need to speak with Renaud. We are friends—I could say old friends—but as only one of us is *that*, it would not be appropriate."

Renaud visibly bristled.

"Is it appropriate to mention age at all?" Greg asked aggressively.

"My, my, the voice of England has a harsh tone! Renaud is old. He is—"

"—a few years younger than me," Greg interjected.

"That I can see," Antoine said.

"What was it you came to say?" Renaud asked, his voice

192

cold. His facial expression was in tragic mode. Was Antoine the bearer of bad news, Greg wondered.

"It's all arranged. That's all you need to know," Antoine said and stood up and stretched. "It's three in the morning. Shall we all sleep in the same bed, or shall I use one of the spare bedrooms?"

"One of the bedrooms," Renaud replied from behind his *Racinien* mask.

"The orange bedroom, the blue or the green?"

"The green," Renaud replied.

"They are named for the constant flowers in them, Greg. Orange actually refers to a pale pink, as in roses, but Renaud likes to call it orange. Green is for leafy plants and a Wildean reference to carnations. The blue is a reference to that ghastly copy of a painting in the living room." He turned to look at Renaud.

"Shut up Antoine."

"Can't I mention it was your grandmother's room? After all, this house is old with memories."

Ignoring this, Renaud asked, "Which evening will it be?"

"I will tell you alone, tomorrow. None of us I feel will be getting up early."

"I am always awake early," Renaud snapped again, and Antoine crept out of the room, literally, an empty smile fixed on his face.

"Well!" Renaud exclaimed, after he had gone.

"Nice man," Greg said, not hiding his sarcasm.

"Antoine is a long story, Greg. Do you still feel unable to sleep? If you are, then I will tell you a little about him."

Greg listened to the (probably fabricated) story of Antoine's thirty-odd years. What he learnt was that Antoine was the black sheep of an Auteuil family who went back as far as Louis XIV. This was most emphatically said, and Greg noticed a great deal of pride in that fact. He also learnt that Antoine had been thrown out of the family nest without money, and it was in this sorry state over ten years before that he had met Renaud, and they had become lovers. As a bonus, the Louis XIV family Antoine came from had Jewish stock in them somewhere along the line, and Renaud found that their relationship shared a mutual hatred for Germans.

"He also has no morals," Renaud added as a postscript. "He can be a gigolo, whore, and very violent at the drop of a hat! He changes his colours constantly and is always entertaining. He can attract anyone, and even the police would not arrest him as he is the son of such a famous family. He also *likes* older men and is possibly a born gerontophile."

"The species does not exist, Renaud."

"Wrong. They just hide, as society is more appalled by them—especially homosexual society, than they are by paedophiles."

"You may be right," Greg replied, and yawned.

"Time for bed," Renaud murmured.

"Can I just sit here for a while? Let my stomach settle. I will follow you up in a while."

"Don't be long, and don't get lost in the corridors."

"Renaud, this is not Versailles. I can find my way," Greg added.

An hour later, stumbling up the stairs, he accidentally opened the door of the green room. As if waiting for him, Antoine pulled him into the room and drew him towards the darkened bed. At the same time, he covered Greg's mouth with a firm grip.

"Don't make a sound. I'm going to fuck you."

Greg pushed away the hand, acute loathing giving him force.

"No," he said firmly, and Antoine laughed; a sniggering laugh that resembled that of a villain in a play that Renaud had probably been in.

"What are you doing with this ancient pin-up?" Antoine asked. "He wiggled his arse on screen when he was a boy, and all Paris trembled, but no more."

"I like him," Greg said, trying to manoeuvre his body away

from Antoine's flesh, which was as serpent cold as the rest of him. "And I am not about to do a *Liaisons Dangereuses* on him."

The sniggering laugh returned.

"Then if you don't want to be fucked, fuck me," Antoine said. As he spoke, he turned on a side lamp and showed his naked body to Greg. "I haven't met one elderly man who could resist me."

"And supposing I have fallen in love with Renaud?"

Antoine languidly began to masturbate himself. Greg did not have an erection, and he felt no real desire. He told Antoine how he felt, and the masturbation stopped.

"So, love him," came the reply. "No one else does. Not anymore. He thinks I do, in what he calls my platonic way. I keep him amused and do his dirty work."

Greg was now intrigued.

"What *do* you do for him?"

"I satisfy him. He also pays well. He's rich. You wouldn't know it, but he got an awful lot of money for a lot of bad performances."

"You still haven't explained what kind of satisfaction this is."

"Well, if the guillotine was still here, I'd probably have my head on the block by now." Then he added in a rather vicious tone of voice, "As well as the Germans I also hate you English. Now that I have had the pleasure of insulting you, go away. I can get plenty of men, young or old."

Antoine then pushed Greg out of the door and onto the landing. Slowly, Greg made his way to Renaud's bedroom. He found him fast asleep and snoring.

Sitting on the bench in the garden of the Tour Saint-Jacques, Greg mentally skimmed over the preceding few days. They had been to the cinema twice. Renaud had chosen re-runs of his so-called better films. One of them was an obscure Italian film set in the USSR. Renaud played a Russian with a scar across his face which added to what was his then obvious beauty and actually made the sensuality of his looks more interesting. The film was graphically violent with much torture of the Belarussians and Greg felt ill.

"That was a bastard of a film," Renaud commented as they left the cinema. "We shouldn't have watched it. They must have changed films at the last minute. I'm sure it said they were showing one of my French films outside."

"Why did you accept to play in it?"

Renaud shrugged.

"I guess I needed the money. I always felt I needed money, despite the fact I was already wealthy. I took cocaine at the time. A lot of cash slipped through my fingers. I was on a lot of the stuff while I was acting."

In his sleep that night, after the film, Greg heard Renaud sobbing. The sobbing lasted a long time, but Greg was afraid of waking him from his dreams. The following morning, Renaud was all smiles, the mask firmly fixed, and they drove down to Chartres. And so time passed until the evening of the eighth day when events changed the dynamics of their relationship for good.

In semi-darkness by the Tour Saint-Jacques, Greg touched again the bag which contained his new belongings. As he did so, images returned. He saw again that night a year before, when Renaud had cried in his sleep. Was it because of the Russian soldier he had had to play? Or was it because of his lost loves, and the young men he had never mentioned, or indeed the older ones? They had all played their parts in the drama within drama of Renaud's life, in the film of his emotions. His masks prevented him from revealing any real truth. But what could truth be to him after the cameras and the endless takes, the scenes that had to be reshot over and over until perfect. The theatre too, mask upon greasepaint mask, the defence mechanism that intensified the rigid poses of tragedy and comedy.

As he sat there on the bench in the garden, he knew he had to consider things carefully. He asked himself, can I really forget Renaud? He had to recall slowly the previous year. He had to remember Renaud's gestures towards Antoine. He had to remember the nod of Renaud's head, signalling approval to Antoine of what should be done with the two young men who were trapped in the room—the two young Germans. And yet, before that dreadful night, Greg had had good days, one he recalled in detail. Both he and Renaud were standing in front of the *Mairie* of the 4th *arrondissement*. Saturday the 25th of August 2018. They stared at the small poster, fixed with Sellotape to the entrance of the *Mairie*. There on the Place Baudoyer they read:

Salon du livre gay
Samedi 25 Août, 2018
De 10h a 18h
Mairie de Paris IV
2, Place Baudoyer, 75004 PARIS
Entrée libre

"Shall we?" Renaud asked.

"I wish Nick's poems had been translated," Greg said. "I wish his work was here. He wrote some very beautiful love poems."

Renaud glanced at Greg and said slowly, "Maybe next year your own work will be here."

"I don't think so," Greg said. "Short stories. I don't think I have that much to offer."

"If you think that, then you should write another book. A book of memories perhaps; of your childhood. Of the way life was."

Greg smiled.

"I'm not sure I still have the force."

"In the comfort of my house; in the quiet there, I would help you as much as I can. I do know certain translators and there are many small publishers in France. I repeat, maybe next year, but why don't we look around now?"

"Homosexual books," Greg sighed. "Do I really believe in them?"

"I don't know. Do you?"

"I want to as long as they are not filled with clichés that kill."

"Kill what?"

"The real situation. Among my friend Nick's collection of books there was an early translation of Jean Genet's *Our Lady of the Flowers*. The title of this early version, American if I remember correctly, was *The Gutter in the Sky*, and to me that title was more fitting than the title Genet had given the book himself. What stranger image is there for us all, but that paradox of the gutter, the filth of the gutter, up there in the sky? Nick said it was poetry itself, that title, and I think I replied, no, no, it is much more. We are saturated, all of us who are marginalised, all of us who are tolerated and given equality, by that gutter splendour, that detritus of self that is in itself such a smell of power and an accusation against the world of those who call themselves normal. We will not go away, neither in the path that leads to the sorrow inflicted by them, nor in the blue sky that is so pure to them. We are in revolt in both places, and however far they may run to escape from the knowledge of us, we will remain the filth at their feet and the shadow that divides them from their man-made heaven."

Renaud hugged Greg to him, and they made their way into the *Mairie*.

"They were looking at us," Greg said of several passers-by.

"Yes, two old men embracing. What a scandal! They do not know how much you and I are joined in hatred towards them. Let's go up and see what is being published about us."

After walking through several gilded corridors, they found themselves in a vast room of civic opulence that to Greg's eyes only the French could achieve with such proud grandeur. Beneath the decorated ceilings, they browsed from book to book and between them they bought several of interest. Greg was especially pleased at meeting and talking with one writer, and her book which was about Jean Genet. Greg talked to her for a long while and Renaud left them alone. The author reflected back at Greg her own sense of marginality and that made the afternoon worthwhile.

The rest of the day was one of what Greg called happiness. A walk by the Seine, stopping at various booksellers. He noticed a poster for a film called *Sauvage* and pointed it out to Renaud. The image of a young man covering his mouth with his hand as if to enclose a tortured scream spoke to Greg. He recognised the face. It was the face of all those who suppress their cries, who are visibly tortured either by themselves or by society, who inhabit their own space between the gutter and the sky. "I like the poster's image," Greg said.

"It would have been death to any film in my time, but I admire it."

"Can we go?"

"Maybe," Renaud said cautiously. "I have read some things about it. I think it may well fall into your area of marginalisation. It opens next week."

"Do you think if you were that actor's age now, you would want to see yourself on a poster like that?"

"I am not that young man's age," Renaud replied tersely. After a pause, he continued by saying, "I cannot put myself into his state of mind. It is certainly not *Plein Soleil* with Delon, half-naked to the waist, taking control of a boat—that was *my* day!"

"Yes," Greg said.

"I hate and love my era. We lived in a false parade of glamour, and we sold our souls to the commodity makers of the day. I never joined the ranks of the great Riva or Seyrig, or the sort of films they were in. *Hiroshima Mon Amour* was not my love, and neither was the splendour of the gardens and house in *L'Année dernière à Marienbad*. That quality of actors never moved in the circle that I was in."

They walked on, and Renaud broke the silence by saying,

"Do you know who the one director is that I would have liked to have worked with? Orson Welles. How I wish he hadn't abandoned and left the *Ambersons* to such merciless hands. And yet, both it and *Kane* are the masterpieces they are said to be. Have you seen either?"

"No," Greg replied.

"Gothic mansions; piles of wealth and stone in both of them. More deadly than the elegance of Marienbad and yet as equally a splendid dream of cinema. Mansions ready to topple under the weight of their ultimate powerlessness. And what is the real treasure in the Kane mansion? The sledge at the end, engulfed in its own secret self! What a stroke of genius. I even got a dog after seeing that film and called him Rosebud. But seriously, let us look and see whether either of the films are showing."

Renaud bought a copy of *L'Officiel des spectacles* at Châtelet, but he could find neither *Ambersons* nor *Kane*.

"I miss *Pariscope*," he said. "This is so bland in comparison. Just like England, we are moving in that direction—only perhaps a little more slowly."

Greg said that it did not really matter, and that he was having a good day.

"We will make it better. We will cross the Seine and go to the Boulevard Saint-Michel. Gibert may have both films on DVD, either new or second hand."

Renaud was right. They did, and he hugged both DVDs to him.

"You know, Greg, you make me want to take an interest in things again. Revisit life."

Greg laughed.

"One old man helps another."

They fooled around as if they were young, and with the weather so good, they delighted in pretending that this was the first spring of emotions, the new clothes of loving instead of what was frayed and perhaps almost beyond wear. Once in the house, Renaud took Greg up to what he now called *their* bedroom immediately, and for an hour or two they continued their game of passion, injecting into ancient motions of technique, a sense of spontaneity.

Lying back afterwards, Renaud asked, "Is it so different, the cock of an old man, the arse of an old man? Is it the final obscenity? Or have we just been brainwashed by others? And I must confess, Greg, there is something that has always puzzled me. Why did nature give us as the focus of our sexual desires the anus and the penis that we both piss and shit out of. Couldn't something else have been invented?"

"I don't see it like that," Greg said.

"But why?" The words were said with an urgency bordering on desperation. "Listen, Greg. Either man or the gods have created a sense of aesthetics in us. Sexual aesthetics. But it's not perfect. Also, ingrained in us since our young years, we have been taught the terror of beauty and its passing. Old age is like a cracked painting, lined and almost cut open, except a painting can be restored, but restoration so often shows." Naked, Renaud got out of the bed and switched on the brightest light in the room. "This cock, here, wrinkled, without beauty anymore and lined with veins has just fucked you. You did not see it, but you felt it. How can a thing of such ugliness give beauty in the act of fucking?"

Greg stared at Renaud's body. He could not lie to himself. It was no longer the body he had seen in Renaud's films. A form remained, and he had felt feeling in that form, then like a blow in the face he realised he was wrong, wrong. He got out of the bed as well and with the setting sun blazing between the shutters, lighting the room even more. He went over to Renaud and took him in his arms.

"Let all the paintings split apart and fall from the walls. Let all the pornographic images we create in our heads, and that includes Michelangelo's wretched David, burn up or crash to the ground. If Nick was here—"

This final unfinished sentence slipped out, and Renaud turned his head away.

"You would love him, if he was here," Renaud prompted.

Greg knew that he had told Renaud too much about Nick, and flustered, he withdrew from Renaud and began to awkwardly put on his clothes.

"It is *you* that matters," he said lamely, trying to cover up what he had said.

"I could share you with him," Renaud said calmly and quietly.

"Could you?"

"Yes."

Renaud dressed as well, and changing the mood, suggested they spend the evening watching both of Orson Welles' films. Dinner would be the interval. The remains of a lobster in the fridge and cold potatoes with tomatoes.

"You know your cinema," Greg said to Renaud after Rosebud burst into flame. "They are great. Not enough people return to these masterpieces, these gothic mansions as you called them, with all their splendour, their neuroses and the most terrifying opera scene in history! How many opera queens watch Kane? I would guess not so many."

"You'd be surprised," Renaud said with a smile, and this, this evening that Greg was recalling as he left the Tour Saint-Jacques and walked further into Renaud's home territory, he shivered, despite the fact that his body was hot, and the sweat of walking clung to him like a shroud. Soon he would approach Saint-Paul and the place to turn up to reach the house. He could still ring the bell. An ache in him wanted a reconciliation of some sort, but two obstacles prevented it: Nick, or the Nick that he wanted to believe was Nick, and that day with Renaud and Antoine almost a year before.

The day came back in all its heat, and the dust of the Paris streets had made his shoes white. He recalled bending down and wiping them with a handkerchief. He was with Renaud, and they had gone out around nine in the morning, to get fresh croissants and special cakes.

"I can do without them," Greg had said.

"Ah, but we can't do without them. Antoine is coming round today."

"*All* day?" Greg questioned.

"He is making tonight's meal. Two people are coming for dinner."

"Friends?"

"No. Fans actually, and they are lovers."

"But why?"

"To meet the once great me, of course," Renaud replied. "They want to brag about me when they get back to their country."

"Foreigners?"

"From Stuttgart."

Greg had shivered then. In the heat, he shivered. He felt faint and grasped at a chair that was jutting out from a café terrace.

"No," he said, and he had no idea why.

"There is no orgy planned, if that's what you are fearing."

"No, I don't have *that* fear."

"You will be witness to a perfectly normal evening, Greg."

"But Renaud, you said so often that you don't like Germans. I don't understand the psychology of all this."

"It will give Antoine pleasure, and they're young. It's different."

"But that film you made, fighting the Germans, you hated the role, you said so. Now you're putting yourself in this situation again but with real Germans, not actors."

"It's nothing," Renaud said, and the coldness in his voice made Greg feel sick. He asked Renaud if they could order some coffee. After drinking it, his first instinct was to say that he did not want to be there with them, but he couldn't. Why couldn't he say it? And then he felt a vibrating shock in his body as if a bolt of electricity had shot through him. Despite the awful sensation he felt stronger. Yes, he *had* to be a witness. He had to be there. He had to witness that nothing went wrong, and it was not Renaud he felt a sense of darkness about, but Antoine. Antoine's *pleasure*. Old though he was, he could stand up to Antoine. The youth from Portslade flared up inside him, a phantom self, alive still and ready with fists and anger.

"I'm alright now. Only one thing I ask—"

"What?"

"That I do not spend the day with you and Antoine. Arrange whatever it is together. Both of you. I will be there for the meal."

"No problem," Renaud replied. "Anyway, I was going to ask you to leave me alone with him. The dinner is different, before the dinner no, it's not for you." He paused then and added, "What will you do with your day?"

"I'll browse for books alone the Seine. I was thinking of someone I once knew long ago, Aurélien. I do not have the Louis Aragon book of the same name."

"*Aurélien?*" Renaud laughed. "*Méfie-toi, le livre est abominable.* It's decades since I read those two volumes, and no one reads them now. Any bookseller will have them. Aragon, the part-time homosexual." He laughed again, and said, "I also knew an Aurélien. Handsome. Arrogant. We did not get on."

"I will stay in the café and rest for a while. Do you mind?"

Renaud got up. "I will pay," he said.

"No, please don't."

"I didn't upset you by referring to an Aurélien I once knew, did I? It would be the craziest of coincidences if it was *your* Aurélien."

"Paris is bigger than it looks," Greg said with a smile. "I am sure it was not."

"Please be at the house by seven. Yes?"

"Yes" Greg said, and silently and swiftly, Renaud walked away.

Paris was silence itself that afternoon. Greg walked by the Seine, following the path that he preferred, going towards l'île Saint-Louis across the river, stopping here and there at booksellers and looking through the old dusty volumes. Many of them were in cracked wrappers which only accentuated their age. His head was full, and it ached. He was full of anxiety, and in this anxious state he bought many authors that he would in all probability not read. Then at a stall facing the Conciergerie, he found *Aurélien* in two volumes. Next to it, a pile of *Paris Match* dating from the late sixties distracted his eye. He put down his heavy package of books and leafed through the magazines, ostensibly to kill time, but realising he had an ulterior motive. Several copies in quick succession had either pictures of Renaud in them or articles about him. The sun was beating down and he felt thirsty, but slowly he read the articles and looked at the photographs.

"Is Monsieur interested?" the woman who ran the stall asked, a clear note of impatience in her voice as he was messing up her magazines and blocking the way for other people to look.

"Yes, Madame, I am," and he carried on turning the pages of one, which hinted at Renaud's homosexuality by observing that he was always seen out with the most handsome young men. In the photograph Renaud was surrounded by a circle of half-naked youths at the Cannes film festival, all with excited faces, holding up programmes and photos for him to sign. In another, was an image of an equally famous actor of the time standing beside him. Greg recognised the features of a rather bored-looking Tab Hunter.

"Has Monsieur decided?" the woman asked.

Greg handed over the six copies he had chosen and was so excited at finding them that he left behind the package of books he had previously bought. It was not until he had crossed to the left bank that he realised his loss. Exhausted by the heat, he sat down on a bench facing Notre Dame.

"I can't go back, I'm too tired," he said to himself and mopped his brow with a handkerchief borrowed from Renaud.

After a while he got up, had a cool drink in a café and then made his way up the Boulevard Saint-Michel to look through the old paperbacks outside Gibert Joseph. There to his surprise he found volume one, then volume two of *Aurélien*. Both were battered with use and only a Euro each. The books seemed to be following him. Turning right at the junction that led into the Boulevard Saint-German he made his way to the Café de Flore. Remembrance of Jean-Louis, Maksim, and yes, Aurélien himself, bombarded his mind with memories. He sat on the terrace and looked at the customers around him. Most of them were the worst of tourists, loud and badly dressed. He began to read Aragon, then put it down, too fatigued by thoughts of the past.

"Monsieur?"

A waiter at last found him and Greg ordered a *Diabolo Menthe*. The waiter left immediately, and Greg noticed an Arab youth standing on the pavement looking in his direction. Greg pretended to read, but feeling the force of a tired sexual interest he looked up again and the youth was still there, standing in the same place with the same fixed stare. He was wearing a pale grey suit with a pale grey shirt beneath and when he noticed Greg looking, he slowly made his way to Greg's table and asked quietly if he could sit beside him. His voice was soft-mannered and pleasing. The youth—for Greg did not think he was older than sixteen or seventeen—was handsome and Greg felt both surprised and shocked by this encounter.

"*Je m'appelle Xavier*," the youth said.

"Greg," Greg replied, and they shook hands.

"*C'est un joli nom*," Xavier said.

"I am tired," Greg murmured.

"You speak English. I speak English, but I did not hear precisely what you said."

"I am tired. *Épuisé*."

"No, do not return to French. I like to hear an English accent. You are English, aren't you?"

"Yes. Sadly."

"Why sadly?"

"Because we live in awful times, and I live in what is fast becoming a third-rate country. A fortress country."

Xavier laughed at this.

"Do you think my name is really Xavier? No, of course it isn't. I changed it because I too come from an awful, third-rate country. France took me in as a refugee, reluctantly, but they did. And now, I am doing very well."

"At what age you arrive?" Greg asked, genuinely curious.

The waiter intervened, and turning to Xavier, asked him what he wanted to drink. There was no *Monsieur* in his question, only a tone of contempt which Greg was all too aware of. Xavier smiled up at the waiter who was definitely not smiling and ordered an orange juice. He then with an equal but quiet contempt towards the waiter, added in French, "If it is not too much trouble, see that the oranges are freshly pressed." With a shrug the waiter walked away. Greg picked up the *Diabolo Menthe* that had been placed on the table.

"One of Marine Le Pen's friends," Xavier said. "How they still hate us. He thinks I am an Algerian, or a Tunisian. I never say where am from."

"Why?" Greg asked.

"Because it is a country of both the poor and the very rich, and it is a country I promised myself never—and I do mean never—to name again. Now I am French, and I chose Xavier."

"It sounds like the name of a character in a book," Greg said.

"What?"

"A character in a book. I cannot remember the book, but I remember the name and was attracted to it."

"A good character?"

"I do not believe in good characters in books. They make very boring reading."

"Surely bad characters do as well."

"Oh, no," Greg said, and stared fixedly at Xavier's brown eyes. "Readers ache for the wicked and hope that they will succeed. Not all readers, but most."

"You are cynical."

"Perhaps, Xavier."

"And will I become a fiction in your mind when we have parted?"

The question alarmed Greg. Was he dreaming all this? Had the sun and the heat of the sun invented this character who he only imagined was sitting beside him?

"May I touch you?" he asked.

"Of course."

Greg reached out and he touched the arm clothed in grey. He pressed, just slightly.

"Do you want to feel my flesh? I can take off my jacket. I am, anyway, too warm in it, far too warm in it. I would do that for you with pleasure."

Xavier took off his jacket and then rolled up his sleeves. His arms were very brown, and Greg tentatively reached out and brushed against the few hairs that covered the skin.

"Very soft," Greg remarked.

"Not soft like a woman, I hope."

"No, not at all."

"So, do you like what you have touched?"

Xavier's smile was wide, and his perfect teeth almost glittered in the sunlight. Greg imagined a pearl light coming from them.

"What time is it?" Greg asked. He had left his watch back in Renaud's house.

"Are you in a hurry?"

"I have to be somewhere for dinner at seven o'clock."

"Then there are some hours still left. Do you want to waste them sitting here, or would you prefer to come to my small room nearby in the Rue du Dragon?"

"I don't have that much money on me," Greg began.

"I like you. I like your accent, and the looks you once had. You were a beautiful young man, weren't you?"

Greg looked down at his unfinished drink. "But surely—"

he began.

"But surely I am expecting money? Yes, usually, but not today. Call this a holiday from work. It would give me pleasure to give you pleasure."

"I am not sure."

"Am I not good enough for you?"

"No, it's just that I am not used to the young anymore."

Xavier took out his wallet, beckoned to the same waiter, and with a cold voice asked him for the bill. He paid at once and touching Greg on the arm, said he was ready to go.

In silence they crossed the boulevard, and soon they had turned down into the Rue du Dragon. Halfway down they entered an elegant building, and taking a lift, went up to the top floor. Facing the lift door was another door and Xavier opened it with his key.

"My home," he said, and they entered a brightly lit room that was in total contrast to Renaud's rather sombre rooms. Greg quite genuinely preferred it. There was a bed with a golden spread on it, a few lamps and a large bookcase with a rich collection of books. A comfortable, if small sofa, completed the scene.

"There is a small bathroom at the end of the corridor," Xavier said, then laughing, he stripped himself of his clothes. All except for his underwear which he kept on. He stood silently before Greg. Greg went up to him and touched his chest, again slightly covered with hair.

"You look sixteen, or seventeen with your clothes on. But you are not, are you?"

"No, I am in my mid-twenties. I dislike my baby face."

Greg touched his face.

"But you shouldn't. It is beautiful. Really beautiful. Many, many years ago, I had a lover like you—"

"And did he love you?" Xavier asked, then reaching forward, he kissed Greg on the mouth.

"Yes. He loved me for a while."

"Why is it always for a while?" Xavier asked, and there

was a wistful sadness in his voice as he asked the question.

"Human nature?" Greg responded, giving question to the question.

Xavier took Greg's hand and led him to the bed.

"Shall I pull down the blind?" he asked, as he passed the window.

"Please," Greg replied. It was not perversity, but he wanted the room in shadow. He did not intend to take off all his clothes. Only his trousers, and then only lowered to his knees. He wanted to be as naked as this beautiful young man was, but he knew that that act of nakedness for him with a youth was impossible. It was as if he was outside himself watching, and he did not have any desire to see that picture. Xavier did not question him about this; once on the bed, he just loosened Greg's shirt and kissed his neck, nibbling at it and exciting Greg with his intimate touch on that central point of all erotic pleasure. Greg then did the same to Xavier, who groaned with pleasure.

"I want you to see all of me," Xavier said and pushed away his underwear. The erect brown penis was as beautiful as the rest of him and Greg lowered his head, thirsty for the taste, thirsty for the liquid. Neither of them were in a hurry for the climax.

"May I say I love you?" Xavier asked, drawing Greg's head away and offering him his mouth instead. The liquid in Xavier's mouth was cool and Greg drew it into him.

"Yes," Greg said, looking into the welcoming eyes.

"I love you. For these brief hours I love you. I could love you for longer, but sadly I know we would tire—"

"I love you too," Greg whispered, and as he said the words, the orgasm was urging itself on, and with a cry, he came.

"Now me," Xavier urged, and Greg lowered his head and within seconds, the liquid drowned out his mouth. The juice was sweet, and Greg relished the taste. Was this all real? Was it happening? Or was he still at the Flore, staring at what he imagined was a young Arab reciprocating his look?

He walked back to the 4th *arrondissement* and rang the bell, not wanting to use the key that Renaud had given him. The memory of Xavier, true or false, was still in his mouth, and the final look between them before parting was sad. He knew the image and the details of Xavier's face would fade as all brief encounters do, except for those who fabricate to keep all the souvenirs of the moment alive. Who, on a brief visit to Venice, or Florence, or even Paris itself, keep an exact picture with them of a building or a square that astonishes? And so it is with the human form, briefly loved.

"Seven exactly," Renaud said with a smile. "But why so reticent with your key?"

Greg handed the bag with the *Paris Match* magazines to Renaud once they were inside the house.

"Memorabilia you may or may not have," Greg said.

Tentatively, Renaud took the bag from him and looked inside. He saw the cover of the first magazine and gasped.

"Lost for years!" he exclaimed. He then kissed Greg hurriedly. "But what of Aragon's *Aurélien*?"

"Forgotten twice. I left them behind. Twice. Once by accident; the second time probably by design. You are right. It is not worth reading."

"*Aragon, pour moi, il est dans les enfers des homosexuelles*," Renaud exclaimed. "Oh, I too am tired. I have been tired all day, and that is making me lazy with the English language, and of course, practising it with Antoine is a nightmare as he finds it pretentious if we use English between us. I try to tell him that on the set of many films I spoke English to other French actors. If we were in a co-production with another country it was quite ordinary. Co-productions are pure commercial merchandise and isn't English the most common commercial language of all?"

"It can be the language of both shopkeepers and poets, just like the French language," Greg said.

"Not quite. You do not hear bits and pieces of French all

over the world like you do in English. English is the language of bargaining."

Greg then asked, "Are we to stay in this dark corridor all evening?"

"I apologise," Renaud replied. "Antoine has put me in a bad mood."

As if intending to confide something, Renaud drew Greg into a side room on the ground floor, a room full of junk and disused objects. It looked like a playpen for grown-ups with piles of broken adult toys. A naked mannequin stood in the centre of the room, with pins stuck in the body. The mannequin had no head and the breasts, half-torn open with time and misuse, accentuated the obscenity of decay. Greg went over to the object.

"Why do you keep this?" he asked.

"It belonged to my grandmother. It was here in this room when I inherited the house. She was about to work on a dress, or a suit, I cannot remember what precisely, when the assassins arrived."

"I am sorry."

"I cannot throw it away. This was her special little room. She would escape here for hours in those first years of the war. My parents kept many of her things, just the way they were. I have done the same. But sadly, the rats too have made their home here. The costume she was about to put on the model you can just make out." Renaud pointed. "See those pieces of brown material?"

In the dust and the chaos, Greg saw various pieces of cloth.

"Did you want to show me this room out of sentiment?"

"It is in this room that my parents told me I would inherit the house. Antoine never comes into it. He thinks it is haunted, and I encourage him to think that to keep him out."

There was a short silence as if in respect for the place, and Greg went and stood at a barred window that looked out onto a dark courtyard wall.

"So—?" Greg began.

"So I want this evening to be as brief as possible. I want the young men to be here for dinner, a couple of drinks and then goodbye."

"Why are you telling me this?"

"It's simple. Antoine likes to torture a situation. He will drag things out, extend the time. He thinks time will bend to his will, that it will allow itself to be stretched."

"How can I help?"

"Greg, I want you to hurry things along. Cough a little. Spill a drink. Make them feel awkward, and if possible, use your imagination to *make* them go."

"I can't do that," Greg replied.

"Try."

Renaud came over to Greg in the cobwebbed room and kissed him.

"This is like a room in the Ambersons' house, or Kane's," Greg said, pushing him gently away.

"Will you promise to try?"

"Let's see how the evening goes," Greg replied, edging towards the door. The room was oppressing him.

In the kitchen, Antoine was putting the finishing touches to the meal. Greg said, "Hello," and stared at the sight before him. On a platter made out of the finest silver, in the midst of a circle of broken ice were cut pieces of cold lobster, glistening red against the white. To one side of this platter were bowls full of potatoes in a froth of mayonnaise. The sight nauseated him.

"I have eaten already," he lied.

"But why?" Renaud exclaimed.

"Hunger. I was hungry at around six. I went into a McDonalds."

Antoine glared at him and said nothing. He was doing something to other vegetables in another bowl.

"Well, if you had to—" Renaud began.

"I had to," Greg replied, then asked, "What time are the guests coming?"

"Eight at the latest."

Antoine said this, knife in hand, held upright, and seeing him like that, Greg had the worst of premonitions. He saw at Antoine's feet, portions of cut flesh; the floor covered with blood.

"I need the toilet," he said.

Antoine laughed, lowered the knife and returned to his job. As he did so he muttered the single word, "McDonalds!"

Once out of sight of both of them and locked in the toilet, Greg sat down on the floor. An obsessive premonition of disaster, of evil, had totally taken control of him. There was a plot against the young men who were about to arrive, and he would be a part of it. Like a recurring nightmare he saw the knife repeatedly fall, and then in his hallucination the knife became a guillotine and the executioner was waiting. He cried out in terror, then buried his head in his hands. There is no death penalty here, no death penalty here, he kept on repeating to himself. Despite knowing it was true, his head was being put on the block and in a moment the blade would—

A sharp knock on the door awakened him from this imaginary horror, and he staggered to the sink and washed his face.

"Greg, come out! They have arrived!"

Renaud's shouting voice echoed in Greg's skull. Another page of madness was being turned in his mind. He looked at himself in the gilt mirror. He looked pale, without life. The dark hollows beneath his eyes showed his age.

"I am ready," he called out and went to the door.

Maximilian and Günter were both well educated, good-looking young Germans. They sat correctly, side by side on the sofa. They had eaten little at dinner and were in conversation with Renaud. Maximilian who was the eldest of the two was talking.

"I am surprised the New German Cinema never considered you," he said.

"I would not have gone," Renaud replied, and Greg noted how haughty his tone was.

"May we ask why?" Günter enquired. He had a sharp, foxy face and Greg found him attractive. Maximilian was more solid.

"But Fassbinder?" Günter insisted.

"Aren't you a little young to remember him?" Renaud asked.

"Not at all. I am studying film. I want to be a director. I am very inspired by what happened in the seventies and early eighties. Take *Heimat*—"

"*You* can take it," Antoine said, and raised his glass to Günter who closed his mouth at once and lowered his eyes. Maximilian, either oblivious or politely oblivious to Antoine's rudeness, carried on where Günter had left off.

"And what about *The Bitter Tears of Petra von Kant*, and that masterpiece *Querelle*?"

"A disaster," Renaud interjected. "Making such a fool of dear Jeanne Moreau like ¹that. I have no idea why she accepted that role."

"That is your opinion," Maximilian politely replied.

"It most certainly is!"

"And what of Wenders and Herzog? Can you dismiss them as easily as Fassbinder? Or Syberberg. You would have been perfect in his *Ludwig* for example."

"Visconti did it more coherently," Renaud replied, and then he got up from the uncomfortable chair he was sitting on and went over to the drinks. "I really, really, do not want to talk about the great directors," he added, staring down at the array of alcohol in front of him.

"I was just making conversation," Maximilian said curtly, all politeness gone. Greg could see how angry he looked.

Greg continued watching the action between the characters in front of him in silence. He watched Antoine especially. There was a fixed and ugly grin on his face. Greg saw only a poisonous reptile.

"Can we talk about the actors you have worked with?" Günter asked, his reddish hair glowed like a beacon in the darkness to Greg. Renaud turned and looked at him, and mechanically reeled off a list of names, now openly showing off.

"You worked with *her*?" Günter asked, surprise in his voice.

"And why not?"

"Magnani?"

"That is her name."

"Was she—?" Günter began.

"She was!"

Greg then looked from Renaud to Antoine, and he saw Antoine slowly nod his head in Renaud's direction. It was made with such emphasis that Greg took it to be a signal. Returning to look at Renaud, he saw that he had his back to them, hiding the drinks and perhaps what he was doing.

"No," he murmured so quietly that no one heard. In one quick gesture, he was on his feet, and deliberately tripping up on the carpet, fell at the German couple's feet. He hurt himself as he fell (I am too old for this, he thought) and then he felt Günter's strong arms raise him up. He saw the gentleness in the young man's eyes as he asked, "You are alright? If you say yes, I do not believe you. You fell hard!"

"We must go," Maximilian said, his full face and cold blue eyes betraying no emotion.

Greg felt Günter place his body beside that of Maximilian on the sofa. Maximilian did not look at him but continued staring ahead at no one in particular. He was a beautiful robot, and with a voice to match, he told Günter to fetch their jackets from the hall.

"But first—" and Günter stared at Greg and said, "What is your name again?"

"Greg."

"Greg is ill," Günter proclaimed with fierce emphasis. Faint though he felt, Greg saw that the young man was angry with the lot of them. Greg excluded himself from the equation.

"I will drive you," Antoine said, and he nodded again to Renaud. "We will take the route by the Seine." The words were directed to Renaud, and not to the couple.

"No," Greg said. "Don't go. Take a taxi."

He knew his voice sounded blurred, dialogue out of sync with the mouth.

"Shut up, Greg!" Antoine shouted.

"Why speak to him like that?" Günter asked. To Greg, the words sounded like a true Teutonic Knight. For the second time that day he was in love.

"Günter," he said. "Don't let them."

Günter looked down at him in pained sympathy.

"My kind English friend, you are really not well."

"He's a sick old man," Antoine muttered, and hurried out of the room.

Renaud came over, and looking down at Greg, murmured, "You're tired, Greg. Don't interfere."

"While we are waiting for Antoine, do you have any music?" Maximilian asked.

Renaud smiled weakly and went over to a collection of CDs.

"Wagner?" he asked.

"That will do."

Greg heard the opening bars of *Siegfried's Funeral March*. The mournful music echoed around the room, and they all remained in their places as if galvanised by the portentous sound. When it came to a close, Antoine returned. Renaud immediately turned off the music.

"The car is ready," Antoine said.

Movements for all of them were swift, except for Greg who was cast aside to watch the action as if he was watching the inevitable outcome of a film.

"Goodbye," Günter said and shook Greg's hand.

"Take great care," Greg replied, "and fight back!

Remember that. If you *can*, fight to the end."

"What are you talking about?" Renaud asked.

"He is really ill. He must have a concussion," Günter observed.

Then they were gone, and Greg was alone with Renaud.

"That is not the behaviour I requested of you."

"Killers!" Greg said.

"What?"

"Antoine wanted you to put something in their drinks? I could not let that happen. I had to stop it. I tripped on purpose. I had to stop it."

Renaud stared at Greg, mouth wide open.

"Are you insane?" he eventually asked. "Why would you think that Antoine—?"

"You hate all Germans. Both of you. Maybe you lure them here often and Antoine does the worst part."

"Enough," Renaud said. "I hate in the abstract, Greg. Do you understand? Am I reaching you? Abstract hate! Is that entering your bruised brain?"

Greg, suddenly outside of himself, looked on. Was this comedy or tragedy? Which of the masks in the play had been put in place? His mind was racing and his ears hissed and thundered.

"If you are both going to kill them or beat them—if you intend that, then I am complicit. I too will have committed a crime. And Günter especially, was good and kind."

Renaud shook him and then held him tightly to him.

"Wake up out of this insane sleep, Greg. Antoine has taken them back across the river to the hotel where they are staying. Do you understand that?"

"No," and Greg pushed him away.

"Probably he will try to seduce them. Why not?"

"No. There were signals between you. Nods of the head as if to carry on. Either with the drinks, or to—"

"—to what?"

"There were signs between you." Greg paused, his mind

circling, his body shaking.

"Stay there. Right there," Renaud commanded.

Greg did as he was told. A crime! Yes, it was in his mind, and his mind, which was out of his body, leered at him; like an old devil on the front of a cathedral, it leered and stared its fixed stare. "Go away," he shouted.

Renaud returned, and holding out a pill, told Greg to swallow it.

"Not me! Not me!" Greg cried, and his voice was now hoarse. He was afraid, and weak though he was, ran to a corner of the room.

"It's Valium. Just Valium! Look!"

"You're lying," Greg said.

"I will show you I am not lying. I will take this pill. God knows I need it." Renaud swallowed the pill without water. He then reached into his pocket and brought out another one. "Now, do you believe me?" He then went over and poured a glass of water from a carafe. "Are you going to take it now? Greg, you have to calm down."

Greg felt he was collapsing from within. His will had gone, his strength. He was too old, too old, and what did it really matter if those two young men were abused or tortured or dead? He let them go, as he let himself go. He sank into that small ball that a child holds within itself; the retreat of the small and the innocent, or the vulnerable who cannot attack anymore.

"Yes," he said.

Renaud came to him and Greg took the pill. He put it in his mouth and as his mouth was dry he accepted the water.

"Now, sit down," Renaud said.

Greg could not walk, so Renaud steered him to the sofa. He sat where Günter had sat. He imagined holding Günter to him and his vision of it was so clear he began to cry.

"Desire. Old. Lost." He murmured the three separate words. He tasted the chemical taste of the drug and felt for a moment that it was stuck in his throat. "More water," he said.

Renaud gave him the water, then sat beside him.

"Antoine brings people back here to meet me. Germans too sometimes. Some I like, some I dislike," he said softly. "It has been like that for years. I flatter myself that I am still recognised in public, and so I do not often meet strangers in public places. Can you imagine it on YouTube Greg? Me with Antoine, and some young man in a restaurant, or heaven forbid, a club? Anything is possible today, and there would be internet gossip, speculation. Antoine would be speculated about as well. Supposing the dialogue was recorded? No, I was too well known, too fashionable, back then to endure gossip now."

"Stop, Renaud," Greg said wearily.

"I am explaining, Greg, why Antoine brings them here. There are no hidden cameras here. Do you know why I did not want you here today? I had people in especially. Respectful people who are experts who checked the house for such devices. The place was practically ransacked for hours."

"You are joking," and Greg began to laugh.

"That's better! A smile at last! Yes, of course it is ridiculous, and it is not true. No one came here, but I am letting you see what paranoia can do. Outside the house I am paranoid. Inside these walls I am not." He paused. "Greg, what are we to do?" and the question was plaintive.

"I don't know. Tell me."

"Do you still believe that those cute and over-intellectual Germans are in any danger?"

Renaud waved his hand in the air as if trying to conjure something into existence. Greg watched the upward, fluttering movements of his fingers. The drug was calming him, but he was not unused to Valium and knew he would not fall asleep.

"You are calm now, Greg."

Renaud stood up and poured himself a drink. Greg stared at him and the gesture of Renaud downing the alcohol in one go made him think of Günter doing the same thing; and then, soon afterwards, collapsing on the floor. Maximilian as well.

In Greg's imagination, they had both taken the drink and were staggering and crying out. The horror was still there, fighting its way to the surface from whatever depths it had remained in, and would probably always remain in, hidden for a while, then return. A crime had been committed.

"I think both you and Antoine have succeeded in the past. Supposing in Antoine's car he has a bottle of alcohol, and it is drugged, and he offers it to them?"

"Enough!" Renaud said, and his voice would have reached the highest balcony in any theatre. "Enough Greg. I have had enough! Antoine with a drugged bottle in the car? What next?" He came and stood over Greg. "Go back to England, Greg. If anything has happened to those stupidly intelligent Germans, there will surely be news of it. Two bloated bodies in the Seine bobbing to the surface! Imagine the crime, Greg—go on, give yourself the luxury! But go. Get some therapy. I will pay for it if you like, but get well, and I will subscribe to *Le Monde* for you, even *Libération*. Every day for a year you will receive a package from me, all the magazines, so you can check for news of the crime. Take a year if necessary. I will still want you—" and he paused, out of breath, "—and then come back to me."

"Yes," Greg said, and he recalled an old French film he had seen in the 60s, where in the middle of the night guards creep into the condemned cell and drag some screaming men to their executions. "Oh yes, the title was *We are all Murderers*." Greg stood up. Momentarily he felt giddy. "I must leave. I agree."

The following morning, he left, and Renaud repeated his promise about packages, money, and the papers. Finally, he reminded Greg of the therapy he clearly needed.

As Greg walked, he recalled his visits to the doctor and then to a therapist. Renaud was punctual with his letters, full of love and encouragement and sent piles of French magazines and newspapers. Greg left them unread, cluttered in his hallway. In the new flat he had chosen to live in, this was the only place to put them. He did not want to read them, just in case there *was* an article about two bodies, but something inside him told him that he must not throw them away. During therapy, he told the therapist that it *could* have happened, that there could have been a murder, and that he was complicit.

"What crime exactly is it that you are complicit in?" his therapist asked.

Mentally, Greg shuddered against this question.

"It never happened."

"Now you are contradicting yourself."

Confused, Greg replied, "I was there. It could have happened. But it didn't. And yet in my mind it has—the awful clinging guilt, the knife falling."

"What knife?"

"Antoine's knife."

The fear was so bad at times, his body was drenched in sweat.

Then, after a while, everything inside him became as still as a lake after a storm. Not a ripple of guilt, not a thought of Antoine driving them to their deaths. And the Seine became a stream in his mind, and no one can drown in a stream. He saw Maximilian and Günter both alive and well in Stuttgart, and knew that neither of them would be giving a second thought to the aged actor they had met.

"I think you do not need me anymore," the therapist said.

Greg looked at him. The brisk man with the wedding ring on his finger, and the beautifully framed picture of his wife and two children on his desk, all said goodbye to Greg. He was dismissed like a long, very long, one-night stand of madness.

"Are you sure?" he asked as he was about to exit through the door one final time.

"I am sure."

The voice was impatient now, as if meaning, when is this neurotic homosexual going?

"May I return if—?"

"If it is necessary. Of course," and the door was closed unceremoniously behind Greg.

Greg recalled his return and his ringing of the bell and the sound of shuffling feet as the front door opened. A white-haired man stared at him, and he too had dark rings under his eyes. Greg could not believe it was Renaud. He was old, old, old, and past repair.

"Greg," Renaud said, only that, and walked inwards, expecting Greg to follow. Greg closed the door behind him. The hallway had a new chandelier, over-bright and gaudy. He followed Renaud into the main living room, its blinds down and airless. For a while, no words were passed between them and Renaud poured out cognac for both of them. In silence he handed the glass to Greg, then sat in the furthest corner of the room.

"Are you better?" he asked eventually.

"It took a while, but yes."

"When was it? Yes, last year. August. And now we are in April. You have been cured in less than a year!"

"There have been consequences. Unfortunately my imaginings have become more acute. I am not as clear as I once was with my memory of anything; of how things were and what really happened in my life."

Renaud sighed. He was so hidden from sight that Greg could scarcely see him. The long room seemed much longer and wider than Greg remembered it to have been.

"I have heard there can be dangers—" Renaud replied slowly. "But you are cured of that one, specific delusion? Did you tell the person you saw about it? About the details? Who I am? Where I live?"

There was anxiety in Renaud's voice as he asked this, and Greg was careful in replying.

"I told him what was necessary."

"Meaning?"

"I did not give your name, and of course, not your

address."

"Not even the *arrondissement*?"

A fly which had either been sleeping or had come in with them began to buzz its way around the room, eventually settling on one of the slats of the blind. This unnerved Greg.

"He was not interested in those kinds of details," Greg said.

"But he must have been interested in the supposed crime."

"Yes, as it related to me and my state of mind. He believed I was imagining—"

"—which you were!"

"Can we talk about something else? It is disturbing me. I must also thank you for your letters and all the newspapers."

Renaud moved then and came further into the room. He went again to the drinks and replenished his glass.

"I drink a lot. I never used to. I too was disturbed."

All the remains of his good looks were gone. Greg stared at Renaud's face as he bent over to pour the cognac. There was a harsh light; the only one in the room, and it illuminated with cruel ferocity Renaud's features. Greg saw how the face had caved in on itself and the contours had disappeared. A puffiness had replaced form and his eyes were smaller. His hair too had turned alarmingly white. As if reading Greg's mind, Renaud said softly, "The past long months have taken their toll."

Greg replied hastily, "I am sure that I too have changed."

Renaud came over to where Greg was sitting and stared down at him.

"I have dreaded a knocking on the door," Renaud said. "I thought you would compromise me, put doubts in the mind of the man you were seeing. It was like some stupid detective novel, false information given, such as what *might* have happened. That man you saw, could have released this information to the police!"

Greg saw Renaud's hands shake as he said this. The words came out in a garbled rush, grammar faltering.

"That is absurd."

"Is it? You could have said that the Germans were in a state of collapse when Antoine took them out of the room, that he had to help them out of the room. You could have said I opened a phial of something that I poured into the drinks. All madness, but then you were mad."

The last sentence was fiercely said.

"Renaud, there is such a thing as confidentiality. And in any case, I said during the first assessment that I was delusional."

"What was the man's name?"

"Does it matter?"

"Tell me. Tell me."

"Dr. Vine."

"And his address?"

As he asked this last question, some cognac spilled over onto the carpet.

"It's not important. It's over. I am here," Greg said.

Hands still shaking, Renaud made his way back to the corner of the room and Greg thought, he is seeking safety. That is his corner now. That is where he hides. It was as if an infection of madness had passed between them and the silence continued; a silence only broken when the fly resumed its buzzing, only to settle once more on a picture rail. How long will it live, Greg thought, and the thought upset him. He wanted to leave the room, to leave the house and to escape from all that had happened, for there was no place in it for him now. How could he even have believed he could have lived with Renaud?

"Where's Antoine?" Greg asked.

This abrupt question, which he had to ask, made Renaud cry out.

"Gone! He left. After all these years, he left! He has disappeared. I tried to find out where, but there were no traces. It happened soon after I told him of your delusion."

"Are you saying I am responsible for his leaving?"

There was a long, very long silence.

"The truth is, Greg, he *may* have slain them. As a final gift for me."

Greg, unable to bear any more, got to his feet, and going to the window, opened the blinds, letting the light of the day flood in. Renaud told him not to do that, but Greg needed the light.

"Why are you saying that? It contradicts everything, Renaud."

He looked at Renaud, huddled in the corner, the small eyes stared at him, and there was a look of terror on his face.

"I didn't mean it," he said. "Will you now go to the police?"

"Renaud, it is over. I was the one who had that thought, and now you? You have taken it from me. Don't you understand?"

"No!"

"But you must. For your own sake. Antoine left I am sure for other reasons. People *do* leave." He paused. "Call it betrayal. It doesn't matter, because Antoine had his own reasons for doing this."

Renaud laughed.

"What do I know or care about reasons? He had a reason, that night and the Germans—he killed them!" He paused. "What a relief to admit it. At last, to admit it." He paused again, shaken after a confession that may or may not have been true. "He left me alone in this house, and there was only you and the endless letters I wrote and those absurd newspapers and magazines."

The ambiguity was too strong for Greg. "Can we leave this room? I am tired. Can I sleep? Is there a room for me?"

"Yes, Greg. Yes of course. I have food as well."

"I'm just tired."

"I understand," and after he had said the word, he shouted out, "It's all true, Greg, it's all true! There is a postcard, somewhere from Germany. It was signed with both their names, and the stamp is marked from Stuttgart." Then Renaud paused, and the agony in his voice grew more intense. "But I am sure Antoine went there, forged their names and sent it himself."

"Where is the card?" Greg asked, and the heavy weariness of this encounter was beginning to overwhelm him.

Renaud replied in a dull, dead voice, "It's no use seeing it, Greg, I analysed the writing. I could see it was Antoine's. A distortion of it, each signature made to look different, but there are certain loops in Antoine's writing that I know so well. They were a tell-tale sign. They were there on the postcard."

It was at this moment that Greg realised the real crime Antoine had committed was to destroy Renaud's mind. He had, in his way, through years of companionship, murdered him.

Slowly they left the room and Greg watched as Renaud shuffled up the stairs, and as he went up them he repeated over and over again, "Why do people do things that cause pain? Why? I have. We all have. Why?"

Greg too left, and quite suddenly. He left behind most of what he had brought with him, taking only a small suitcase, and now as he sat at the Bastille café table, he recalled how every day, in Renaud's house the inquisition of self had continued. Like a torturer who cannot stop, Renaud tore at his mind, and after trying to undo the harm he had done, he tore at the gaping wounds of false memory again. Only once did the process stop, on the last evening of Greg's stay. They had eaten a meal, and Renaud went to his DVD collection and brought out his favourite of all the films he had been in.

Greg had sat there watching the incoherent plot. It was a heist story. A film from the mid-sixties. Renaud was one of the plotters and the clichéd robbery was mainly planned by him. It was in the same tradition of *Rififi* by Dassin, but it did not have either the suspense or the style. The characters were given bad dialogue, and the leading actress was vulgar and overwhelmed Renaud's performance.

"Aren't I good?" Renaud kept asking.

"Excellent," Greg lied.

"I mean, look at the competition I had. Some of the best names in the business. And she was an icon in those days. Adored for her voice and her wonderful Italian accent. Gay men adored her!"

"They adored you as well," Greg said, eager after the torment of the past days, to please.

"Yes, but a woman is adored more. Every woman in the audience wanted to be her and every straight man wanted her. And as you surely know, French men are basically all straight. They marry, have children, discard their former lovers, and in the process destroy themselves, or do you think they are happier married? I mean Antoine. Did you know that he is married? He's bisexual. Maybe that is why he left? Do you think that is the reason?"

"Hush, Renaud. Watch the film. Calm your mind."

Renaud who had been staring intently at Greg looked again at the screen. He edged his chair forward as close as he could. He put out his tongue as if he wanted to lick at the flickering light that resurrected his former self. He looked like a child, full of wonder that this heist anti-hero was himself.

"I want to touch him," he murmured, and Greg realised again the power of the disintegrating mind. The dying mind that wants so desperately to embrace its former capacity of recognition, of acceptance. Then finally, the end credits came up and Renaud put his head in his hands. He did not want the images to come to an end.

"I am—" he said.

"Brilliant. Quite brilliant," Greg replied, and then went to turn off the television.

"No, not yet," Renaud cried out. "Let us watch it again."

"But I am tired."

"Please. Just for me. It is my best performance. My face is so handsome. I want to look at him again. At that stranger

228

who was me."

The way he said the word *him* hit Greg in the stomach. He could not stay. But for the moment he had to be the adult. He had to convince Renaud that there was another day, another possibility of viewing. He had to gently explain and lie that he would always be there for Renaud, that he would always return to him.

"Think how happy you will be tomorrow when you put on the DVD. He will be there again."

"Yes," said Renaud, and with a slow gesture of defeat, he waved his hand at the screen. "Let him go, let him go."

"For tonight, yes."

"I know."

Those were the last words Greg said to him. He helped Renaud up the stairs to his bedroom and, like a passive creature that has been cornered and given in, he allowed Greg to undress him and put him to bed. Greg switched off the light and silently went back to his room. The following morning, he was gone.

The taxi arrived at the Rue La Fayette, stopping a few houses away from where Nick lived. Greg paid the driver who had been talking to him all the way about his mental problems and how he lived to drive by night, knowing that his wife was asleep, and that when it was his turn to sleep, she would be out. He told Greg love did not exist.

As he walked towards the house, Greg tried to clear his mind. He knew that love existed and that he loved Nick. So why did I run from him? Why was I so frightened, even appalled, at what I saw? Before he rang the bell, he had to come to terms with what he had seen. It had been Nick's body. An old man's body with slashes of red scars all over his flesh. He had been attacked by knives, and his face was marked as well. A vivid scar showed on his forehead and to the right of his face, and whoever had done it, had been merciless. The red stood out against the green of the light, green because Nick had thrown a thin green cloth over the top of the lamp. "I did not see it in the café," he said to himself. "I did not see it in his home, and while we talked, I saw Nick, young, beautiful, not with white hair and mutilated skin."

Standing by the house, but in shadow, he saw that the front door was open and that a few yards away an old woman was calling for her cat. Her call was loud, and she had her back to him. Unnoticed, he slipped in through the door, and instead of using the lift, he slowly made his way up the stairs. The higher he got the louder her calls seemed to be. Arriving at Nick's door he heard music quietly playing. A woman's voice and an aria that sounded like a hymn. He rang the doorbell, and the music stopped. Very cautiously the door opened, and there Nick stood, dressed in an old sweater and baggy corduroy trousers.

"Greg," Nick said, "I was thinking of you just now. I think better when I play music."

"What was it? It sounded very fine."

Greg focused on making his voice as natural as possible.

"The end of *Un Ballo in Maschera*. I don't like opera much—"

"Neither do I," Greg replied, "but that was exceptional."

"Yes." Nick paused, as if lost in thought, then said, "But come in. The place is untidy. I haven't washed. Well, you are here."

Greg closed the door behind him, and he no longer saw the old man he had seen in the bedroom. Again the vision returned; will beauty never go away? he thought. Why can't I see Nick as he is now? He looks in my mind like a student in those faded grey corduroys, in that red sweater.

"It's late—" Greg murmured.

"—and you have been walking. I can see that you are tired."

To make conversation, Greg explained how he had got into the house. Nick was preparing a tisane for both of them, and he explained that the old woman was the concierge, and her cat was all she had in life, but the cat did not like her and tried at every opportunity to escape.

"That's sad," Greg said. Then he noticed the Rilke book of poems. He picked it up and read *The Panther*. Nick came over and saw the poem he was reading and laughed that laugh that Greg remembered so well from Islingword Street.

"Another kind of cat behind bars," he said making light of it.

"I thought there were no concierges left in Paris," Greg said replacing the book.

"I call her the concierge, but she no longer is. She still has her rooms. How she can afford to pay for them now that she no longer works, I do not know. I see her son sometimes on the stairs. I expect he helps."

Greg sat down and asked Nick if they could talk.

"But aren't we talking," Nick questioned.

"No."

"Should I ask why you have come back?"

"Yes, to begin with, aren't you surprised? I mean, after the way I ran?"

"Everyone runs," Nick said, and handed Greg his drink.

"I thought I saw something, and it shocked me."

Greg did not want to explain what had seen and for a moment he thought it had been his imagination. Nick *is* as young as I thought he was in the café and during our time in this room. It was *my* hallucination; the wave of my fears falling—breaking up, crashing over me. He sipped at his drink.

Nick was quiet now and sat on a single chair. He leant forward and then he did something that only a magician could do. He made a gesture with both hands in the air, then drew them down again and covered his face with them. He made the motions of clawing at his face, and like white paper his skin seemed to fall between his fingers. Greg wanted to cry out but controlled himself. He wanted to beg Nick to stop, to say that it did not matter, that he did not care, but instinctively he *knew* that this was what Nick had to do, and that there was a reason in the savagery of the gestures why the truth should be revealed. Then at last the hands fell away and the full extent of the damage to his face was exposed.

"Look, Greg. Am I still Nick?" he asked.

The face was a patchwork quilt of cuts, and the scars were there, one on the right side of the face cut downwards, the other, horizontal along his forehead.

"Yes," Greg said. "It is you, but what—?"

"And you saw them on my body?"

Greg nodded his head.

"I have hallucinations, Nick. Since I left you, I have had the images at the back of my mind, not brought forward, but there. And there, in that recess of the brain I refused the truth; I knew, or told myself I knew that I had invented this—"

"—atrocity," Nick said.

"But how—who did this? And why is there this white skin on the floor, scattered like real skin? Is it a mask?"

Nick smiled, and the scar on his cheek twitched, and blood seemed to pulse beneath the surface of the wound. He got up and walked to the window. The blind was not down, and he looked out over the tracks. In the silence, an early train was heard entering the station.

"It is paper-thin, but it covers the worst. A make-up artist makes them for me. The cuts are too deep not to show, and I do not want any operations, despite the fact my doctor says there could be hope of making it more—let us say—more bearable to look at." He paused and drew in his breath. "Just like the old horror films. I remember the posters—"

"Yes, so do I," Greg said. "I remember you kissing me during a monster film. I wasn't ready for it. But then, that was our childhood."

"Did I? Did I love you even then?"

"As a child can," Greg replied.

"It always lasts when it is in childhood," Nick said, and he then turned and faced Greg, and the words, the wild cry of words, exploded with pent-up passion from his mouth, "*They did it to me*. In that village, outside of placid, peaceful Angers. A group of them in their teens with knives and anything that could cut in their hands. One used a broken shaving mirror. My memory has almost gone, but I can remember the slashing and the twisting in, and the blood soaking my clothes. I was young! I was young! I am not Nick, Greg. I am Nicolas Ghéon from Angers, put there God knows how or when! I was a youthful man, approaching middle-age, but young in mind, full of inner mental pain that I can no longer recall, but I existed. I could look in a mirror without shuddering, hold a glass to my lips and drink red wine without thinking of blood. I have no recall of those youths' faces. They are getting old themselves now—"

This last note of bitterness hurt Greg the most. But who *had* put him, as Nick expressed it, in the region of Angers? Or was it true that this was not his Nick at all?

"Can you really not remember any more?"

"No. Nothing." Nick turned again and once more looked down at the tracks. "I will go into the bedroom, and when I come out, you will see a flat surface. You will see the thin mesh that covers the worst. It is, as I said, paper-thin, and I've been lucky. The man who makes them for me is one of a kind; a specialist of specialists. Some drag queens go to him, and they say his masks are better than the truth."

Greg watched as he left the room, and then went over and put on the last track of *Un Ballo in Maschera*. The words soared upwards, quietly but with gentle power. He heard the simplicity of loss, the prayer over and above death—*per sempre—Addio!* and the final chorus of *Notte d'orrore; notte d'orrore*.

Nick returned into the room. He was smartly dressed, and his features belonged as they always had, to Nick, to the Nick of Brighton. Greg loved this man. It was simple now, and with the chorus receding, like the overhanging wave of his panic, he went and kissed Nick, or Nicolas, on the lips.

"Does it matter *who* I am?" Nick asked.

"Not anymore."

"Then let us go and watch the trains come in. Or are you too tired. Am I being selfish?"

"We will sleep late," Greg said.

"Always?"

"Always. I want to stay. I want to be with you. I love you."

Part Four:
Happiness

"Did Greg suffer?" Karel asked the doctor.

"I would say he was delirious, but not in pain. He spoke your name once, and we found your details in an address book he had in his pocket. I will make sure it is returned to you. Will you be making the arrangements?"

"Yes. I will make sure he finds his resting place here."

"I am sorry you arrived too late to see him. Perhaps we took too long in contacting you."

"How was he at the end?"

"As I said, he had no pain, but the turmoil in his mind cast up many images and conversations that may have been real or unreal, true or false. Do you have any idea why he came to Paris?"

"No, I'm sorry, I don't."

"At the end, just before he died, he smiled and murmured, 'I love you.' Then his heart simply stopped. It was not distressing."

"Yes," Karel paused. "Perhaps it could even be called happiness."

"Was he happy before?" the doctor asked. "Was he happy back in Brighton?"

"He shut himself away. I think he wanted to confront himself."

"And were you his lover? Excuse me for asking."

"I was. Once. In our youth."

"And were you happy?"

Karel did not reply but looked deeply into the doctor's eyes. The doctor paused and nodded before speaking again.

"I think I understand. Speaking from my own experiences as a black man, I know how hard it is to be different or on the margins of society, no matter whether you're black, Jewish, or homosexual. Sometimes I think it is the world that should stop breathing. To die. And then, after a long while, renew itself with other people; better people."

"Perhaps," Karel replied.

Once outside the hospital, Karel glanced at the sun. It was a warm day with a warm breeze. He felt Greg beside him, and it was good. He felt happy.

We walk in parallel worlds, he thought, and smiled. What do any of us know?

✱✱✱✱✱

Thank you for reading *Greg at the Station*.
The next book in the series, provisionally titled *Karel & the Chelsea Lighthouse Café*, is in preparation.

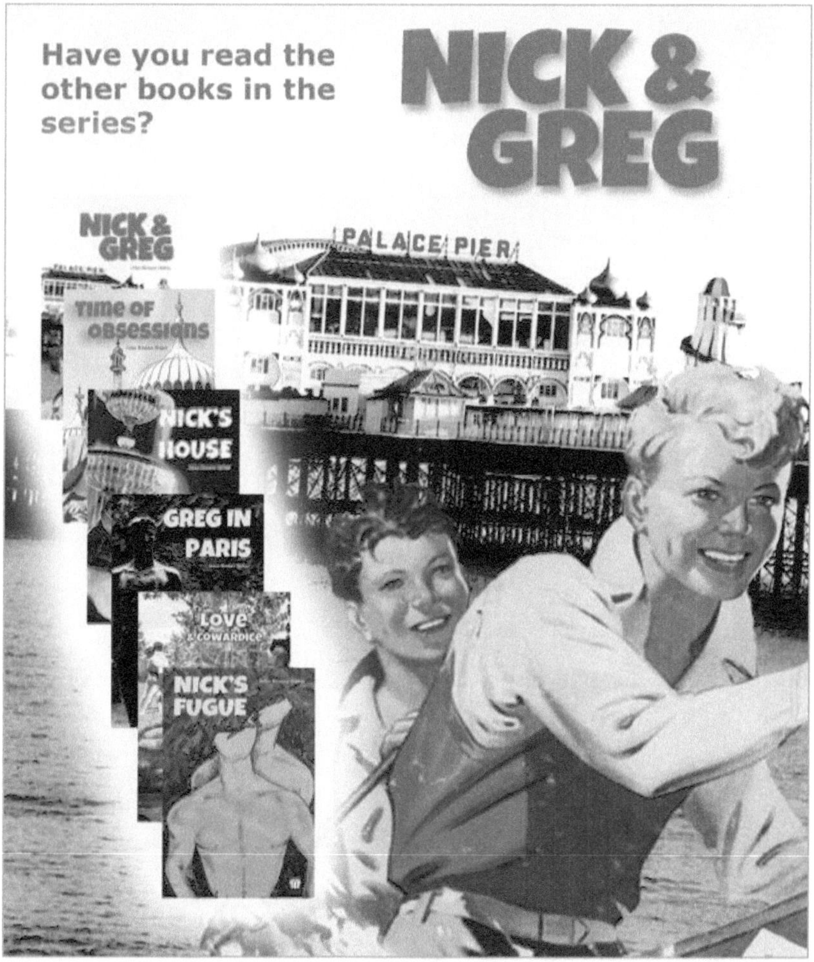

Have you read the other books in the series?

NICK & GREG

www.ingramcontent.com/pod-product-compliance
Lightning Source LLC
Chambersburg PA
CBHW022010170626
46808CB00001B/354